Sycam

Sycamore Glen

Brad G. Leech

Brad Leech

2016

Copyright

For Connie
The beautiful red haired girl I married on a
warm summer day in 1973 that seems like yesterday.
Proof that there is such a thing as love at first sight.

~ Acknowledgements ~

Being a first-time author, I need to thank several people for helping make Sycamore Glen happen at all.

John Barmonde came to me with an idea he had about a golf story. I must thank John for encouraging me in my efforts. Although the end result probably was not what John had in mind when we began discussing it, he has supported me throughout the process.

I also need to mention my wife, Connie, for her patience while I worked on Sycamore Glen. When I started, I think she may have thought that this effort was beyond my skills, but she never actually said it. I recall her laughing when I told her that - 'Just because I only got "C's" in English class - It didn't mean I couldn't write a book.' As she read my material, I think her opinion may have changed a little.

I don't consider myself a writer, but I've had a little taste of what a true writer must experience when he sees some enjoyment in a readers' face while quietly reading his material. That will stay with me always, and makes this experience priceless.

Thank you, Connie.

Finally, I also need to thank the handful of relatives and close friends who read Sycamore Glen while I was writing and re writing it. Your opinions have been invaluable, I listened to everything you had to say. You, also, encouraged me to stay with this effort. I hope the sequel I'm working on is of equal interest to you.

~ Contents ~

~ Brad Leech ~

~ Preface ~

All that follows occurred in the south, but not that far '*South*'. When I say to you that someone visited from the north, that's not to say they were from the *'North'*. These are just points on a compass.

These people were really where you and I are from, and maybe, not so different than either of us.

The story could take place anywhere. Anywhere there is a stream and some nearby sycamore trees.

A place like Sycamore Glen

~ Brad Leech ~

~ Prologue ~

It had been weeks since school ended during the cooler, early, days of summer. Like the anticipation of children starting their summer vacation - then becoming bored, it too had ended. Now it was just plain hot. The summer sun was boiling the macadam on the well crowned, two lane rural road. The center line had long ago worn away and probably wouldn't get repainted anytime soon. There were few improvements that would ever happen in Clark County. The one thing that would happen, today, for sure, is that the weeds along this road, would be kept at bay.

Svisssh.

Svisssh.

Svisssh.

BaoOOOOOM! The sound of the shotgun echoed off into the distance, jolting the birds in the adjacent fields into silence.

"Cletus, what in thee Hell are yaul doing back there?"

"Got a real nasty one back here Boss! I'll get her tho!"

Shaking his head and muttering to himself, 'Yep, just like always.' To everyone else, "Jest keep iiiiiit moving …!"

Now you have to understand something about southern chicory. This is not a small roadside weed like in other parts of the country. It is a bush. I've seen baby rabbits seeking shade under them. Left unattended, they will scrape the paint off a car that strays too close to the edge of the pavement. While it does not grow as fast as kudzu, it is infinitely more devious. Some idiots think it makes good coffee. It's even able to pass itself off as a pretty blue flower.

Something to be plucked, put in a 'co cola' bottle and given to a mother on her day.

Svisssh. Another blossom neatly severed with surgical precision from halfway up the anterior portion of the spine.

Svisssh. A small seed pod taken from underneath an overhanging blossom. The blossom left untouched.

Svisssh. This blossom taken from …

"Jeeesus Cletus, I thought I told you to get a move on back there! Ahhh! I just know your Mamma raised a deaf boy. Damnation, we got us a road to clear today!"

Swiiiiick.

The entire plant taken off at exactly one eighth of an inch from the gravel shoulder of the road.

"Moving up Boss."

Swiiiiick.

Exactly one eighth of inch, just like every weed today. Just like every weed, every day. Day after day …

A car rushed by. The driver steering the car down the left side of the road, well clear of the crew, raising his hand in a nonchalant, thankful, salute to the men hacking down the weeds in the boiling sun. They looked up as he waved, and watched the unmistakable, brilliantly red, wildly finned, brand new, 1957 Chevrolet convertible recede into the distance.

~ 1 ~

Cletus stood outside the administration building for the Clark County Detention Center. It was midmorning and the clerk inside had said there would be a bus coming through before noon, heading north to the small town of DeLong. Cletus was fidgeting, restless to get moving. Get moving with his life. He stood and stretched for about the tenth time, and looking south for the bus, he started walking. Not a shuffle, but confidently striding. It felt good. He wasn't sure exactly where he was headed but he had to move.

His crime was not a major one, but he'd deserved what had been handed to him, and he accepted it, fully. Deep down he was actually thankful for how he'd spent the last two years of his life.

Growing up on a farm, he was no stranger to hard work. The truth was, that he loved being outdoors. Rain or shine, he was an outdoorsman. So, when he was assigned to one of the road maintenance crews, he was in his element. The days were long and the work was tiring, but he loved it. He was more than a model prisoner and had turned down other jobs that were both less strenuous, and less 'supervised'. He had always been in good shape physically, this job turned him into a machine.

He sat his duffel bag down to roll up his shirt sleeves, it was just starting to really heat up. No prison tattoos for him. As he moved his sleeves up, all you saw were golden brown forearms. While he'd never be mistaken for James Dean, he could probably play the part. His hair was a lot lighter than Dean's, his eyes a more brilliant blue. His smile was what probably attracted the most attention, from girls, anyway. He'd had a lot of friends, but that was all. Most seemed too – 'organized'- if you could call it that. His life had been a little scattered, not so well defined, and he couldn't blame anyone but himself if that kept him from getting really close to anyone. He didn't think of himself as a drifter, he was just ... well, maybe he was a drifter. Was. That was changing right here, right now – he continued – south.

~ 2 ~

Dan was a golfer. No doubt about it. And he let everyone know about it. Every opportunity he had. If you met Dan by chance, your first impression of him was that he was a car salesman. And you'd be right. Dan was nothing, if not transparent. But he loved golf even more than selling cars. He had long ago learned that to succeed in sales you had to be absolutely honest with your customers. If someone came to him looking for a blue, two door coupe – that was exactly what they would leave the dealership driving. Maybe the customer would wind up with a set of chrome hub caps that they didn't think they'd get – but they hadn't paid anything extra. Dan had made sure they were more than satisfied with the deal they had just made. And when they drove off in their new car, Dan was guaranteed that in three or four years they would make the pilgrimage back to his dealership to get the next car of their dreams.

Each fall, after the frenzy of the new models being released by Detroit, Dan would jump in his new Chevy convertible and head south for a golf weekend to relax before the hectic sales routine began at the dealership that was sure to follow in the coming weeks. His car had to be a Chevy, and had to be red. This years', 1959 model had these giant, laid back fins. How could they top this next year? His route south took him over smaller country roads, the interstate highway system was just beginning to be widely used. He preferred slower roads through a string of rural communities that had become so familiar to him on these outings. With the top down and the wind roaring in his ears he was a man moving between his two worlds. As he cruised through the countryside he was vigilant for the occasional stray heifer wandering along the edge of the road just around the next bend or the frantic movements of a chipmunk insisting on playing tire tag with his new car.

He had passed the county jail a while ago and was moving into an area where the trees crowded up close to the road when he spotted the hitchhiker. He had almost missed seeing him and was somewhat startled as he made the abrupt transition from bright sunlight into the semi darkness of the overhanging trees where the hitchhiker was standing. He pulled over onto the shoulder and waited for the young man to jog up to the car.

"Where you headed son?" he said as he leaned over toward the passengers' door and swung it open.

"Well sir I'd just like to get into town to find out what buses might be leaving today."

"Well hop in and we'll get you there in no time at all."

"Thank you, sir. I'd appreciate that – although there's no real rush about it." The young man dropped a duffel bag into the back seat before settling into the front seat.

"I thought so. Seeing where you've been. Just thought I'd help out. 'Always like a little conversation when I'm on the road."

"Well I'm not much of a talker sir, but I do appreciate the ride, so I'll try to hold up my end of the conversation."

"I'm on my way to Jasper for a couple of days of golf. Are you from these parts, you know about the course in Jasper?"

"Well I grew up nearby in Jacksonville and I've been to Jasper once, but I don't know about the golf course there."

"Man, it is some layout. I came down a couple of years ago, and discovered it. Now I come down every chance I get. I play at a lot of courses but this one just suits my game. I don't claim to be a good golfer, but I do enjoy teeing it up."

The boy had relaxed a little and was easing back into the spacious seat and began taking in the surroundings as the car floated along the road. You just could not beat the suspension in these big old lumbering brutes from GM.

"If you don't mind me asking, why were you in there?" as Dan jerked his head backwards towards the prison.

"Well I got into some problems over some money. It's not like I hurt anybody or anything like that, so you don't have to worry. Truth is, I hurt myself worse than anybody else. I see that now. I had a little time to think about it."

" 'Nuff said. I see a lot of people in my line of work and am a pretty fair judge of what I find in them. Seems as though you're handling this okay. What's next?"

"Well sir I need to find some work. That's why I'm going to take the bus to Franklin. Maybe there's work there I could do. I've tried my hand at several things, there may be someone there who'll give me a chance. I'm a hard worker, but saying it is one thing, being able to prove it is another."

"Anything in particular you'd like to try your hand at?"

"Well sir I've been outdoors a lot, so I'm going to try and find something in landscape work, maintenance work of some sort. I like it outdoors, I don't know how I'd do inside. I don't ever see myself in an office or somewhere closed in. That's nothing to do with – back there." As the boy waived his hand that had been resting on the right-side mirror. "I've always worked outside."

Dan nodded in agreement. "Me too. I'm lucky. I'm outdoors a lot with customers. Did I tell you I sell cars? There's a lot of paperwork I have to do, but that's just a part of the job. When I'm inside with a customer, I can sense when they feel crowded or pressured by the closeness. Outside, everyone changes – that's a big part of golf. The courses are so wide open compared to my sales lot. Even the courses not so well known."

The car rumbled over an abandoned railroad crossing. Jasper wouldn't be too much farther. The houses that were so few and far between began popping up more frequently. The large fields were giving way to the sprawl of Jasper, if you could call it that. Dan pulled into the first gas station that appeared, a Gulf station. The attendant came out and asked what he needed.

"Fill her up with No Nox please. Restroom key inside?"

"Yes sir, just inside the door and the restroom is around to the right".

Dan got out, took several steps towards the station then backtracked. He leaned inside towards the boy with his hand and said – "By the way, name's Dan – Dan Steele. Plumb forgot to introduce myself. Be right back, just need to stretch a bit."

The boy took his hand – "Cletus Armstrong, a pleasure to meet you sir."

~ 3 ~

On his way back to the car, Dan saw that while the attendant was checking the oil, Cletus was chatting with him. The attendant had already cleaned the windshield of the layer of late summer bugs that had so quickly accumulated on the new car. Cletus nodded a thank you and got back in the car.

Dan looked at the pump as he walked to the attendant and handed him a ten-dollar bill. Dan thanked him and told him to keep the change and got back in the car. The attendant thanked him for the generous tip, a rare event in his life.

"Man, can you believe it, seven dollars for a fill up, incredible." Dan said as he started the car and moved away from the pumps.

Cletus nodded back towards the attendant, "He said I just missed the daily bus to Franklin. Leaves at eleven during the week."

"Well Cletus, it's getting on towards lunch time. How about I treat you to a sandwich while you figure out what's next?

"Thanks Mr. Steele, but I have some money, I should treat you for getting me this far."

"Nonsense Cletus – please, it's Dan, and besides, we're eating at the course. I want to get there early and get a tee time for tomorrow morning if I can."

The car lurched out onto the road and into Jasper. Driving through town, Dan's car received some serious stares. He'd only had it a couple of days and the full-blown Detroit blitz of advertising had obviously not yet found its' way to Jasper. They moved past the town square with its' requisite statue to their hometown Civil War hero and a bandstand with banners that was touting the annual Harvest Festival occurring in several weeks. Dan would not mind living here, but he would exhaust the car buying pool of customers quickly.

As they moved out of the town proper, they passed the first sign for the Jasper Country Club. The turn off was just ahead and moved them up into some rolling hills that would never have made for great farming. Grazing maybe, but not crops. With so much flat fertile land nearby, this area wasn't threatened by the farmers. While you could not call this suburbia, there were quite a few houses scattered about Jasper. Obviously, enough people lived nearby to support the Jasper Country Club.

They began to pull into the drive that led towards the clubhouse. Not a magnolia lined lane leading to a pillared hall, but sycamore trees that had naturally flourished along the stream that dictated the course of the roadway, as the stream meandered down from the clubhouse. No matter how many times Dan came up here he, he found himself swerving slightly to miss both the entrance sign and the first massive sycamore tree. The road was fairly narrow as it followed the stream up the hill. Dan had already played chicken on more than one occasion with someone headed in the opposite direction. The clubhouse itself was all about golf. While seeming to crawl out in several directions, it was just the result of the club growing throughout the years and accommodating the growth as best it could.

Dan wheeled the car into the adjacent parking area and jumped out. He motioned for Cletus to follow and together they headed straight for the pro shop so Dan could get his tee time for tomorrow morning. Dan was home. The shop was busy for a Friday. People were moving past in different directions, each on a mission.

One group was getting ready to tee off but obviously, someone was missing. He was making his excuses from afar, to his playing partner in a phone booth in a corner of the room. A number of people were heading into a dining area which is where Dan and Cletus would be, after he made his tee time.

As Dan stepped up to the counter in the shop, the attendant immediately recognized him and greeted him warmly. "Mr. Steele, what a pleasure to see you back so soon!"

Dan shook his hand. "Thanks Curtis, it's great to be back. Any chance of a tee time sometime tomorrow morning?"

Curtis pulled the reservations book closer and confirmed what he thought. "You're in luck Mr. Steele. We had a group cancel their 7:00 tee time and we're putting together a foursome to fill the slot. You're our third so far. How does that sound?"

"Fantastic Curtis! Say, you're not sending a lamb into a den of lions, are you?"

"No sir. The two gentlemen in the group are very much like yourself and I'm sure I'll fill out the foursome with someone that plays equally well."

"Great. I'll swing back through after I've had lunch. Thanks again."

Dan moved away from the counter and Cletus joined him as they walked back through the entry hall and crossed over into the restaurant.

MacGregor's was the Jasper Country Clubs' idea of a Scottish pub. Dan had been at enough 'Scottish' golf course restaurants over the years to realize these people had gotten it right. Maybe it was the food, which wasn't entirely Scottish. Maybe it was the bar, once again, not entirely Scottish. It probably had a lot to do with the man behind the bar, and his daughter, walking across the pub to seat Dan and Cletus.

~ Brad Leech ~

~ 4 ~

"So Mr. Steele, you and your handsome young friend here have driven allllll the way down from the Big City just to litter our fields of gorse and pollute our pristine streams with your errant tee shots then? I'm supposin' you need some nourishment before you take on that herculean task this afternoon, so I'll be showing you to a table."

With that, she stalked off towards a table by expansive windows that looked out over the practice green and nearby pond. The pond had once been larger, the reservoir for the mammoth water wheel powering a mill that was the original structure at the site. Now it was smaller, just decoration, like the wheel. The undershot wheel turned slowly governed by the trickle of water escaping the pond, headed beneath the clubhouse, and down the hill away from the course. As some of the water fell back from the bucketed blades of the wheel, it musically plumped back into the pond – the notes drifting through the open windows back into the pub.

As Dan and Cletus took their seats, Dan winked at Cletus and spoke to the waitress, "So what you're saying then, Mary, is that this young man here, is more handsome than I am?"

"Now Mr. Steele, you don't have to get surly with me. I was merely trying to ascertain your plans so I could direct any women and children to the nearest shelter, should you and your friend here, decide to move to the tee box. Let me get you some menus." With that she turned to move away from the table, bending her head downward slightly towards Cletus with a wink that turned into a dazzling smile, she continued towards the kitchen.

"That, Cletus, was Mary MacGregor! Oh, by the way, you can breathe now."

As Dan looked towards the bar, Ian MacGregor was smiling, offering up his white bar towel as a truce flag for Dan to use. Dan shook his head and softly yelled back "Not necessary, but thanks."

Ian spoke back, "You know best sir!" But to himself as he turned back to the bar, 'I'll keep it handy, you may need it later.'

As Mary went through the doorway into the kitchen she turned just enough for Dan to hear her say, "He is."

Ian had met Mary's mother, Katherine, when she came to Scotland to visit relatives with her parents. Her parents were elderly, Katherine was a late addition to the family. Her mother didn't think she would ever have a child, then …Katherine had come along. Katherine and her parents had stayed in Scotland during most of the summer of 1926. It had been a whirlwind romance. Ian and Katherine had married and returned to Katherine's home, Jasper. Katherine's parents had died, not long apart, while the war in Europe was grinding down to an end. Katherine had been Ian's only true love, Mary became the jewel of his life. Mary had a fierce independence, much like Katherine, and she acted upon it – regularly! After Katherine's death, Ian sold the farm and opened MacGregor's at the course. There was never a chance that Mary would stay on the farm. After college, MacGregor's Pub offered Ian the chance to maybe keep Mary close for a little longer. As MacGregor's established itself, more and more of Ian's homeland became a part of it. Sure, some of it was just for tourists, at least at first. But, over time, that had dwindled and the pub had become more than a place to eat and drink, it had become home. Ian and Mary had their own apartments, Ian's in the basement of the pub and Mary's out in the old stone section by the wheel. They each had enough space to live their lives in a little piece of Scotland.

The hills surrounding the course were not unlike Ian's homeland. The forested areas here dwarfed the sparse stands of trees on the ancestral fields that Ian's family had farmed for centuries. Mary had visited once, but preferred the sycamores of home and not returned. There were few relatives left in Scotland, they treated Ian and Mary more as tourists than relatives and Ian no longer felt comfortable there either.

The big change came when Mary went off to college. She could have attended on a scholastic scholarship, but chose a school offering her a chance to play on their golf squad. She was developing into a formidable player when a knee injury brought all that to an end. Not long after college, she came home and began helping her father with the pub.

After that, there was never really any question of who was handling what at the pub. If Ian was the 'businessman' behind the pub, surely Mary was its' soul. She had developed her skills to the point where it was not a business to her any longer, it was her life. She moved through the pub effortlessly. While there were others working at a whole range of jobs, you had a sense that Mary was 'handling' everything, all the time. And it was not at anyone's expense, she brought out the best in everyone and they loved her for it.

Mary returned with the menus. As she handed one to Dan she said, "I've already put your pie in the oven so don't be changin' your order. You just let me know what you want to drink."

Over at the bar Ian offered up the towel yet again. To him, Dan just put his hand up in 'never say die' defiance, to Mary – "Just a coffee please." Cletus was struggling with the menu, not because of the sprinkling of unfamiliar Scottish terms, but because of the proximity of Mary. It wasn't that he had not been around a lot of women for a while, Mary just engulfed you with …

"Cletus this is Mary MacGregor. Mary, meet Cletus Armstrong. Cletus is a fellow traveler headed down that road of life with soooo many twists and turns. He's just trying to decide which route is best."

"Pleased to meet you Miss. Mr. Steele here, Dan, was kind enough to bring me into Jasper and offer me a lunch."

"Well take your time with that menu Cletus. Mr. Steele can point out some things you might like. I've got to get back in there to check on that pie, I don't have a full staff coming in until later. I don't want Mr. Steele, here, complaining about something getting burned. Not good to have people talk about the restaurant that way." As she walked back towards the kitchen, Ian looked over at Dan and just shook his head. No towel this time, just a serious 'I told you so!' look.

~ **5** ~

As Dan and Cletus ate their lunch, the pace of people coming through the pub picked up noticeably. Golfers that had played their rounds in the morning were returning for lunch and others were drifting in that weren't golfers at all. They just liked the food. While there was some drinking at the bar, you had a sense that Ian wasn't going to let anything get started – or he would finish it - quickly. All the locals knew this and it was probably why MacGregor's was so successful. It didn't take long for visitors to learn this either.

The game pie that Dan had devoured was good. It didn't consist of all the traditional ingredients, wild critters with unpronounceable names that you might find in Scotland, but it certainly was not a frozen, chicken pot pie either. Over time, Mary and her cooks had tweaked their recipe to appeal to the local palette, then just for good measure, added a bit of mystery. This was part of the game between Dan and Mary. He would guess at the ingredients and she would, without a definite commitment, shrug off his guess and return to the kitchen to ask the cook. Dan suspected that he had already nailed it, she just wouldn't admit it.

"So, Cletus, what did you think of the ham sandwich?"

"It was really good Dan. How about your pie?"

"Cletus, it was … fair. Too much … paprika!" this just as Mary was passing by the table.

"Noooo." was all she softly said as she swung off in another direction.

"Listen Cletus I have to get into town and find a place to stay before everything fills up. What do you say about staying over until you can get your bus schedule figured out?"

"I don't know Dan ..."

"Listen - I don't mind advancing you a little money. Truth is, I like you and wouldn't mind helping you get things sorted out a bit. Besides, do you fish?"

"Sure Dan, every chance I get." With a smirk to remind Dan of where he'd just been 'camped out'. "Why?"

"Well you know that you have to use the right bait to reel in the fish you're after. Right?"

"Yeah I suppose so. What's that got to do with anything?"

"Well Cletus, I need you to stick close by, so that when I see that fish approaching, you'll jump on the hook. I saw the way Mary looked at you."

Smiling a little sheepishly Cletus said, "Well if it were just a day or two I wouldn't mind. I like it here. I'd like to look around a bit. If I could get some work ..."

"First things first, we gotta find a couple rooms. Things fill up fast on the weekend in a small town like this. The one good thing is that Jasper's not that close to the interstate so we shouldn't have any problem if we get started now."

Dan got up and moved to the bar to pay Ian for the meals. "Ian, you think we'll have any problem getting rooms at Delancy's?"

"No sir. Still too early for most travelers. I can call ahead and check for you if you'd like?"

"Thanks, but we'll just head down there and see what they have. We'll stop by later. Do you have anyone playing tonight?"

"Sorry not tonight. Tomorrow though, we've got some music."

As Dan and Cletus moved to the door to leave, Cletus scanned the room. With a smile, Dan said, "Cletus, she's not going anywhere. She'll be here tonight."

Cletus turned back to Dan, and before Cletus could say anything, Dan told him, "Cletus, now is not the time, or place to be jumping on the hook! Not unless you're the one doing the fishing. I only came down here to golf. You're the one who claimed he knew all about fishing."

Going back through the entryway Dan remembered to stop back by the pro shop.

"Curtis, you been able to fill out the foursome?"

"Not yet sir, it may just be a threesome unless we get a single tomorrow. But seven's a little early for that."

"Here's a thought Curtis. How many caddies do you have here?"

"Not many sir, and they're already booked – you know – the members."

"Well how about this. Suppose I ask you to get me a caddy, and suppose you ask this gentleman here – Mr. Armstrong, – to be my caddy – and just suppose Mr. Armstrong agreed – do you suppose that might work?"

With a smile, Curtis agreed, "You know Mr. Steele I suppose that might just work. If Mr. Armstrong hasn't had a lot of experience caddying, I suppose you could probably show him the ropes, couldn't you?"

"I suppose you're right about that Curtis. See you bright and early in the morning."

As Dan and Cletus went through the doorway out towards the parking lot Cletus confided in Dan. "Dan I really don't know anything about golf."

"Well, the thing is Cletus, anybody you talk to who says he's a golfer is learning something about golf every time he tees it up. If he doesn't believe that then he's not really a golfer. And if he can't admit it, then he's lying – even if it's only to himself. And that's the worst kind of lie."

The car swung out of the parking area and started down the hill. Dan turned to Cletus – "Cletus, tomorrow you'll learn a little about golf, and maybe a little about yourself."

~ 6 ~

Delancy's did have rooms for Dan and Cletus. The huge Victorian house was just off the town square on a quiet side street. While not on the town square proper, you could see all the buildings that did border the square. The courthouse was the largest, and oldest building. It had been rebuilt after the Civil War when the town had been the county seat and still commanded enough attention to warrant spending the money to replace the burned-out relic that had been originally built in the heyday of the farming town. Since then, the county seat had moved to Franklin, which was larger and more prosperous than Jasper. Almost all the town services were now housed in the courthouse.

Across the square from the courthouse was the Methodist church, which really said a lot considering where Jasper was located. But this community was a conglomeration of several waves of immigration and had crested many economic surges that moved through the countryside.

The truth is that Jasper was not doing well. While its' lifeblood had been the many farms and associated businesses, it just wasn't keeping up. Places like the Jasper Country Club were needed because of the work it provided for the residents. While everyone still seemed to be getting by, it was tough. Community planners had a number of ideas, but none seemed to make it out of the planning stage.

Everyone thought the interstate would help out, but it seemed to only carry everyone 'by' Jasper more quickly. Things were changing, not everybody seemed to really grasp it.

Another building facing the square, was Bartlett's Hardware store. Bartlett's had everything. I mean they had it all. Anything. This is where Dan and Cletus were headed after they had checked into Delancy's. Dan had taken a look at Cletus's duffel bag and determined that quick action was necessary.

Golf is a strange sport. It seems to the casual observer, in other words 'non-golfer', that golfers are 'clothing challenged'. There appears to be little difference between a weekend golfer and a scarecrow. Both are sure to frighten birds away, the golfer has the added benefit of being able to scare off small children and unwary adults.

Dan had Cletus try on some appropriate clothing so he could act the part of a caddie. The clothes were more understated than what Dan had brought to wear, and Cletus had to have a comfortable pair of sneakers to wear.

"Dan this is a lot of money you're spending. You sure you want to do this?"

"Listen Cletus, looking the part is most of game. The rest is easy to learn. Believe me, you look the part already. Tomorrow you'll get the details about the game – no problem. But right now, we should get a move on because I'd like to get one of those steaks back at MacGregor's before they're all gone. Trust me, they don't last long."

Cletus changed out of the golf clothes and they hopped back into the Chevy and roared out of town back towards MacGregor's.

The late summer sun was setting earlier now but it still was a sight to see as they climbed back up the hills towards the course. It wouldn't be long before the sycamores started to turn colors with the approaching fall. But they didn't turn like the more vibrant maples and oaks that you see further north. They would still be beautiful in their own right. For now, though, the bark was the attraction. The wide flaps of the outermost bark of the trees were continuing to curl, and as the mottled white and brown bark pulled away from the trunk it began to reveal the light green layer of newer trunk growth. The trees sprawled overhead as they drove up the winding road with large splotches of the sun filtering through their lower limbs. Water was never very far from a sycamore and the light that made it through the leaves created a dazzling display in the water as it tumbled alongside the road down the hill.

As Dan pulled into the parking area he swung wide away from the entry toward the massive wheel on the opposite end of the building. On a balcony reaching out over the stream was Mary, lost in the pools of light on the water bubbling up from the flow beneath the building. The setting sun catching her hair and turning the long, soft, auburn curls a more vibrant red.

Cletus felt guilty for staring, as if he was somehow intruding. Mary never noticed, only realized that soon she had to get back to the restaurant. More customers were arriving, she'd just heard the crunch of tires in the lot and more would surely follow.

Dan could almost taste the steak.

Cletus knew his life would never be the same.

~ Brad Leech ~

~ 7 ~

Dan pulled into a space next to a Cadillac. Man, this was an automobile! He got out and walked around it, admiring it as only a true enthusiast could. He'd read the literature, but his dealership hadn't received any vehicles yet. They were on back order. He knew it would be a while before he could sit behind the wheel of one, so he just drank it in. It was all he could do to keep himself from popping the hood to explore the engine.

As he and Cletus were heading across the main entryway towards MacGregor's, Curtis came out to meet them. "Mr. Steele, I was hoping I'd see you tonight. The two gentlemen I paired you with tomorrow, just came in for dinner. If you'd like, I'll introduce you and your 'caddy' to them."

"Excellent idea Curtis, lead on."

The three of them entered MacGregor's and headed across the room to a table overlooking the patio. Below MacGregor's a spit had been set up on the patio. It was turning slowly as a cook continuously basted the pig rotating on it. There were more tables set up near the spit to accommodate the Friday night crowd that would slowly filter in.

"Excuse me gentlemen, let me introduce you to your playing partner in tomorrows' round. Mr. Steele this is Mr. Robinson and Mr. Jefferies, who like yourself, journey down to Jasper for the occasional round of golf. This is Mr. Steele's caddy, Mr. Armstrong."

With a wink to Dan, Curtis excused himself and headed back to his office.

"Please gents, the name is Dan and Cletus here is more of a companion than a caddy. Just can't call him a golfer yet since he's never swung a club, or so he says."

Jim Robinson stood and shook hands with Dan and Cletus, "Dan, it's Jim. Nice to meet you Cletus. Just to be clear, this fellow here," as he motioned towards Jeffries, "is *my* pigeon, Dave Jeffries." Jeffries chuckled and stood shaking hands. "Jim here treats everyone as fodder for his game. I put up with it only because I'm usually the one pocketing all the money coming off 18."

"I don't care, as long as he takes care of me in the bar afterwards." Chimed in Jim. "But just to show you how wrong he is, Dan, Cletus, what'll you have?"

Dan thought for a moment, "How about a pint of Ian's bitter. Cletus?"

"Well sir ... Jim. Just a draft beer for me."

Jim glared down at Dave, "And of course a Scotch and Soda for you. Be right back."

Dan motioned Cletus over a little closer, "Cletus why don't you head out there and make sure they haven't given our steaks away to anyone else?" As he glanced down toward the spit.

"Sure Dan. What is it I'm asking for? It looks as though they just have a pig roasting out there."

"Well, just do your best. I'm sure you'll find something to your liking. Just tell them to make sure my steak isn't burned to a crisp! I'll be down in a minute."

As Cletus turned towards the doorway to the stairs that led down to the patio, Dan noticed Mary giving some instructions to the cook about the spit. "Great," he muttered out loud to no one in particular, "I'll bet my steak gets burned."

Dan headed off to the bar to help Jim with the drinks. When he reached the bar, he separated his drink from what Jim was collecting and said to him – "Give me a second here. I just want to say hi to Ian. Don't let your food back there get cold." Jim left as Dan sat down.

"So, Ian, how's business, how have you been?"

"Good Dan. How was the trip down?"

"Pretty much the same relaxing drive it usually is. Bumped into Cletus, there", with a nod down towards the patio where Cletus and Mary were talking near the spit. "Seems like a nice young man don't you think?"

"They always do …speaking like a father of course." Said Ian with a similar nod towards the patio. "Her mother, Katie, wouldn't feel that way of course. I don't think Katie ever felt anyone had a bad bone in their body. She could look past anything and find the best in someone. Mary too. You see the way she is around here. This is her place, not mine. As much as she tries to convince herself that she's helping me here, it's the other way 'round." With another nod towards the patio as Mary had turned to speak to group of people that had arrived for the roast.

"We'll talk later Ian. I have do get down there before she ruins my steak!" Ian looked down at the patio, Mary had turned back to Cletus.

As Dan swung by the table he collected Cletus's beer and motioned with the drink towards the patio "The kid's letting my steak burn out there. Be right back."

When Cletus had come down to the spit, he saw there were no steaks anywhere in sight. Just as he began asking the cook about this, Mary appeared by his side, close. "I can see you were expecting something other than this fine pork that Terry here has spent most of the afternoon preparing."

"Well Miss MacGregor, Dan told me there'd be steaks here and not to let his burn."

"First off Cletus, it's Mary …please. And secondly, Dan knows I've always got a couple of steaks in reserve – just for him he believes. Don't spoil it, let him continue with that. I'll get one for you as well and that will really confuse him." She motioned to Terry who left to get the steaks, handing Mary the basting brush.

Grasping for conversation Cletus barged ahead, "Thanks …Mary. This is really nice down here. Do you have this roast often?" …. What a feeble attempt.

Mary was trying hard not to smile, but, "Really, is that the best you've got?"

With that, Cletus had to laugh. Which started Mary laughing.

"I'm sorry Cletus, you look like you're trying so hard. Relax, be yourself, I don't bite."

"It's just been a long day. A lot's happened. All for the good. I started out to just get on a bus and look where I am." As he waved a hand around the patio. "Nothing like this has ever really been a part of my world. I know I can't begin to explain it to you, and maybe you don't want to hear it, but as much as I might envy you for having all this – it's probably not for me. Most of it anyway."

Terry had returned with the steaks and dropped them on the grill alongside the spit, and retrieved the brush from Mary.

"Cletus, I've got to keep circulating with my other guests. We'll talk some more." She moved away from him a bit then turned and said, "Which parts of it are for *yew?*", with just a hint of a smile.

"Kid they're ruining our steaks over there! Look at the flames." As Dan brushed by Cletus on his way to the spit, practically spinning him like a weathervane in a tempest.

Dan calmed down when he saw that Terry had just put the steaks on the grill adjacent to the spit. He began giving detailed instructions to Terry as Cletus stood motionless trying to absorb what had just happened. The slightest hint of a brogue had slipped out and crept into Mary's voice, the first he'd heard from her, making the question seem much more personal.

~ 8 ~

Over dinner, Dan and Cletus got to know Jim and Dave. Dan wasn't interrogating either man, but he learned a great deal about them. In Dan's line of work, it was second nature to learn as much about an acquaintance as quickly as possible. Dan's technique was tried and true. He genuinely wanted to hear what you had to say and made you feel like you could tell him anything.

Jim and Dave had known each other for years. While they had met on a golf course, their friendship had endured all manners of golf course chaos. Their games were similar so neither dominated the other on a regular basis. To Dan they appeared to be successful in their businesses and needed the regular golf routine to keep their lives in balance – just like him. As the dinner progressed, the golf stories got lengthier, more involved and although maybe a little hard to believe, definitely funnier.

In a break in the conversation Cletus glanced at the empty glasses around the table and excused himself to retrieve more from the bar. He hadn't spoken to Ian yet and it was not lost on Cletus that Ian watched over Mary closely – as any father would.

"Mr. MacGregor, could we have another round of drinks? I think you know what everyone is having."

"Just give me a minute Cletus. I can call you Cletus, can't I?"

"Of course, sir. Please"

"Well you'd better be calling me Ian then. I know you're a customer and all, but being around Dan ...well everybody just feels like 'friends' pretty quickly."

"If you don't mind me saying so sir, I'd say the same about Mary, I mean Miss MacGregor, sir." Ian looked up from mixing the Scotch and Soda. "I mean, I see how she is here with everyone, and it seems to me, they mean more to her than just being a paying customer."

"True Cletus, you'd have to be blind to think otherwise – and maybe deaf, too." This as there was some hearty laughter to something Mary had just said to another table full of diners back further in the room.

"As I was telling Dan, earlier, Mary is her mother's daughter. I'm not just saying that because she's my daughter, but the two of them are so much alike. Here look at this." Ian reached up behind the bar and retrieved a small bowl inscribed 'Katherine MacGregor – Women's Champion – Jasper Country Club – 1947 – 204'. He sat it carefully on the bar in front of Cletus. "She tore into golf like everything else in her life. What you don't see here is, that same year the Men's Champion shot 207. The fact is that one of her three scores included a 65 which is only one off the course record. And she played from the back tees – same as the men." I thought by now I'd have a collection of them with Mary's name on them. She was a great golfer, maybe better than Kate. But After Kate died, when Mary was away at school, Mary never played the game the same way. She injured her knee that year but I don't think that had a lot to do with it. Kate and I didn't push her into golf. She'd tag along with Kate. Not just on the course but all over the farm. Our farm was further up the hill beyond the course. She'd sneak out on the course when she thought no one was looking. Of course, everyone here knew. It was probably the worst kept secret. Truth is, even then, everyone loved Mary."

"Well, your drinks are getting warm and I'm sure you don't want to hear me rattle on. Best get back to your table."

Ian turned to put the bowl back up behind the bar and when he turned back Cletus was still there. Cletus was watching Mary at the table with Dan. The look on Cletus's face said it all. Ian and Cletus were going to become more than friends.

~ Brad Leech ~

~ 9 ~

After dinner, Dan and the rest of his foursome moved down onto the patio next to the pond. The cook had cleaned up the spit and others had taken down the dining tables that were scattered across the patio. There were some smaller tables close to the water. The fireflies had come and gone for the season, as had the mosquitoes. There weren't so many bugs that you couldn't sit out and enjoy the warm evening. There were, however, some near the water, drawn by the reflection of the torches on the opposite side of the pond. You could hear a slap every now and then as a trout would rise for the meal. The ever present, steady, plup, plup, plup of the water wheel being more vocal as the rhythm of the activity around the patio and clubhouse quieted down.

Up in MacGregor's, the tables were being cleared and the pub had filled with diners looking for another drink to stretch the evening out a bit more. Ian had a helper on Fridays and Saturdays so things were under control in the Pub. The rest of the staff would clean everything up so it could all happen again tomorrow. Ian looked across toward the pond and saw a couple of groups at the tables in the flickering torchlight.

Dan, Jim and Dave were starting in on the real whoppers now. Cletus was getting a real education about golf. If you thought fishermen were the only ones that talked about the one that got away, you'd be wrong.

From Jim - "I'm telling you Dan, I know that putt was going in the hole. I woulda' had a 79! I know the hole was crowned when they put the cup in! Just wasn't fair!"

From Dave – "Sad thing is. He missed the putt coming back! I'd a bet that was going to happen but nobody would have taken the bet. It was that close!"

Jim chuckled as loudly as the rest. He had learned not to take himself as seriously as he took the game when he was on the course.

To Dan, this was as much a part of the game as anything done on the course. Maybe more. So, he couldn't drive the ball 250 yards or make it spin back 10 yards on a green, but he enjoyed trying, and he enjoyed talking about it afterwards. As he was starting in on his next story, he looked over towards the wheel and saw Mary. He nudged Cletus and asked him to see about one last round of drinks for everyone. They had an early tee time and he wanted to get a good nights' sleep.

Cletus started back towards the clubhouse and noticed Mary over by the wheel. With only a little hesitation, he veered off course towards her. Dan saw, and smiling, dove off into another story.

As Cletus neared, Mary looked up and waved him over to the bench she was sitting on. Her shoes were off and her feet were up on the small table in front of the bench. The wheel was a lot louder over here but it failed to block the sporadic laughter from Dan. The continual flapping sounds of the blades entering the water … Mary looked up at Cletus who was looking out at the wheel before he sat down next to her.

"We tried keeping a pair of swans in here but I think the wheel kept scaring them out of the water. They just didn't like it. So, no swans. The trout love it though. When no one's looking, I drop a line in the water from up there." As she nodded up to a small deck cantilevered out over the water. "I've caught a couple nice trout. Dad likes them once in a while, reminds him of home."

Cletus was lost. Mary was stunning in the light of the partial moon that was just rising. The light was reflecting off the pond. The torches having just been extinguished. Mary noticed him looking at the reflection – "You know this will probably be a harvest moon in a couple weeks. It's the middle of the month and I think we've already had another full moon. Besides, we've lost a couple boys in the pub who have to help now with the harvest on their family's farms. I think a couple of the groundskeepers are also going to be off until all the crops are in. So, it seems to be the right time for the moon."

Cletus could not have agreed more. "I grew up on a farm also. This was the tough part of farming. At least for a kid like me. We didn't have a very big place, but, with just me and my dad it was all we could handle. Long, hot, days to get everything in before it turned rainy in the fall. We worked well past dark sometimes. It was hard, well, just like tonight." As he nodded up at the moon.

Mary quietly chuckled. Cletus was quick to say, "No wait, that didn't come out right. The moon, I meant the moon. The harvest moon I recall was always red and large when it fully rose. It meant that you'd succeeded for another year. It meant your heavy farm work was almost done for the season. You could take a breath." Cletus looked back toward the patio and realized they were alone. Everyone had retreated to the pub.

Mary spoke, "I know what you meant Cletus. I remember the relief my father felt when fall arrived and the backbreaking summer work was behind him. I helped as best I could, but he had some of the local boys working for him so I was spared most the work that I'm sure you did. I don't think Dad was ever cut out to be a real farmer. We did okay, the farm was profitable. But I just don't think it was in his blood. Not like the pub anyway. After my mom passed away there was nothing to keep him on the farm. I'm sure he knew I wouldn't take over. I had other dreams. Places to go. Things to do. But after all that, I came back here. This is my home, I never doubted it. I was, you know, just curious."

Cletus nodded in agreement. He too felt the need to move on, probably never returning.

Mary broke into his thoughts, "Well I've got to call it an evening. Big day tomorrow. It's always busiest on Saturdays. Besides don't you have an early tee time?" With that, she leaned over and gave Cletus a fleeting kiss on his cheek before she grabbed her shoes and headed back up to MacGregor's for a final check to make sure everything was ready for tomorrow.

Cletus didn't move except to turn and watch her climb the stairs. He turned back and looked out across the pond as the moon kept rising up over the sycamores. The wheel kept plup, plup, plupping. 'Peepers' from the nearby fields joining in as a full chorus of night time activity commenced, including an occasional brrrrrupppp from a bullfrog somewhere along the edge of the pond.

~ 10 ~

The pub was starting to clear out. Some diehards wouldn't leave for a while, or until Ian 'excused' them. Dan was left by himself. Jim and Dave had headed back to their motel. They would reconvene in the morning. Dan headed over to the bar and nodded towards the coffee pot sitting on a hotplate behind the bar. Ian reached for a cup, and after filling it and sliding it towards Dan, poured one for himself.

For a moment or two there was an awkward silence until Dan began. "Ian, are things here really going okay?" Ian had expected a comment about Mary and Cletus, and for an instant he thought that was what Dan meant. Realizing Dan meant something else he said "Oh, I thought you meant something else. Looked like it was going okay for Mr. Armstrong." Which he said with a knowing smile. "You mean the pub, don't you?"

Dan had to chuckle for a moment, and nodding toward the patio, "Yeah, that looked like it was going okay." But in a more serious tone, "Jim and Dave back there seemed to think the course is struggling a bit. I think they're here more often than I am, and they say play is falling off on the course."

"Dan, I just run the pub and our business has been good. But you're right. I look out on the course every day and it just doesn't seem to be filled like it used to be. We have a pretty small operation here," motioning around the room with his hand, "nothing like the course. Do you know what it takes to maintain a course? And not just the money, it takes a large crew to do everything out on the course. We have a lot of kids here, and they're good workers, but this time of year they're needed at home on the farms. So, for a while, we'll be stretched thin. It's hard on everyone. The really sad thing is, that when they go off to school, they probably won't return. It's not just the golf course, it's the whole community. The course and MacGregor's need each other. If something were to happen to one, the other wouldn't last long."

"I thought so but I just wanted to hear it from you. I mean, I see some of that at the dealership. Not that times are so bad, maybe it's just a change in how we live. Most kids I meet are rushing off to school, then work – usually in a city, then a family. It's gotta' be hard on a community like yours to watch that happen."

"It is. We take it a day at a time. We work hard. It's all we know."

"Well I didn't mean to strike a sour note, but I was just curious. I know this'll sound strange but this … *place* … means something to me. If you want to know the truth, I'm a terrible golfer." With a smile, he added – "Keep that to yourself. But this place *feels* like it's more than golf. And I've been around enough to know that can be kind of hard to find – *anywhere!*"

Ian smiled, "What you are Dan is a philosopher."

Dan responded with, "Touché."

Ian noticed the kitchen door opening and said to Dan, "En garde, mon ami." As Mary passed thru into the bar area behind Dan.

Dan turned slightly towards a woman further down the bar, to address Mary, and said "Basil!" It came out more like a yell and the woman flinched upward in her seat spilling the drink she held in her hand.

As Mary leaned in close to Dan – "Never!" and continued out through the door towards her apartment.

With that, Dan turned to go and find Cletus, raising a hand in an exiting salute as he crossed the floor, they had an early tee time.

Ian smiled as he watched Dan stalk off. One heck of a car salesman for a philosopher.

Cletus was out in front of MacGregor's. He'd needed some time to think. A lot was happening and he was having a little trouble processing everything. He'd walked around the pond on a path that circled back to the front of the clubhouse. The path wound through some of the larger sycamores that closed in around the clubhouse before following the stream back down the hill. There was a small footbridge across the stream just back from the wheel. The water pushing past the wheel, dropped down into a small pool of water before flowing under the bridge. As Cletus climbed up the rise from the stream to the parking area, the reflection of Mary's light blinked out in the pool. The plupping noise from the wheel was the only sound.

"There you are kid!" We gotta' get a move on, big day tomorrow, early tee time!"

Cletus rallied with "Yeah Dan, big day tomorrow." To himself he muttered 'Today had been a pretty big day also. What would tomorrow bring?'

~ Brad Leech ~

~ 11 ~

Cletus awoke to a thumping noise at his door. Dan rasping, "Kid, get a move on or we'll be late. Kid you awake in there, or what?"

Cletus mumbled back, "Yeah, yeah I'm coming. I'm awake." He got up and opened the door for Dan to enter. Dan had a cup of coffee in each hand. Black. Steaming.

"Here you go Cletus, this'll get you started." Cletus nodded a thank you as he carefully took a sip. "Dan give me a chance to get dressed and shaved and I'll be ready to go."

"Sure kid, meet you down at the car." As Dan moved out the door, fully awake, ready for golf.

Dan went back downstairs and out onto the veranda that engulfed three sides of Delancy's rooming house. There was almost no movement as he looked out towards the square. The sun was now rising a little later in the morning, there was a perceptible, dewy, haze settled across the square. A newspaper boy had thrown a paper up towards the door earlier. Dan retrieved it and settled into a chair to get caught up with what was happening in Jasper while waiting for Cletus. The air was so crisp, almost sweet tasting. The mixture of smells here, so different than the initial impact of asphalt and gasoline around the dealership that was Dan's normal start to his day. The front-page news included a reminder to everyone that the Fall Harvest celebration was only two weeks away and included a schedule of all the events with emphasis on the mid-morning parade. In smaller print, he noticed that there would be a picnic luncheon on the square starting at noon, and a gala supper up at the Jasper Country Club later in the day. Fireworks would follow at both the course and here in town. Hmmph. Too bad he'd miss all this. Sounds like fun.

Cletus came out the door quietly, almost noiselessly in his new sneakers. Yup Dan thought, 'I remember when I'd get a new pair of sneakers, nothing felt like it.'

"So, kid, let's go golfing."

On the way back to the course neither spoke much. For Dan, it was the start of another adventure. Cletus was still trying to wake up.

They pulled into the parking area and Cletus was surprised to see so many vehicles. After they parked, Dan popped the trunk and pointed to his bag. "There you go kid." Cletus stared into the trunk at the misshapen piece of luggage that Dan called 'his bag'. Cletus dragged it out of the trunk as Dan grabbed his golf shoes and moved away from the car towards the clubhouse. Cletus put his arm through the strap and lifted it as he closed the trunk. It was heavy! This was not starting out being as much fun as he thought. By the time Cletus made it through the doorway, Dan had disappeared. He came up to the counter, crashed the bag down on the floor and looked around. No Dan. No Curtis. He looked across at MacGregor's. Open, but no one in sight. A couple of moments later Dan and Curtis came around the corner from the course offices to the front desk.

"Cletus, we're all set here. We just have to go downstairs and check in with the starter. Cletus manhandled the bag back up on his shoulder as they went down the stairs to the starter's desk and checked in to let him know they were at the course. There was a coffee pot on the end of his desk and he motioned that they should help themselves. Dan poured a cup and offered one to Cletus, who shook his head – no. "Dan, my throat is still recovering from the first cup."

Jimmy, the starter, looked at his list and said to Dan, "Mr. Steele, you're playing partners aren't here yet, so you have plenty of time to putt while you wait." As he nodded out in the direction of the practice green.

Dan watched Cletus struggle yet again to get the bag on his shoulder and fight his way through the door. After passing through to the outside Dan said, "Cletus why don't you throw the bag on a cart over there before you hurt yourself."

Cletus mounted the bag on a cart like the others he saw nearby and walked back to Dan. Dan said, "You didn't think I was going to have you lug that thing all over the countryside, did you?"

Cletus laughed, just a little, "Yes, actually, I thought that was exactly what your plan was. It's not that heavy, just a little awkward to get it balanced."

"Now what fun would golf be if you were struggling for a couple hours with something like that on your shoulder?"

Dan had been carrying his golf shoes and sat down on a bench to put them on. He went back inside for a moment to leave his regular shoes with an attendant who would find a locker for him. When he returned, he motioned Cletus to the cart and they moved out towards the practice green. Dan got out and retrieved a couple of balls from his bag and dropped them on the edge of green. "Cletus. First rule of golf – it's a pretty quiet game – at least some of the time. When someone is addressing their ball ...okay ...getting ready to hit the thing, give him a little quiet time. Usually it's not more than a couple of seconds, but it allows him to focus. Seen a lot of chatty golfers, and that's okay with me – just not while I'm swinging. Okay?"

This was about as serious as Dan had been since he met him. "Got it Dan – no talking."

"Well no Cletus, not exactly, just not when … you'll see. It's not a big deal but it affects everyone about the same … you'll see. If you golfed, you'd understand."

Now I'm just gonna' putt a little out here to get the feel of the greens. I haven't been out in a couple of weeks so I just want to loosen up a bit. You know, I forgot to grab a scorecard. Why don't you see if you can find one inside before Jim and Dave show up?"

Cletus nodded and went back to the clubhouse to find a card. On his way back into the building, he met Jim and Dave on their way into the locker room. They'd played yesterday and just needed to change into their shoes before meeting up with Dan. Cletus asked the starter about a card and a pencil which were a little further down the counter from his book and the displays of golf balls you could buy in three packs. Cletus picked up a couple of cards, a pencil, and headed back out the door towards the green. Jim and Dave were close behind and they too began a little putting when they reached the green. Dan had moved further away and was practicing short chip shots onto the green.

~ 12 ~

Jimmy came over to Cletus who was watching Jim putting and told him the foursome should move to the tee box on number 1. The group ahead of them had moved ahead on the hole and they could tee off.

Cletus mentioned this to Jim and walked to Dan and Dave who were on the far side of green chatting, to tell them. Everyone moved to the carts and then proceeded to the nearby teeing area for the number 1 hole.

Jim insisted Dan tee off first. Dan looked down the fairway to see where the golfers were that were playing in front of them. They were well beyond his range so he teed a ball up.

His swing was a little unusual, but hey – it got the job done. He hit it about 200 yards down the right edge of the fairway. Jim and Dave were both impressed. Cletus assumed this was a typical drive for Dan. He watched as Jim and Dave both hit their opening tee shots. Jim was next and he hit a high tee shot that didn't quite match Dan in length, but it was almost exactly in the middle of the fairway. Dave's shot was the longest. His had also been hit higher than Dan's but as Dan explained it was a 'draw' which tended to travel a little further. It had a graceful right to left arcing flight that landed in the fairway and ended up close to the left edge of the fairway.

As they got into their carts Dan yelled out, "Well boys, we've got this one surrounded." And off they went.

On their second shots, everyone hit up near the 100-yard marker on the hole. Dan had pointed out that 100 yards from the greens you'd see red birdhouses on posts along the right edge of the hole set back from the fairway so as not to interfere with the golfers. At 150 yards, the bird houses were white, and at 200 yards the birdhouses were blue.

While both Jim and Dan hit their third shots onto the green, Dave hit his into a sand trap on the right side of the green. After Dave hit it out of the bunker, Dan gave Cletus a quick lesson in how to rake the sand trap after a shot had been played from it.

Dave joked that this took a little sting out of being in the bunker. Normally he'd have to rake it himself. Later he explained that when he and Jim played, they rarely used caddies. They preferred to play a little quicker than most golfers and sometimes a caddy slowed you down.

Not so with Cletus. He got the hang of it very quickly. As play moved from hole to hole he fell into the rhythm of what was expected of a caddy. He couldn't recommend any club selections because he'd never swung a club, but his opinions on yardage in spots that were out of range of the birdhouses appeared to be extremely accurate. All three of the golfers had played long enough to be very consistent with the distance they hit their iron shots. If they weren't comfortable with their own estimates about distances, Cletus removed all doubts with his.

Dan was impressed. He wouldn't tell Cletus, but Cletus would have made a great caddy. He had quickly adapted to the activities you'd expect from a caddy around the greens. Holding the pin when needed, standing in spots that didn't distract the golfers, and being quiet.

Cletus had thought Dan was kidding about being quiet, but he saw what Dan meant when the competition started heating up between Jim and Dave. While all three of the golfers were competing against each other, you could see that, between Jim and Dave, there was a little extra ferocity in their match against each other.

When they approached the tee box for number 8, a little trash talking started between them. Jim told Dan he was getting a little thirsty. Dan agreed, he told Jim he'd take care of some drinks when they came to the clubhouse after the ninth hole. Jim told him not to worry, Dave would have it covered. By Jim's calculations both he and Dan had lower scores up to this point than Dave. All this occurred as Dave was teeing up his ball on the par 3 hole. Jim and Dan had already hit. Their balls were clearly visible on the green. After Dave swung, his wasn't. "On the beach" was all Jim said as he marched back to the cart. Dave had a scowl as he passed by Cletus and slumped into the cart alongside Jim. "Asshole" was all Cletus heard as their cart roared by him as he waited for Dan to get in their cart.

Sure enough, when they walked off the number 9 green and approached the clubhouse, it was Dave who asked what everyone wanted to drink. They pulled their carts up near the patio and climbed the stairs up to it. There were umbrellas opened above all the tables on the patio. Dan, Jim and Cletus dropped down onto the seats of a table while Dave went off to get a round of large lemonades. He came back shortly and the group enjoyed their drinks. There was a steady movement of golfers on the course. They stayed at their table and let the group that had been playing behind them, pass on through to the number 10 tee box. Nobody here was in a big rush to finish playing golf. They would try and drag it out as long as possible without slowing down the play on the course. They had already let a twosome play through earlier.

~ Brad Leech ~

~ 13 ~

When they finished, they moved back out onto the tee box at number 10. This brought them around to the 'hillier' half of the golf course. You could look up and see the holes woven around clumps of trees on the hillside. Number 10 was an uphill par 4 that doglegged to the right around a clump of the trees.

Jim teed off first, followed by Dan and finally, Dave. All three hit good shots that carried up to the dogleg. No one was able to get their second shots onto the green. Dave had come up short in front of the green, Dan was right of the green, and Jim found himself in a sand trap on the right side of the green.

As they came up to where Dan's ball had been hit, Cletus noticed another ball lying in the rough only a couple yards from Dan's ball. Dan got out of the cart and joined Cletus in looking at the ball. As he looked up he saw a group of golfers playing number 12 which was a dogleg left hole, coming down the hill towards them. The green for number 12 was about fifty yards away, uphill. One of the golfers motioned with his arm to get their attention and let them know it was his ball. Dan and Cletus walked back to Dan's ball and waited while Jim and Dave both played their shots onto the green.

Dan chopped his ball out of the rough nicely and had only about a twelve-foot putt to score a par. As they were preparing to putt, a cart from the group playing number 12 approached the green and stopped. They remained seated while everyone putted. Dan missed his par putt as did both Jim and Dave. They walked off the green over to the cart that had pulled up.

"Judge, I thought I saw you out there ahead of us." Said Jim as he approached the cart and shook the driver's hand. The Judge nodded in Dave's direction and said, "Nice to see you too Dave. I see Robby fixed you up with another twosome."

Jim introduced Dan and Cletus, the Judge introduced his cart mate, Bill Morgan. Everyone quickly shook hands, but nobody was immediately behind either group.

The Judge got out of the cart and picked his ball up. Jim said to him, "You should play it from here and save the penalty stroke."

The Judge said, "No I'll take my medicine and drop it back where it crossed out of play on the edge of the fairway. Cletus had noticed the red stakes placed between the two greens to indicate that shots played past the stakes on either hole were considered to be in a lateral hazard which incurred a penalty. This area was often wet with water draining from the course which was why the grass was so thick.

"I'm not that good with my wedge in this thick stuff." He said with a mock frown towards Bill. "It takes some strength in the forearms to really muscle it out of here." He pointed to where his ball had been. "Besides I've held your game up enough already."

Jim looked around and said, "No one's pressing us. Come on, give it a try. Just to see if you can. Go back and drop a ball in the fairway after you try, use it for your score."

The Judge dropped it into the deep grass. He used a wedge on his attempt. The ball went about twenty yards, remaining in the thick rough between the two greens.

"See." was all he said to Jim.

Jim dropped a ball into the rough. He pulled a wedge from his bag and attempted the shot. It went about fifteen yards. Dave started laughing. Jim said to him, "Hey, the Judge is right, this stuff is thick in here. The shot is harder than it looks!"

Dave wouldn't let it drop. This was his first opening to take a dig at Jim that he'd had in a while.

"You know Jim, I'll bet that Cletus here could hit a better shot than that. What do you say Cletus, do you want to give it a try?"

Cletus looked at Dave, "Dave I'm no golfer."

Dan had been watching Cletus, "Come on kid give it a shot. If you do better, Dave will never let Jim hear the end of it." Dan took a ball from his pocket and dropped it into the grass. He went to the cart and came back with a pitching wedge and handed it to Cletus.

Cletus gripped the club lightly, he turned to address the ball to get it headed in the general direction of the hole. There was no waggling around, no practice swings, no real movement of any kind. Except the swing …Swiiiiick!

The ball lifted cleanly out of the grass, flew up high, straight toward the pin on number 12. It plopped down softly on the green and rolled to within a foot of the hole.

The others were stunned. For several moments, no one said anything. Jim's mouth was open. Dave just stood there shaking his head. The Judge was staring at Cletus as was Bill. Dan was looking at Cletus not in awe, but ….trying to process something else. The way Cletus had swung the club. It was not … Well it wasn't a golf swing at all. It was …Then it came to him. He smiled.

"Great shot kid!" said Dan breaking the silence. The other two golfers on the number 12 green applauded.

Jim said, "One incredibly lucky shot. I can't believe it. Fantastic shot." And then he made a mistake.

"I'll bet you can't do it again!" he said, laughing.

Dan waited a moment, "You're on. Five bucks!"

Dave was quick with, "I'll take that bet too. Five bucks also."

The Judge and Bill were laughing, how would this play out?

Cletus said, "Hey, I don't want to risk anybody's money. That wouldn't be right."

The Judge said to Cletus, "It's just a friendly bet Cletus. Let them have a little fun. Personally, I'd just like to see that swing again. Come on son, give it a try." Bill agreed also.

Dan retrieved another ball from the cart and dropped it in the grass.

Cletus looked at Dan, Dan gave him and wink and said, "Come on kid, take a whack at it!"

As before, Cletus turned back toward the ball and swung at it with a flicking motion. Swiiiiick! The ball rose up cleanly from the grass, arcing up into the air toward the green and hit a couple of inches from the other ball laying there. It rolled up to the edge of the hole and stopped.

Well, now the hooting and hollering really began. The Judge just shook his head in amazement, Bill was still processing what he'd just seen.

Dan really got everyone going when he said to Cletus, "I thought you said you weren't a golfer kid. How long have you been playing?"

Cletus was still looking at the two balls on the green when he said, "Never Dan, I've never swung a golf club until now."

Now there was disbelief. In the confusion, the other two golfers came down from the green. The Judge introduced them to everyone. Steve Kennedy and Ed Timmons were lawyers that knew the Judge. He'd invited them to play a round with him. Everyone quieted down and said they'd meet in MacGregor's after the round to carry this discussion further. There was a group coming up number 10 and they all realized that they would be holding up play if they stayed there any longer.

As Dan and Cletus rode up to the next tee, Dan said to him, "Quite some shots kid. The swing looked a little unorthodox, but mine looks worse." Then he continued with a smile, "But I didn't have the advantage you've had – whacking all those weeds on the side of the road!"

~ 14 ~

As Dan and his foursome headed from the final green back into the clubhouse, Curtis came out to meet them. "Mr. Steele, might I have a word with your 'caddy'?" Dan turned to Cletus and said "Cletus, we're going to the locker room to change and clean up. We'll meet you upstairs in a bit."

Curtis motioned Cletus back towards the stairs, Cletus followed him back to the front desk. When they got there, Curtis reached beneath the upper ledge of the desk that faced Cletus, to retrieve a handful of money. He gave this to Cletus, saying, "Here's the caddy fee that Mr. Steele insisted you receive for helping him with his round of golf. I thought you'd like to receive it privately."

Cletus was stunned. Looking at the money, he saw five, crisp, ten-dollar bills. Without hesitation, he handed it back to Curtis. "I can't accept this Curtis, it wouldn't be right!"

"Cletus, Dan said you'd say that. That's why he gave it to me to give to you. He thought I'd be able to convince you to keep it."

"Curtis, what do caddies usually earn when they 'work' for a golfer like I just did?"

"Well Cletus, carrying a single bag, eight dollars. If they carry double, like some of the bigger boys do, twelve dollars. Then there's the tip. Unless they've done something really unforgiveable, most golfers add a five or ten-dollar tip."

"You see Curtis, that's the problem. I don't think I earned any of that." As he nodded to the money Curtis was holding. "Look, here's what I think we should do. I noticed on the bulletin board downstairs, just outside the locker room, that you have a caddy scholarship fund. Why don't we just put the money there?"

"Well Cletus, I don't think that's what Dan had in mind, but if that's what you want – I'll see that the money gets there. This is really very generous, thank you."

"Curtis I'm sure this is the best way of handling it, and – can we keep this between ourselves? Dan's already been very kind to me – I don't want to risk doing anything he might think is an insult – okay?"

"Mr. Steele won't hear anything from me!"

"Thanks Curtis" Cletus said shaking his hand. "I gotta catch back up with my foursome." He turned and went back down the stairs towards the locker room. He passed Dan, Jim and Dave who were headed to MacGregor's. Cletus said he'd join them as soon as he'd washed his hands.

Curtis turned to look out at the course through the windows behind his desk. It was close to noon time and, as some of the golfers coming off the course were making their way to the clubhouse for lunch, a couple of the groundskeepers were also stopping work for lunch. Curtis strode down the stairs to catch up with them. He called out to Jeff – "Jeffrey!"

Jeff turned to him, "What's up Curtis?"

"Jeffrey if you see Teddy, could you have him stop by if he can. There's something I need to discuss with him."

"Sure Curtis, I just saw him a couple of minutes ago, I'm sure I can catch him before he goes back out on the course." And Jeff rushed off towards the tables outside the maintenance building that the other workers were eating at.

Curtis went back up to his desk to help the golfers just arriving for their afternoon tee times. Most went straight down to the locker room. Others veered off into MacGregor's, which was filling up fast. He looked back towards the course, and spotted Teddy trudging across from the maintenance building.

Steve Trasker was the course foreman, responsible for everything happening out on the course. He'd been here longer than Curtis, and was a fixture on the course. He managed an ever-changing crew that consisted mostly of seasonal workers – boys really – full of energy and not afraid to work some long, hot, hours before returning to school in the fall. Each day the course woke up when Steve arrived. He did not live nearby, he had almost a thirty-minute drive to get to the course. By example, he knew that if he could make it here on time, so could everybody else. And they didn't disappoint him.

He was over six feet tall, with massive forearms and a ruddy outdoorsman's complexion. While he was somewhat 'barrel chested', there was not an ounce of fat in his body. When there was work to be done, he was usually right in the middle of it. He led by example. But, he was beginning to slow down a little. All the years of working such a physical job were starting to take their toll. That, and the fact that he had twin teen aged daughters. His wife Mavis would prefer that he find ways of spending a little more time with them before they were gone – off on their own, in school, then to who knows where?

He couldn't disagree, he was trying. It was just hard to back away from something you had done for so long, and enjoyed as much as he did.

When Steve had brought Mavis to their first 'employees' cookout so many years ago, she had yelled over to him using her pet name for him – 'Teddy'. That was all it took. No one called him Steve after that. Not that it bothered him, he did look a little like a big Teddy Bear.

He came up the stairs and turned to Curtis. "Curtis? Jeff said you needed something."

Curtis said, "Just a quick word with you. I know you probably want to get right back out there."

"Yeah, I'm working along the creek, up by the shed on number 14. I need to keep working on that mess."

"I won't keep you long, but there's someone here I think you should meet." With that, he pulled Teddy in tow across the entryway towards MacGregor's, speaking quietly with him as they walked along.

~ 15 ~

Curtis and Teddy walked into MacGregor's. Curtis motioning Teddy over towards a large table with a waitress taking an order from eight people. Chief amongst them was Dan. He had already started in about the round that *just barely* slipped away from him today. Dan paused when he saw Curtis approach the table, "Curtis, I hope I wasn't getting too loud over here. Looks like you've bought the bouncer in to throw me out!"

There was a long pause as everything became quiet. Cletus was just beginning to get a little uncomfortable when Dan rose and said – "Teddy. I didn't see you out there. You sleep in this morning?" With that everyone broke into laughter, Cletus managed a smile.

Teddy's frown broke into a broad grin as he shook Dan's hand. "Mr. Steele, nice to see you again. I thought I heard a ball rattling around the trees out there on number 15."

Curtis said, "Mr. Steele do you think we could borrow your 'caddy' here," nodding towards Cletus "for a couple minutes? It looks as though your meals won't arrive for a while yet."

"Sure Curtis." Said Dan. "I'm only on hole number 3 'here'" as he waved around the table. "The really good stuff didn't start happening until number 8."

Cletus was still a little confused but got up and moved away from the table to follow Curtis and Teddy out the door. Curtis led the procession down the stairs and out on the patio to sit at an empty table.

He motioned to Cletus and Teddy to sit down with him and he began with Teddy. "Teddy, meet Cletus Armstrong – Cletus, meet Teddy Trasker. Actually, his name is Steve although I've never heard anyone actually call him Steve."

Teddy chuckled, "Teddy will do just fine Cletus." Teddy shook Cletus's hand and received the same firm grip that he, himself, always put into a handshake.

"Nice to meet you Mr. Trasker." Said Cletus somewhat cautiously.

Curtis began. "Teddy, Cletus here just caddied for Mr. Steele this morning. My guess is that won't happen again, will it Cletus" as he added a smile.

Cletus returned the smile and said, "Not likely."

Teddy spoke next, "Curtis here didn't think you really looked like a caddy. Not that we don't have some caddies older than most of the lads out there." As he motioned towards the course. "The thing is, we already have enough caddies. Curtis thought you might be suited to my line of work 'out there'." As, once again, he motioned to the course. "You strike me as someone who's spent some time outdoors and aren't afraid to get yourself dirty. Am I wrong?"

Cletus answered, "No sir, you're not wrong. I'm certainly not a caddy. I enjoyed it out there with the others this morning, but that's all. I'm not a golfer either. I've bumped into Mr. Steele and he seems to think I'd learn to like the game the way he loves it. You really do have a nice course here, not that I know much about a golf course. But it does seem that it was designed to be a part of the land and not an intrusion upon it. I see that, further up the hill, you have some hardwoods that could have been cleared out, but were left intact. Seems as though someone here really takes care of things like that." This last bit was said looking directly at Teddy.

Teddy liked this young man. He returned the look at Cletus and said "Why don't you come in here first thing Monday morning. I'll have some time to show you around and you'll see what we do. But if you want to work for me you have to call me Teddy." With that he rose to shake Cletus's hand again. "I've got to get back out there. I want to keep working on 14. Nice meeting you Cletus. Six o'clock Monday." With that he started to walk back towards the maintenance building but did turn back to yell, "Thanks Curtis" to Curtis.

Curtis and Cletus got up. Cletus managed to say "Thanks" to Curtis also as they headed back inside the clubhouse.

~ Brad Leech ~

~ 16 ~

Mary had just come out of the kitchen and noticed her father looking down at the patio. She heard him mumble "Wish I could read lips." He saw her looking at him and nodded downward towards the three people sitting at the table.

Mary looked down and saw Curtis, Teddy and Cletus. While she watched, everyone stood, shook hands and left the table. Curtis and Cletus were coming back inside. She stood there for a couple moments more, and without saying a word, went back into the kitchen.

Ian turned back towards the bar. This wasn't that complicated, was it? He didn't need to be able to read lips. This seemed pretty straightforward didn't it? Then he recalled the look on Mary's face and thought, 'Yeah, this is getting complicated'. But he smiled anyway, he liked Cletus too.

~ Brad Leech ~

~ 17 ~

Dan's morning exploits were still the topic of discussion when Cletus returned to the table. Dan finished and turned to Cletus, "They didn't see you swinging that club out there, did they? Try to charge you for a round of golf instead of paying you to caddy, did they?"

Cletus turned to Dan and said, "No Dan they didn't catch me golfing. Curtis paid me. And I told him I'd never caddy again. It's not that it's hard work or anything. It's just tough watching someone struggle like you did out there with your game." Cletus said seriously as he winked toward Jim and Dave who sat across the table. Then his face broke into a wide smile as everyone began laughing, including Dan.

Their meals had been delivered earlier, everyone but Cletus had finished. Dan pushed himself from the table to excuse himself, he needed a coffee and didn't want to wait for the waitress to return. The dining area was filled, but there were fewer people waiting to be seated. He walked up to the end of the bar and nodded toward the coffee pot. Wordlessly Ian poured a cup and sat it in front of Dan. There were only a few people at the bar. Most were just picking up something to take out on the course for their afternoon round. When the noontime crowd finally thinned out there would only be a short lull before the afternoon rush began and after that, the dinner crowd.

Dan said somewhat vaguely to Ian, "Well, I guess things may be working out okay. What do you think?"

Ian said, "I agree, maybe things are working out."

Ian took a sip of coffee from the ever-present cup that was in front of him. "Seems a little strange though. Curtis and Teddy seemed to think that Cletus might be the man for a job around here. A job requiring somebody to do some hard work outdoors. Wonder how they'd get that idea? Somebody would have to know a little about that young man over there." Said Ian as he nodded back towards the table.

Dan said, "Well I don't know about that, but Curtis has always impressed me as someone with good 'people skills', someone who could size up someone else pretty quickly. You ever get that impression?"

Ian began carefully, "Yesss …now that you mention it. That probably is one of Curtis's strong points. He meets all sorts of people at the desk. Some are real characters I imagine."

"I Imagine so." Was all Dan said as he got up and headed back to the table.

Their table was far enough back into the room so that you could also look back out towards the parking area. As he neared the table, Dan let out a quiet, low whistle. "Boys will you look at that!" Most heads turned, but not all. "That is some sweet machine!" A pure black colored Corvette had pulled up into the reserved parking just outside the front door. Dan was mesmerized while a woman in a tennis outfit extricated herself from the two-seater. Her hair was blonde, almost as white as the tennis outfit. This was a golf club, but hey, you had to love tennis too. Dan lost sight of her before he turned back to everyone else and sat down at the table.

Jim said with a smile, "Dan I'm going to stop you right there."

A puzzled look crossed Dan's face. Before he could ask the question, the Judge, who had not turned to look out the window said simply, "Obviously, Claire has arrived."

As Dan was taking this in, everyone around the table made moves to rise while Claire Townsend joined the table. She passed by the Judge who remained seated giving him a quick peck on the top of his head saying, "Daddy", while she headed to the end of the table opposite Dan. Dan tipped his chair backwards somewhat as he tried to jump to his feet. Cletus caught the chair before it hit the floor.

At the bar, Ian was doing all he could not to laugh, 'Yes' he said to himself 'Claire has arrived.' He had seen this so often, it had turned into one of his favorite forms of entertainment. Let's see who would fold next at the table. Dan had been predictable. But he hadn't even seen her coming. Most of the others at the table already knew Claire – so nothing to be gained by watching them. Cletus was the only real question; how would he react?

The Judge introduced Dan and Cletus to his daughter, everyone else had already met her. Cletus just said a simple "Nice to meet you ma'am."

'Very impressive' thought Ian.

Dan paused, before starting to say something, jusssst enough to lose the momentum …

Claire started in with, "And you Mr. Steele must be the owner of that very nice, red, Bel Air parked out there. Aren't you? Please call me Claire … everyone." As she looked around the table.

Ian came out to Claire's side and sat a club soda with a slice of lime in front of her. "Afternoon Claire", was all he said.

"Ian, thank you. It is a beautiful day, isn't it? If Mary is around, we need to talk. I just wanted to stop by and say hi to daddy and his friends."

Ian said, "She's in the kitchen. I'll let her know you're here." And he left to find her.

Claire continued, "Gentlemen, I can't stay, but Jim, Dave - We are planning on talking a little later aren't we? Mary and I have a couple things to finalize about the dinner here during the festival.

Then I thought we'd discuss our business, I'll come find you after I've talked with her, okay?"

They both nodded 'okay', Dave said "Sure Claire, we'll be outside when you're done with Mary."

Claire spotted Mary heading her way after exiting the kitchen. She stood and said "Gentlemen nice seeing you all again. Cletus nice meeting you. And, Mr. Steele, nice meeting you too. Maybe you'd like to take a closer look at her?", Nodding toward the Corvette and dropping the keys on the table in front of him. "Being a lover of convertibles I'm sure you're curious about how she handles." And with that she was off.

Ian was laughing at the bar, Claire never disappoints.

At the table, everyone was staring at Dan. Before he could say a word, the Judge said, "I know how you're feeling right now. No need to say anything. Everyone else here except Mr. Armstrong has gone through this."

Cletus could not help himself, "Dan, it's okay, you can breathe." Which is where everyone lost it and began laughing … except Dan.

There were few things and fewer people that had ever caused Dan to fumble for words. Claire was one of those people.

~ 18 ~

Mary walked with Claire out through the entrance to MacGregor's and crossed into the office area in the clubhouse. Claire had an office just down the aisle past Curtis's desk. They entered the room, Mary closed the door and they both settled onto the couch. Mary had brought much of the paperwork she'd prepared concerning things that had to happen for the festival dinner.

She said to Claire, "So, what do you think of him? He's pretty cute, isn't he?"

Claire responded, "Mary he's adorable. He's everything you ever said he was."

Mary was confused. "Claire, I just met him yesterday, what are you talking about?"

After a momentary pause, they both started laughing.

Claire Townsend had been Mary's mothers' closest friend when growing up in Jasper. She was a little younger than Katherine, but not much. You could say the years had been kind to her. But it was earned. She worked hard at everything she did, and played just as hard. She was no golfer but excelled at everything she tried. She had married quite young – to an equally young businessman – Charles Townsend. He and the Judge had purchased the golf course from the previous owners. Charles was the minority owner with forty percent of the ownership, while the Judge owned the other sixty per cent. It was a good arrangement. Charles ran the course, while the Judge continued his career within the court system.

Unfortunately, Charles had died in an auto accident not long after Mary's mother passed away. They had not had any children. They both led such busy schedules. They just thought they'd have time 'later' for children. She thought of Mary more as a niece or maybe a younger sister. She had never really been a part of the business at the course but threw herself into the Jasper Chamber of Commerce. She was a natural. She could work with people and develop connections amongst them to everyone's advantage. She was a big part of the reason that Jasper had held itself together like it had. You would not have guessed it based on her actions, but there really wasn't any room in her life for men. She had turned flirting into an art form. And she enjoyed it. Not all women know what they do to men. She knew it and had fun with it.

Currently she was working on something really big, maybe her biggest deal ever. If she succeeded, Jasper would be so much better off. And not just in the immediate future. There would be long lasting effects for the entire community.

Mary started with, "Okay Claire, enough about men. Let's talk turkey. How many do we need? What's the estimate up to for attendance at the dinner?"

"Mary, so far out of four hundred invitations I've got about two hundred thirty positive responses. Can we handle that many people?"

"I think so." responded Mary "We've had as many as three hundred fifty people here for other events." Mary was doing some quick math in her head. "The big problem, is anything we have to bake. We have limited oven space so the turkey is the big question. Is everybody indicating turkey, or do they want steaks?"

"Right now, Mary, it's pretty evenly split."

"Good. We'll keep the full barbecue set up outside and reserve the kitchen just for the turkeys. We just have to hope the weather holds up or it could be a problem with the steaks and the side dishes. I'm thinking, though, that I could ask Teddy to move everything out of the maintenance building for the day so we could move the barbecue inside at the first sign of rain. We'll just have to wait a little longer for the forecast."

Claire said, "Okay, I think this is moving ahead pretty well. We can handle it, no need to panic just yet." With that they both laughed, just a little.

"Now", Claire said, "Let's talk about Cletus. I agree, he is cute. What do you know about him?"

"Well" Mary said, "Dan dragged him in here yesterday … and there's just something about him …. I don't know."

Claire asked, "Is that an 'I don't know' and *maybe* I'll find out. Or an 'I don't know and I *really* want to find out!'"

Mary thought for a moment, "I *really* want to find out!"

"Me too." Chimed Claire – "About Mr. Steele that is. Maybe he's got his breath back by now." She said as she got up to leave.

Mary laughed. You just had to like Claire. Maybe Dan would also.

~ Brad Leech ~

~ 19 ~

The golf conference in the dining room had broken up. Jim and Dave had headed outside to the patio while Dan and Cletus followed the Judge and his playing partners out into the parking lot. His partners wandered off to their cars while the Judge, Dan and Cletus hovered over the Corvette. Dan had the keys. He was going to just leave them with Ian but Cletus encouraged him to go out to the car and start it so they could hear how the engine sounded. With the Judge standing beside him he was reluctant to sit in the car and start it up. The Judge gave him enough of an indication to start it – without saying anything.

Dan squeezed himself into the car, but had to slide the seat back a bit to clear the wheel. When Dan turned the key, and touched the gas pedal, it roared to life! As the car settled back into an idle, Dan just beamed. What a car! His dealership had sold some, but he had always enjoyed the "bigger" ride, so he let the younger salesmen deal with the sportier cars.

Cletus and the Judge stood silently watching Dan with the car. Finally, the Judge said, "You should take it down the hill and get it out on the road if you want a real thrill!"

Dan turned the car off. Got out and said to the Judge, "Maybe later. She's a beauty all right but I'd hate to be driving someone's car and have anything happen."

"Well suite yourself Dan." Was all the Judge could say, but he added "She can be a little temperamental so be careful if you do take her out on the road!" The Judge winked at Dan as he moved towards his Lincoln parked in the shade out near the maintenance building.

Dan and Cletus headed back inside to leave the car keys with Ian. They walked up to the bar, and Dan looked down at the table with Jim, Dave, Claire – and Mary standing there with a tray containing some drinks. Ian looked over at Dan, Cletus having joined him, looking downward also – 'This end spot by the window was getting crowded.' He thought to himself.

Dan turned back to Ian and said, "Here's Claire's keys. I figure this'll be the first place she checks." As he handed the keys to Ian who placed them behind the bar.

"Dan, it's not the first time she's left them here." Ian said to Dan, not with a wink or a chuckle but just a simple man to man statement. Obviously, Claire meant more to Ian than just a long friendship with Mary's mother. Dan knew this without being told. He turned to Cletus and said, "Hey kid, do me a favor and take Claire's keys down to her for me." Cletus nodded and took the keys from Ian. A polite dismissal that Cletus was only too happy to comply with. "Sure." Ian and Dan watched as he walked off.

Dan spoke first, "Listen Ian if I've …" Ian cut him off with a raised hand. Quietly Ian said, "Not needed." Emotionally he continued. "Claire is one of the first friends that I made when I came here." Moving his hand outwards towards the course. "She was not only Kates' best friend, but has remained my closest friend. It's a friendship I'll always have. I wouldn't risk it by letting it become anything else. I think she feels the same way. Mary probably wanted it to become more, but she's past that now. Look at the two of them down there and tell me they're not sisters!"

Dan looked back to the patio and studied the two of them. Their body movements confirmed what Ian had said. They had a closeness and easy way of being near each other that you don't often see in women that aren't sisters.

As Cletus approached the table, Claire gave Mary an almost imperceptible nudge, a communication – 'Here he comes'.

Dan turned back to Ian. "What's going on out there Ian? I met Jim and Dave and played with them this morning, but they didn't mention anything about any business meeting. You have any idea about this, anything you can say?"

"Well Dan I know a little. But you should ask Claire, or maybe your playing partners out there. They have something in the works that they want to bring to the festival … well the dinner that we're putting on here the week after next. I don't know much more than that. Don't get fooled by her though, she's a shrewd businesswoman.

~ Brad Leech ~

~ 20 ~

Mary turned to smile at Cletus as he approached. Cletus handed the keys back to Claire and said, "She's really some car Miss Townsend."

Claire said, "Did you and Dan take it out on the road?"

"No. Dan said he'd wait and maybe you'd take it out with him when you're done here, if you have the time. He's upstairs now with Mr. MacGregor. He asked me to come down with your keys and give you the message so he wouldn't miss you." They turned to look up at MacGregor's. Dan was standing in the window, he just raised his coffee cup in a salute. Cletus nodded back at him and smiled.

Mary was watching Cletus, watching him smile. She loved his smile. This one appeared to be a little bit mischievous. She turned to Cletus and said, "Cletus, we should let them finish their business here. Come on back up to MacGregor's with me."

Claire stood up, as did Jim and Dave and said, "Dave, Jim, I think we're all set here. Aren't we? I know we still have more work, but that can wait. We can talk on the phone until you're back again next week. How's that?"

"That works for me." was all that Dave said.

Jim added, "I may not be able to make it next week, but I'm sure we can settle everything else on the phone that we're currently facing."

As everyone left the patio, the kitchen staff began setting up the equipment they'd need for the evening cook out. They weren't using the spit tonight, just the wide grilling pit covered with racks to put chicken, fish and steaks on. There were still some golfers coming off the course, but most had finished their round. Some would make the trek back up the hill later tonight for the cookout.

Jim and Dave excused themselves so they could return to their motel. Neither was staying over to Sunday. They had traveled down to Jasper together and both needed to return home.

Claire, Mary and Cletus came back into MacGregor's and approached Dan who was still chatting with Ian at the bar.

As Claire came up beside Dan she looped her arm around Dan's arm and said, "I like your idea of a quick spin!" Dan turned slightly towards Cletus and gave him a slight, frowning stare. But he recovered quickly and answered Claire, "I thought we could just take it down on the main road for a couple miles. If that's not going to hold you up?"

Claire responded, "Nonsense. I have plenty of time. I just have to get back home in time to change so I can return here tonight. They're having some music and a cook out. It will be nice. You're staying, aren't you?", as she looked at Dan then Cletus.

Cletus answered for both of them, "Of course we are ma'am. Dan, they're having chicken out on the grill. You wouldn't want to miss out on that, would you?"

Mary was silent but she noticed that Cletus was flashing another smile. And not just at Dan, but her also.

All Dan could manage was, "Of course kid. I noticed you had a pretty good time here last night, down by the grill too."

Cletus's broad smile eased back into a slight grin as Marys' face flushed a little.

Dan continued, "Don't wander too far off while I'm gone Cletus. Because we gotta' get out of these golf clothes too. Nobody wants a stinky golfer hanging around them."

With that, Dan left MacGregor's with Claire on his arm. Mary went back into the kitchen with her tray leaving Cletus and Ian at the bar.

Ian quietly said to Cletus, "I know those two." nodding out towards the Corvette "They won't be back for a while. Why don't you go downstairs and ask Robby, who handles the locker room, for a towel? He'll show you where everything is down there. You look a little uncomfortable and I thought just a quick clean up would make you feel a little better."

Cletus said, "Thanks Ian, I would like to wash up. Dan's right, nobody wants a stinky golfer around them. A stinky caddy either."

Ian continued, "Besides, if you're going to be working here, you need to know your way around and meet everyone."

Cletus looked at Ian. Ian was quick with, "Cletus it's a small business. Everybody pretty much knows everything about everyone else. It's a family. Probably the biggest reason it's lasted this long. I can't speak for Teddy, but I think you'll fit in. Now, get down there, get cleaned up a little, and come on back up here. We'll talk some more."

~ Brad Leech ~

~ 21 ~

Claire and Dan came down the hill scattering gravel each time she turned the wheel. At the end of the drive she naturally swung out to the right before stopping at the main road. She had done this thousands of times. She muttered, "Just wish that tree wasn't right on top of this intersection." She turned and pulled out onto the paved road and continued to head east, away from Jasper.

Dan studied her. She was a smooth driver. She handled the car effortlessly. When she got on the gas a little, for Dan's benefit, the roar of the engine increased noticeably. They were flying. Claire's hair was swirling around, the soft blonde curls of hair bouncing against her cheeks. She came up on a curve pretty quickly but barely decelerated as she downshifted and guided the car through the curve without any tire noise or moving out of the lane. Her movements were precise, she was in command of the car.

She said, "I don't like to drive really fast, but I know men, and they like to go fast."

Dan replied, "Speed's okay. But to me, it's the way the car handles. I've had a lot of cars, and the ones I've liked the best have been smooth handling cars. The car's got to be built with a lot of things done right, to provide a really good ride. I mean, you can have a great engine, such as this one, but the suspension, the steering, the tires – the way the weight's distributed – all of it has to be just right ….for the ride.

She had eased back on the gas and they were just cruising now as the fields blurred by. They were continuing east along some bottom land. There were some crops along the strip of land between the creek and the roadway, but not like the fields they'd just come past. The land here was more undulating and the car bobbed over the rises in the road.

They had driven over twenty miles in what seemed like no time at all to Dan when Claire eased off the car and they pulled into a roadside 'rest stop' that was on just enough of a rise so that you could look across the creek to the northeast and more farmland. There were more buildings in the distance, obviously, a small village or cluster of businesses.

Claire turned the car off and they studied what was laid out before them.

Claire said to Dan, "Isn't it beautiful out there? As she motioned to the wider plain beyond the creek. "It's some of the best farmland in this part of the state. Over to the east there's Bingley. It's not much of a town, smaller than Jasper actually. But the people are the same. Mostly farmers. Some with cattle, most are dairy farmers. We have some farmers growing cash crops but most have stuck with dairy farming. Too bad though, this land would be perfect for crops that do well in this type of soil – it's really rich soil – it could support onions, lettuce, carrots – even potatoes and tomatoes up on the sides of the valley where it's a little drier."

Dan spoke to her, "Sounds like you've given this more than a little thought." Turning to face her a little more directly he said, "What are you going to do about it?"

She turned to him with a smile, "Jim was right. You're a lot more than a car salesman, aren't you?"

Dan said to her, "Sure, I sell cars, lots of cars. But that's not who I am. I could probably sell anything. But I happen to like cars, so that's what I happen to be doing now. I didn't really set out in life to be a car salesman – for my whole life."

Claire could see that he was serious now, choosing his words a little more carefully. He didn't want her to misinterpret anything he was saying.

He continued, "As much as I enjoy what I do, selling cars, I also know I could do more, contribute more, have a more satisfying life."

Dan stopped. He was absorbing the words he'd just spoken. Hearing himself say the words out loud, finally … had an impact on him.

Claire saw the change in him. She'd often felt the same way. As much as she loved her community, she often felt stymied by, what she thought, was an inability to really have a positive effect on it. All the work she did at the chamber of commerce and the charities she helped with was important – but how tangible was most of it.

Dan broke the silence by saying, "Hey, we should be getting back. You've got some things to do, so do I. And besides, I don't want people talking, getting any ideas, especially that Cletus."

That made Claire laugh, the first genuine laugh that Dan had heard from Claire. He laughed a little too.

But Claire turned to him and said, "Not just yet. I've got plenty of time. There's something I'd like to explain to you, if you have the time?"

~ Brad Leech ~

~ 22 ~

Mary came out of the kitchen to find Cletus seated in the 'employees' booth just outside the door of the kitchen. It was beyond the end of the bar in an awkward location that wasn't as nice as the other booths and tables, so it was permanently 'reserved' and the employees used it when they came up to grab a quick meal.

Mary said to Cletus, "You sure you want to sit there? There's no view of the course!"

Cletus looked up to see Mary smiling at him. "Yes, yes I do. Besides, the view here is better than anything I'd see out there." As he motioned to the windows beyond the bar. He too was smiling.

Ian had come up to the booth and said, "I had Robby show him around downstairs. Teddy told me he'd be starting Monday, but I figure he should know his way around." He sat a cup of coffee in front of Cletus. "From now on, the pot's over there when you need one." As he nodded to the coffee pot at the end of the bar. "Mary, I thought maybe you'd show him around a bit more when you have some time. I know it'll pick up in here before long, but you've got some time yet."

"Sure dad." With that, Mary motioned Cletus to follow her. He got up and they headed out the door into the main entryway.

Ian looked back at the booth and saw the untouched coffee and thought 'I better get used to that, at least when the two of them are together.' He brought the cup back to his sink and dumped it out.

Curtis watched as Mary led Cletus through into the office area where she pointed out the several offices and who occupied them during the day. She showed him the Judge's office but explained he was rarely there. Teddy, Curtis and several others ran the course on a day to day basis. The Judge was pretty much a 'hands off' owner.

On their way back, passing by Curtis, he leaned closer to him and said quietly, "Did you have anything to do with this?"

Curtis's response was, "Sir, I'm sure I don't know what you mean!"

Cletus said to him, "Two things Curtis. One I don't believe you, and two… thanks!"

With that, Cletus moved to catch up with Mary who was headed downstairs. They moved out on the patio because Mary wanted to check on the progress of the setup for the cooking area and the small musician's platform being moved into place against the back of building beneath the overhang of MacGregor's.

Mary said to Cletus, "I wish we didn't have to go through this all the time. It's really a pain to set everything up and take it down every night. But there's just not enough room to leave all this set up. During the day, the patio out here is where most of the golfers congregate and at night the room up there just isn't big enough if we have a good-sized crowd of customers." She looked up towards MacGregor's then back to the patio.

"Sorry Cletus, but I've got to cut our tour short. There's other things here that I've got to get started with."

"I understand Mary. I'm sure Dan will be back before too long, we've got to get back into town to get cleaned up for tonight."

"Well get going then. When you see Dan tell him this is a chicken barbecue tonight – No steaks!" With a flash of her smile she was off to see Terry about getting the charcoal started in the grilling pit.

Cletus went back into the clubhouse and was discreetly looking around for Dan. No Dan. He must have gotten lost out there somewhere with Claire. About the only place he hadn't checked, was in the parking area.

When Cletus went out through the door he saw the Corvette across the lot, alongside Dan's car. Her car was idling as Claire prepared to leave. Dan leaned in close to say something to Claire then straightened up and patted the car as he stepped back, signaling he was clear and she could blast off.

There weren't too many stones flying as Claire moved through the parking lot and exited. Dan watched until she was gone, then looked back toward the clubhouse, motioning Cletus over to his car. "C'mon kid." He yelled. "We gotta get a move on or we'll be late for the party!"

Cletus rushed over, piled into the car and they were off.

~ Brad Leech ~

~ 23 ~

The cookout that night at the course was essentially a time for all the employees to get together at the end of the season. The big dinner in two weeks was a little more formal, there would be a lot of guests that had been invited for a lot of reasons. Tonight though, was more about just getting together and letting everyone know it had been a good season. Soon the weather would begin changing and it would be harder to call everyone together. Most of the harvest work was yet to be done, so many people would be unable to attend. The more strenuous golf course work would happen also. As the golfing began winding down because of the weather, the course workers could spend more time on the course, not interfering with the fewer fall golfers.

Tonight, would be fun for everyone. While MacGregor's would be preparing the food, everyone understood that those workers also were here for some fun. So, everyone was encouraged to try their hand at preparing their own meals, and that might mean cooking their own meat on the grill and spelling Terry from time to time so he could enjoy a little of this with his family.

It was expected that others would also come to the cookout. It was actually hard to distinguish an employee from a guest golfer. Many of the golfers here spent almost as much time at the course as any place else. The true 'members' of the course were paying for everything tonight. The guests were asked to make contributions to several funds to help the children of the employees, as well as the caddies, attend college after finishing school in the spring.

Teddy was at a table with his wife and daughters. Mavis was speaking to them, Barbara and Susan, pointing out where things were and what they might like to eat. As if they hadn't been through this before. They'd settle down, once more of their friends showed up and they didn't have to be seen with their parents. Teddy motioned to Mavis and pointed out Dan and Cletus as they came out onto the patio. He'd mentioned to her earlier that Cletus was going to begin work here on Monday. Her immediate thoughts had been, 'Finally, Teddy will get a break. Maybe this will mean a little more time with us, with the girls.' Teddy had told her that he thought Cletus looked like someone who could handle the strenuous work. Someone he wouldn't have to watch over constantly.

Mavis walked over to them and introduced herself. "Mr. Armstrong, it's so nice to meet you. Won't you and your friend come sit with us?" as she motioned back towards Teddy and the girls.

Cletus politely shook her hand. "Mrs. Trasker, this is Dan Steele." Dan shook her hand also, then said, "Sure Mrs. Trasker. We'd love to meet the rest of your family." And they walked back to the table. Teddy stood up to shake hands with Dan and introduced Barbara and Susan. Barbara sensed where this was headed, so she tugged at her sister to follow her off towards some of their friends that were arriving.

Mavis began, "So Mr. Armstrong, Teddy tells me you'll be starting here on Monday."

Cletus responded, "Well Mrs. Trasker, Mr. Trasker asked me to come out and see what I thought about the work that needs to be done. To see if I'm able to do it. I …"

Mavis politely cut him off, "Mr. Armstrong, I know all about what Teddy does here, and I'm sure you're capable enough. The kids here are okay, they work hard, but you know, they're still kids. Please call me Mavis, everyone here does. I can call you Cletus, can't I? Every time somebody calls me Mrs. Trasker I expect Teddy's mom to pop up somewhere behind me. You too Mr. Steele. I've heard about you from Ian … "

Dan saw an opening so he quickly jumped on it, "Mavis, please call me Dan." Teddy looked relieved that someone had gotten the conversation back under control.

Dan went on, "You see Mavis, Ian – up there …"As Dan nodded back up towards the windows in MacGregor's, "Well, he sees all the antics of the golfers as they come through his place. I think he likes to study his customers. When Mary starts in on them, he's enjoying himself. So, yeah, I guess you could believe most of what Ian's saying about me. Mary, on the other hand, I'd watch what she says about people." Dan nodded toward Cletus, "For example, don't believe anything Mary says about him. Her judgment's impaired." As Dan winked at Mavis, then a quick scowl at Cletus.

Cletus stood and said to Mavis, "Excuse me ma'am, but I think I'll head over to the grill to see if they're having any steaks along with the chicken. Some of us prefer chicken, while some of us prefer steak."

As Cletus headed toward the grill, Dan said to Teddy, "Teddy, the kid's going to work out. He just needs someone to give him a chance." Dan looked toward the grill to find Cletus chatting with Mary. "One thing though, Teddy. We've been staying down at Delancy's, and I have to get back to work. I'm leaving in the morning. Cletus can probably stay there for a while, but … it's a little pricey for his budget. I was wondering if you knew of something maybe more within his means."

Teddy looked at Mavis and thought for a couple moments. Then he looked back at Dan and said, "You know, I have a room, that I've fixed up for myself over in the maintenance building. I use it once in a blue moon when I've had something big going on here. I really don't like leaving the girls all alone overnight." Mavis nodded, she really didn't like Teddy here, away from home. "I'll take him aside sometime tonight, see if he's interested. It's nothing special, but he wouldn't have to worry about much of a commute."

Dan looked over again at Cletus and Mary. He said to Mavis, "Yeah he'd be close. Although maybe a commute gives you time to think, to keep things in perspective." He motioned toward Cletus and Mary. With a smile, he asked Mavis, "Think those two kids over there are keeping anything in perspective?"

~ 24 ~

Cletus came up to the grill and said hi to Terry. There was a child next to Terry, Terry was explaining to the child how to see that the chicken was cooking properly. He was rotating a number of chicken halves, moving them back from the coals as they continued to cook, making room for more meat. He had several steaks cooking farther down the grill, keeping the two areas separated and only for what was already cooking. Someone came up and inquired about fish, Terry showed him a fish rack that could be used on a section of the pit that was fully exposed to the coals. He demonstrated how you could lay the hand-held rack onto the grill and across to the edge of the pit so the fish could be flipped easily allowing the meat to cook through without burning.

Mary came up beside Cletus and said, "You know those steaks are already spoken for, don't you?"

Cletus turned to Mary, smiling, "Yeah, I thought that might be the case. I like steaks as much as the next person, but I have to say those chickens look inviting."

Mary said, "Well I know Dan is a 'steak' person, but missing a steak once in a while might do him some good."

Cletus chuckled, "I'm sure you're right about that. I just wouldn't want to be the person that tried taking that steak away from him though. How about you? When do you get to eat?"

Mary explained, "Well tonight is a little different than what normally happens out here. Once everything's underway I'll have something to eat – I want to make sure dad also eats." She nodded up towards MacGregor's. "I see you met Mavis. She's really sweet, isn't she?"

"She sure is." Agreed Cletus.

Mary looked around, returning to face Cletus. "I don't see Bill around here anywhere yet." Cletus looked a little confused. "Bill, Bill Morgan. You met him at lunch. One of the Judges playing partners."

Cletus chimed in, "Oka…y, Bill. Yes. Bill Morgan. I met him at lunch. Does he work here too or is he just a friend of the Judge?"

"Both" said Mary. "He's a very good friend of the Judge. And he manages the golf course."

This surprised Cletus, "He manages the golf course?"

Mary said, "Well this doesn't surprise me. Bill likes to play golf, but the trouble is, he's usually pretty busy. So, when the Judge asks him to play, he jumps at the chance. He's a pretty good golfer too. But he doesn't want anyone here to think he's a slacker. You'll never see him out on the course unless he's with the Judge."

Mary could see the wheels churning in Cletus's mind. She said, "Relax, Cletus. I'm sure you made a good impression on him. Otherwise, he wouldn't have said anything to Curtis *or* Teddy!"

Cletus did relax. Noticeably. There was so much more at stake than a job.

~ 25 ~

Up in MacGregor's, Ian was watching the patio as several mini dramas were playing out, when Claire joined him. He was watching Mary and Cletus when she said, "How much do you know about him?"

Ian turned back to Claire, "Not much really, seems nice enough, more polite than a lot that come through here. We've spoken a couple times … I like him. How much do you suppose a father has to know?"

Claire showed some mock exasperation, "Not him Ian, him!" And she pointed to the table where Dan, Teddy and Mavis were seated.

Ian smiled. 'Okay, I see where this is headed' he thought. "Oh, you mean Dan. He's been coming here for the past couple years. Surprised you haven't bumped into him before now."

"Well Ian, I haven't been driving a car like the Corvette before. That's what he's interested in. He's probably been in here and I just didn't notice."

"Claire you're a terrible liar!" as he continued to chuckle. He continued, "If you were throwing a party, Dan could probably be the sole source of entertainment. Look at him out there. And right now, he's keeping it tame – the kids and all. You should see him in here after even a bad round of golf." Then in a little more serious tone he added, "But there's a lot more to him than that. I suppose someone could hide behind that kind of behavior. I don't think Dan's hiding, I think maybe Dan's looking. Problem is, he may not know it himself."

Claire was staring at Dan. She thought, 'Ian you're good. Maybe better than just good.' She looked at Ian, not saying a word. Ian smiled back, he too was silent. As he continued smiling at her, a little more broadly, then raised his eyebrows in a questioning manner. As if asking, 'Well, your turn – next question.'

Claire redirected her gaze towards Dan, "Ian, I never doubted how much you loved Katherine. And I don't know how many times she explained to me why she loved you, but you keep showing me more reasons."

As Claire was silently looking out at Dan. After a long moment, Ian said, "Two peas in pod I'd say. Wouldn't you?"

Claire looked at Ian then out towards Mary and Cletus. "Oh, you mean them." With a slight nod.

"Them too." Was all Ian said.

~ 26 ~

Most everyone had made it to the grill for the chicken and to the other tables where the side dishes were set up. Corn on the cob was abundant. The torches were burning on the opposite side of the pond, drawing the few insects still out, to the flames, rather than the food. Ian had come down from MacGregor's when Mary motioned to him that she had a plate for him. He joined Mary with Cletus at the table where Dan, Teddy and Mavis were seated.

Dan had found a stray steak in a small cooler, put it on the grill and went through the motions of cooking it – that lasted about three minutes.

At a nearby table sat, the Judge, Claire, Bill Morgan and his wife, and Curtis and his wife. Bill looked over to see that Teddy and Mavis had finished eating, and motioned them join him. Bill said a couple things to Teddy leaning in close after Teddy and Mavis had sat down. Teddy nodded in reply.

Bill scanned the patio a little more, was satisfied that this was as good a time as any. He stood up and said in a voice loud enough to carry across the patio, "Everyone. Everyone can I have your attention for a couple minutes?" The conversations around the patio quieted down a little.

"I won't take long here. I don't want anything to get cold. I just have a couple things to say. First – Thanks Terry, everything here's great. I know you, Mary and everyone else at MacGregor's worked hard putting this together, thanks." He applauded a little and everyone joined in.

"I also want to thank all the guests and members who could make it here. I know quite a few of you had to travel a bit to get here. Everyone here welcomes you, thanks for joining us tonight – without most of you, this wouldn't be possible. You come here to play golf, we enjoy having you, but you mean so much more to us and the rest of the community. We also want to thank those of you who are able to help out with the funds to help out the kids who work here. Kids? Look at them - they're hardly children any more. Soon they'll be off to school – helped along by you!" At this there was applause, when it stopped, Bill continued, "We also want to thank all the club members for providing this" and he waved his arm across the patio, "we truly, appreciate it. It gives us an opportunity to get together as a group and thank everyone at the club for all their hard work during the season." More applause followed.

"Since we're all here, those of us who work here want to thank the members, not just for this cookout, but for all the support you've provided. I know we see you out on the course but we probably don't thank you often enough for everything we're able to do, thanks to your generosity."

As the applause continued, the Judge stood up, nodded to Bill who sat down.

The Judge began, "I'm not going to say much. Bill pretty much said it all. I just wanted to add a couple things. Claire and I wanted to thank Bill and his staff here" as he motioned down to the rest at the table, "for all their hard work. I don't think it's hard working *with* anyone here. It's just a lot of long days during the season. I also want to say that I'm glad everyone has stayed safe while working this year. I know that we have some dangerous equipment and accidents can happen. Maybe not so often, if everyone makes an effort to work safely. Last thing, is this Harvest Festival dinner in two weeks, hope everyone can return. I think we'll have some fun. Everyone loves a parade. That's at ten in town. Lots going on in town – and of course later the dinner here. Try to make it. That's all. Claire, want to add anything?" Claire shook her head. "Okay then, let's finish this food. I think we've got some late season watermelons over there that we ought to cut into!" There was more applause as the Judge sat down, but it was short lived as everyone resumed chatting at their tables.

The others at the table headed off to get some of the watermelon. The Judge turned to Claire and said, "Nothing you wanted to add Claire, that's not like you."

Claire smiled, "No dad. You and Bill covered it all. Charles envied you. Did you know that? He loved listening to you speak. Not just to large crowds like this, even in court. Did you know he'd sneak into the courtroom sometimes when you were reading a ruling, giving an opinion?"

The Judge said, "Oh, I'd see him there once in a while. I thought at first, he was just trying to catch me between sessions about the business. But I realized it was more than that. You know Claire, I miss him too."

Claire was misty eyed, not quite crying when she looked the Judge. She said, "Look around dad. Charles helped make all this possible. He hired Bill and Teddy and Curtis too. Oh, I know you could have said no, a couple times. But did you ever?"

"Claire, I trusted Charles with everything. Was I wrong? I don't think so. I don't have to look around, all I have to do is look across the table at you."

Tears were coming down her cheeks now. The Judge reached across and put his hand on hers.

~ Brad Leech ~

~ 27 ~

Mary stood up from the table and said to Cletus, "Cletus, help me get some plates of watermelons for everyone here."

Cletus got up and followed Mary to a long table that was being filled with slices of watermelon on paper plates. Between the two of them, they were able to carry enough back to the table, thanks to some creative stacking by Cletus. They passed the plates out so everyone could enjoy what might be the last good watermelon of the season.

Dan had picked up his slice and bitten into it as it dripped all over. He was almost finished chewing the first piece when, uh oh, seeds. He tried to casually glance around to see if anyone was looking. Mary. Busted.

Mary said, "Mr. Steele! If you're thinking what I think you're thinking. You're right! These aren't seedless watermelons. Let's not get carried away by starting any competition with the children. But we are planning on washing off the patio when we're done tonight." As she continued with a wink and a smile.

Cletus was eating his watermelon. He wasn't dripping. He tried chewing around the seeds, letting them squirm out back onto the plate. The seeds he wound up with, he swallowed.

Teddy had finished his when he said to Cletus, "Cletus when you're done, there's something I want to show you."

Cletus swallowed the last of his watermelon, he looked back at Teddy and said, "Sure."

Mary nodded for him to follow. She picked up several of the emptied plates and headed off to throw them in a trash container.

Teddy led Cletus off in the direction of the maintenance building. While they walked, Teddy explained, "Cletus, Dan mentioned he was cutting his trip short this time. He has some business back home. I know the two of you have been car-pooling and you're staying down at Delancy's. Dan asked us if there was any place you might stay until you get settled a little better. He thought Delancy's might be a bit of a stretch on your salary at the course."

"He's right Teddy. I haven't thought too far ahead, a lot has happened really fast. I can stay at Delancy's though. At least until I get squared away."

"Well, the thing is Cletus, without a car it's near impossible to get up here. I know anyone coming up here would give you a ride. Most live in town so it wouldn't be a big problem, but I've got a better idea."

They'd entered the building through a side door. The main face of the building was filled with several overhead doors to let the larger equipment enter. Teddy turned the lights on and they walked past several pieces of equipment; fairway mowers and smaller mowers with rollers to work on the greens. Against the back wall were a series of rooms. Several were offices, one was a storeroom. In the corner was a room that Teddy had turned into something approaching a studio apartment. He opened the door and turned on the light as they entered the room. The room was nearly what you'd find in an apartment. The only thing lacking was a bathroom. This wasn't necessary because there was a full bathroom and shower just down from the storeroom. This let the workers clean up here rather than interfering with the golfers in the locker room.

"Well Cletus what do you think? I know it's not much, but it's my home away from home."

Cletus was stunned. Someone he'd just met was offering all this to him. "Teddy, I couldn't …"

"Look Cletus, the fact is, you'd be helping me out. Mavis hates that it's too convenient for me to stay over here rather than come home. This'll force me to go home every night. Not that I need my arm twisted." He said with a grin as he gave Cletus an imploring look to answer his question.

Cletus didn't take long, "Alright Teddy, you've convinced me. But you've got to let me pay you something for all this."

"Not possible Cletus, it's not mine, belongs to the course."

"Well thanks Teddy. I'm still going to talk to somebody about paying rent."

"Well good luck with that Cletus. I've offered myself, but been turned down. Maybe you can convince someone though." He turned back towards the door. "C'mon let's get back out there."

As they walked back, Cletus said to Teddy, "I'll be sure to thank Mavis for her not liking your apartment so much."

Teddy laughed. This kid might just work out.

~ Brad Leech ~

~ 28 ~

When they returned to the table everyone had scattered. Mavis was tracking down her daughters. Mary was helping clean things up around the grill. Ian was gone, probably back behind the bar upstairs.

The Judge's table was almost empty. Claire, Dan, and the Judge were deep in conversation. Cletus wondered how long Dan would stay but didn't want to interrupt him. They looked like they were in a business meeting. Dan was still joking a little bit but this wasn't about golf stories.

Cletus went to the grill to help Mary and Terry. All the cooking grills were being removed so they could be washed down. The litter containers were being filled with trash and the plates and utensils were being loaded onto carts that could be rolled back into the clubhouse. When Robby had shown Cletus around the basement area, he pointed out the service elevator they used to move things from MacGregor's kitchen, down onto the patio. He also showed Cletus where Ian's apartment was, opposite the elevator.

About the only thing left to do was take care of the coals in the pit. There was still some life in them. Terry asked Mary if he should extinguish them, but she said no, maybe the children that were still here would have roasted marshmallows or s'mores. These supplies were still inside but could be brought out if there was enough interest in it. Mary walked off to mention it to several girls and asked them to spread the word. That's all it took. Before long the pit was ringed with children. Terry hovered nearby, the coals were still hot enough for a serious burn. His kids were there also.

Mary was still looking around wondering what needed doing next. Cletus had scanned the area also. Looking to help someone if they needed it. Everything was returning to normal on the patio. Most of the people, like last night, had found their way up to MacGregor's, at least those without children.

Mary turned to Cletus and said, "I think we're the only ones out here without children."

Cletus glanced around, "You know you're right." He moved in close to Mary and softly said, "You know what I haven't had in a long time. Something I've really missed?"

Mary's heart raced, just a little bit. Her eyes scanning nearby – who was watching? Who was listening? She leaned closer to him and carefully said, "What's that Cletus?"

Cletus carefully, quickly, pulled a skewer up between their faces – with a marshmallow speared on it. "These."

She started laughing which then turned into a broad smile. "You know, I was having, exactly, the same thought!"

Cletus picked up another skewer and several more marshmallows. They moved to the end of the grill where a couple children had finished, heading off home with their parents.

At the Judge's table, Dan and the Judge were continuing their conversation while Claire watched Mary and Cletus at the grill. 'How long, has it been, to be like that', she thought. 'Those two don't even know they're falling in love'. She looked at Terry with his children who were having what must have been about their tenth marshmallow. While Terry was watching everyone around the grill - he's seeing this happen also. She turned back to Dan.

"Daddy, let's go in. You two can continue up in MacGregor's. I'm starting to feel a little chilled out here." Dan and the Judge agreed.

They got up. Dan took his jacket off and put it around Claire's shoulders as they leisurely walked across the patio.

~ Brad Leech ~

~ 29 ~

By the time Mary and Cletus found their way into MacGregor's there were only a few people left. Dan and the Judge were sitting at a table off to the side of the room. Claire and Ian were drinking coffee at the bar. Mary and Cletus settled into chairs at the bar. Ian held his cup up in a gesture to Mary. She nodded, 'yes'. Ian looked at Cletus and motioned him to the coffee pot, with a smile. Cletus walked around the end of the bar and poured coffees for Mary and himself, returning to his seat with the cups.

Mary motioned towards Dan and the Judge, "How long have they been at it over there? I didn't think it took that long to fix a ticket!"

Claire laughed, "It started out with some golf stories, but I think it's moved beyond that."

The conversation broke up at the sound of Claire's laughter. Dan and the Judge came back to the bar. Dan motioned to Ian that a coffee might be nice. Ian was already headed towards the pot. Ian looked at the Judge who shook his head, no.

Dan turned to Cletus, "Cletus give me a chance to have a couple sips of this and we can head back to Delancy's. I don't know about you, but I'm bushed."

Cletus agreed, "I feel the same way. Caddying is hard work!"

There was some chuckling and general agreement. Everyone here had seen caddies coming off the course and into the clubhouse. They usually looked pretty beat. Few would go out on the course for a second round of eighteen holes in the afternoon.

Dan said to Cletus, "I'm going to head back home tomorrow Cletus. I talked to my manager at the dealership and he thinks there's some things I should get on top of. He's great when I'm away, but, this time of the season there's always issues with the shipments of the new cars. I wish I could have gotten in a round tomorrow, but it's just not possible. How's tomorrow shaping up for you Cletus? What are you up to?"

Cletus smiled, "Well there's some things I've got to take care of as well." He continued smiling, "If I'm coming in here on Monday to look at what Teddy has planned for me, I've got to get some work clothes and other things I've been putting off."

Dan said, "Well, I'll have breakfast with you at Delancy's tomorrow morning then head out. I hear they fix up a real nice meal."

Mary joined in, "Cletus if you give me a call here at the restaurant around ten o'clock, I'll probably be able to get away to retrieve you. There'll be a rush, early, but by mid-morning it's pretty quiet here, on Sundays. That'll give you some time in Bartlett's, since they'll be the only store open. You should find what you need in there for the time being."

Cletus said, "Yeah, I looked around there yesterday. It shouldn't be a problem. I need a good pair of boots. Thanks for the offer."

Mary said, "Well this will give you a chance to poke around here some more and learn where everything is. I should have a little free time in the afternoon too."

Dan spoke up, "Well then it looks like everyone's set then. Cletus why don't we leave these folks alone so they can finish up here and call it a day. Looks like we're the last one's here anyway." Dan looked around, and they were the only ones left in MacGregor's.

"Judge nice talking with you. Claire – Hope you had a nice evening. Mary, Ian always a pleasure. C'mon Cletus let's make a mile."

As he turned to leave, Mary said, "We'll see you Dan, it's too bad you missed the Festival that's coming up in a couple weeks."

Dan turned back to face Mary, "Yeah I should have delayed this trip by a couple of weeks. But then I wouldn't have met this fella here." As he nudged Cletus. "You know I think I might just come back for the festival!"

Mary's face lit up a little.

Dan winked at the Judge, then said, "Besides, I want to see how this kid works out here – If he's still around!" He gave Ian a quick, knowing, look and smiled a little more broadly at Mary. "C'mon kid we're keeping these folks up!" And with that Dan began hiking off towards the door with Cletus close behind trying to say good night to everybody and keep up with Dan.

~ Brad Leech ~

~ 30 ~

After Claire and the Judge left MacGregor's, Mary came back up to Ian at the bar. She had picked up the last of the tables that her staff had left uncleaned when she told them to go home. They would have time in the morning to finish what little needed to be done. Ian was tidying up behind the bar.

"Dad, what was going on between the Judge and Dan? They spent a lot of time together tonight."

"Mary, I really couldn't say. They talked quite a bit, but you know Dan ..."

"Those weren't some of Dan's golf stories, the Judge's either."

"Talk to Claire, Mary. She's probably in on it. She didn't say anything to me about it tonight. She didn't really seem to be herself tonight. Anything bothering her? You talked to her earlier."

"I don't think so dad. When she talked with me this afternoon, she seemed liked she always is, you know ...just ...Claire!"

"Well I'm going to get some sleep. You should too. Dan was probably just trying to convince the Judge to switch from Lincolns to Cadillacs. Come on, let's turn the lights out in here."

"Sure dad. You go ahead, I'll shut things down here in a couple minutes."

Ian left, trodding across MacGregor's out to the stairs leading down to his rooms. It had been a long day. Maybe he was starting to feel his age.

Mary closed up the kitchen and turned off all the lights in MacGregor's except the small light in back of the bar which they left on all the time. She leaned forward looking out the window down at the pit. There were still a couple bright red embers left.

She smiled then headed back to her apartment.

~ 31 ~

The next morning, Cletus met Dan in the dining room at Delancy's for breakfast. They had large breakfasts, Cletus insisted on treating Dan to a full meal before he left to head back north, home. They had finished eating and were enjoying the coffee, this wasn't instant coffee but was a drip coffee that had brewed a while ...strong.

"Dan, I can't begin to thank you for everything you've done. It's too bad you couldn't stay – get in another round of golf. I'm no golfer, but I wouldn't mind caddying for you ...anytime!"

"Cletus, it was great meeting you. I've really enjoyed spending a little time with you here. If I thought you could sell cars, I've have you working with me back home. But that's not what you are, is it?"

Cletus shook his head, "Dan, you're right, that's not me. There's a lot of things I could do, but sales – like you do – would be way down the list, maybe at the bottom."

Dan got up from the table, followed by Cletus. He walked out onto the porch, stopped, looked out onto the square. There was a lot of movement. People were arriving for church. A small town waking up and settling into the daily rhythm. Dan drank it all in. The air had that sweet smell again. There were enough fields nearby, with cut hay, laying, waited to be baled. The aroma was nice.

"Okay kid I'm outta here." He reached out to take Cletus's hand. "I think you'll do fine here. If not, there's always the bus station over there - somewhere." As Dan nodded away from the square. They never had found it, they had never even looked for it.

"I think you might have found what you're looking for up there!" He nodded towards the golf course.

Cletus didn't argue, just nodded as Dan moved to his car.

As Dan drove by when leaving he yelled back to Cletus, "See you in couple weeks kid! Take care of yourself." Waving as he drove off.

~ 32 ~

Cletus rummaged through Bartlett's finding work clothes, some dressier casual clothes and some boots. Steel toed construction boots. He also managed to find other items that he'd need for the time being, such as towels and other linens that Teddy didn't keep at his room.

He'd have to buy a hotplate if having meals at MacGregor's became complicated, but he didn't think that was the case. He was a pretty fair cook, so he was sure things would work out.

When he was finished, the clerk boxed up everything. It was more than just a couple of bags. He hoped there wouldn't be a problem moving everything in one trip. He called MacGregor's, Ian answered. Cletus asked Ian to pass a message to Mary that he had finished, and she could pick him up at Bartlett's when she was able to break free long enough for the round trip. It was just past ten o'clock so he told Ian he understood if she couldn't make it until after the lunchtime meals had been served. He'd find things to do in town, Bartlett's could hold his purchases until she arrived.

When Ian found Mary downstairs in the storage room and gave her the message, she left immediately. It wasn't really busy yet. She thought she'd replenish some of the kitchen supplies until she'd heard from Cletus. Ian owned a station wagon which he shared with Mary. As a business, MacGregor's also owned a panel truck. They used it to pick up supplies from a variety of nearby farms. They had also done a little catering for small events. Mary thought it would be a good source of income, but that part of the business hadn't really taken off - yet. If they had a larger kitchen it would be a lot easier juggling the golf course work with a separate catering business. Mary told Ian she was taking the wagon and would be back in half an hour.

She made it into town in fifteen minutes and found Cletus on a bench in front of Bartlett's. Boxes were stacked around Cletus, as was his duffel bag.

He came around to the back of the car as Mary lowered the tailgate.

"Thanks Mary, I really appreciate this."

She smiled, "Cletus, you're welcome. But, you don't have to keep thanking me."

Cletus smiled back, "Okay, I'll try to stop. It's difficult because you, and everyone else …have been so kind."

Mary said, "I've got to pick up some supplies here that I asked Ralph to put together for MacGregor's." As she moved into Bartlett's. Cletus followed closely.

"Do you have to ask?" was all he said with a smile.

They loaded the two additional boxes into the vehicle and began the trip back to the course.

On the way, Cletus was quiet. Looking at the several small farms they were passing.

She said, "You're quiet this morning. Something bothering you?"

"Nope, just enjoying the scenery." was all he said.

They continued driving, getting back to the clubhouse just before eleven. Mary parked out past the clubhouse near the maintenance building – Cletus's new home.

Cletus spoke first, "Mary, let me carry your things in for you. My stuff can sit here for a while." He got out, walked to the rear and opened the tailgate to pick up the first box. "Leave that." He said to Mary as he nodded at the remaining box. "I'll come back for it."

They walked around to the back of the clubhouse to enter through the lower doors, nearest the store room. Cletus put the box on a worktable just inside the door.

"I'll be right back with the other one." He said as he exited.

Mary yelled after him, "Come up for some lunch before you get started with anything else."

Cletus retrieved the other box and came up through the clubhouse to MacGregor's. As he passed the front desk Curtis nodded a good morning, "Morning Cletus."

Cletus smiled back, "Morning to you too, Curtis. Busy today?"

"About the usual. Tends to be a little slower on Sunday. You know, church and all. We'll see some activity in the afternoon."

Cletus said, "Well I'm going to have something to eat. I'll be around. If I can help with anything give me a shout."

Curtis nodded in thanks as someone came through the doors and approached him.

Cletus went into MacGregor's heading for the booth by the kitchen door. Teddy was sitting there having a sandwich. Cletus attempted to ask if he could join him, but Teddy was already waving for him to take a seat – while munching on what looked like a chicken sandwich.

When he could speak, Teddy said, "There's some chicken left from last night. Terry thought I'd like a sandwich of it. There's a lot more left back there" – as he nodded into the kitchen. "Just poke your head in there and tell Terry."

Cletus got up and gingerly opened the door, seeking out Terry. Terry looked up at the sound of the door opening.

Terry said, "Let me guess. Teddy says we're giving away free chicken dinners in here – right?"

Cletus responded, "Well something like that. He thinks maybe there's enough for another chicken sandwich."

At about the time Cletus finished saying that, Terry was finishing placing a sandwich on a plate with some salad and a pickle. He handed it to Cletus.

Terry said, "Well there's more than a little left from last night. I've been making sandwiches since I came in. Here you go."

Cletus thanked Terry and returned to the booth.

Teddy began, "After you get settled in this afternoon, maybe you can take a little hike up the hill along the creek and see what you're facing tomorrow."

Mary came out of the kitchen with another plate containing a chicken sandwich and salad. She sat down next to Cletus.

Teddy continued, "Just stay on the far side of the creek as you walk up there. That way you won't be a nuisance to anyone playing those holes that follow the creek. When you get to the second hole along it, hole number 14, watch yourself. There's a spot along the trail in there that seems to be a target for everyone slicing the ball off the tee. Damn fools try crossing the creek there to retrieve the balls – fall in the creek pretty often. The water's only ankle deep, but the rocks in there are really slippery. Watch yourself if you get in there."

Mary was following the instructions. Teddy looked at her as if to say, 'That goes for you too!', then back to Cletus and said, "Okay?"

Cletus said, "Okay. It's only going to take a couple trips from the car to move my stuff into the room. Then I'll head up there to see what I've gotten myself into."

Teddy said that he had better get back out there and got up to leave. As he looked at the two of them, he focused on Mary.

He looked at her and said, "Just be careful if you're taking him all the way up to the pond. Okay? There's a couple spots in there that are dangerous until we get it cleaned out." He finished with an imploring look – waiting for her to agree.

"Understood Teddy." was what she managed in a slightly military tone.

"Seriously you two. Watch yourselves up there." And with that Teddy strode out.

~ Brad Leech ~

~ 33 ~

When they had finished their lunch, Cletus left to move his belongings into his room, while Mary went off to change. It was quiet enough in MacGregor's to allow her to spend a little time with Cletus, showing him the path up the hill. She changed into blue jeans and put on a pair of waterproof boots.

It only took Cletus a couple trips to move everything into his room. He left everything packed up except for his new boots which he changed into. He came back to the clubhouse and found Mary waiting for him on the patio.

Mary nodded toward the pond and Cletus joined in, making their way around the pond and across a small bridge over the creek. Cletus had been on this part of path Friday night. The main path continued downstream past the wheel, crossed back over the creek and led into the parking area in front of the clubhouse.

They veered off the path, following the creek upstream away from the pond and the clubhouse. The path was maintained, but much of the area they walked through was still left bushy and untouched to discourage any golfers and guests from exploring. As they moved uphill past the finishing hole, number 18, things cleared out a little. A small service road joined in with the path. This allowed small vehicles to make their way up the hill without affecting play on the course just opposite the creek.

As they continued up the hill, Mary explained this was the number 17 hole. Number 17 was a big, sweeping dogleg right coming down the hill. The tee shot would take the golfer along the creek to the dogleg, which, turned away from the creek. Cletus remembered the hole.

A couple hundred yards further along the path Mary pointed out the danger from the number 14 tee box. The path came in quite close to the creek, there were almost no trees to stop a ball from crossing over from the hole. Apparently, this was just about the distance that a weekend golfer could carry their tee shot. As they walked along they spotted a number of golf balls.

When she saw the balls, she said to Cletus, "I'd come down here every day when I was little. I'd carry a bucket and always returned home with enough balls for me and my mom to play without worrying about losing a ball or two. When my mom was teaching me to play, she always told me not to worry about hitting over water, not to worry about losing a ball. All I had to do was walk down the hill in the morning!"

Cletus was listening to Mary talk while they slowly made their way up the hill. He noticed that there were now limbs down. Some near the path. Most had been cleaned out, but mainly, just to allow a cart through. More work would be needed to really clean everything up.

They continued up the path and could see the green for number 14. This was about the furthest point from the clubhouse on this side of the course. They continued walking a little further and the path split away from two ruts that served as a 'roadway'. Mary motioned Cletus to follow her along the roadway away from the creek, away from the green. They had only gone a short distance when a small shed appeared.

Mary explained that this was a storage shed for some tools and other items they used on the course. It helped, having them close by, saving time running up and down the hill for common items. She opened the shed and showed Cletus what was there. She also pointed out a cabinet with first aid equipment in case anyone was injured. There was also a phone which was just a direct line to the front desk, not a phone you could dial out on.

She picked it up, "Curtis? Yes, it's Mary. Just checking the line from the shed on number 14. No. Yes, I will. Bye."

Cletus looked at Mary, Mary explained – "Curtis just wanted to know if there was any problem. Then he reminded me – Just like Teddy – to be careful!"

They left the shed and returned to the path. Mary took Cletus's hand and they moved further upstream beyond the golf course.

Cletus liked the feel of her small, delicate, hand in his. She was continuing to talk, he wasn't focusing on her voice, just her touch.

Mary said, "So the club owns all this land up past the course to the top of the hill. We'll walk up a little further so you can see the real damage from the storm that came through here."

The other, smaller, trees had thinned out leaving only larger beech, oak, maple and the ever-present sycamores along the creek. Many more limbs were down, as well as some whole trees. Curtis could see what Teddy was concerned about. A number of limbs were in the creek and everything was becoming very tangled. Once the fall leaves began dropping, it wouldn't take much for water from the creek to jam everything together into a real snarled up mess. The longer this stuff laid around, the more difficult it would be to cut it up and move it out away from the water.

Cletus said, "I see what Teddy meant. This is bad up here! The longer it sits like this, it's going to become a lot harder to get it cleaned up.!"

They were off the path now, just walking through the woods. Mary was leading them up the hill, unable to use the path, but paralleling the creek. The creek bed was contained in a large, bowl like, amphitheater of trees. Although the beech and oaks were much larger here than down below, they couldn't match the sheer grandeur of the sycamores. They were massive.

They had just cleared a small rise when Cletus heard the waterfall. Mary gripped his hand a little tighter pulling him forward. The ground had leveled out a little, and in front of them was a small waterfall in the creek. It wasn't very tall, fifteen feet at most, but the water splashing into the small pool below it, made quite a sound – enhanced by the absolute silence of woods surrounding them.

Mary turned to look at Cletus, to see what he thought of all this. The smile on his face was her answer. Cletus had seen beautiful things in his life before, but not like this. The vibrant woman holding his hand, the aroma of the forest, the waterfall …

Cletus let Mary's hand fall away as he reached up to her face with both hands, drawing her face to his, and kissed her.

This was not some fleeting kiss, brushing her cheek, but one that drank her in. A man showing a woman he cared for her.

Mary returned his kiss with passion. She had sensed that there was so much more to Cletus than his good looks, his shy humor. She was right.

~ 34 ~

Ian was at the bar filling an order. He looked up to see Claire enter. She came straight across to him near the end of the bar. Ian finished with the drinks and sat them in front of the group seated at the bar. He came down to Claire. She had poured herself a coffee and noticing that Ian didn't have one, made one up for him as well.

Claire remained quiet. Ian spoke first, "Afternoon Claire. Didn't expect to see you back here so soon." He expected this would coax something out of her. He remained quiet. He looked out across the floor to see if there was anything that needed looking into. He looked back at Claire, still waiting.

Claire responded, "Afternoon Ian." As she sipped her coffee. She stayed silent.

'Wow', thought Ian. 'I've gotta do something here' – "Beautiful day, wouldn't you say?"

Claire paused then said, "It's a gorgeous fall day Ian" Another sip of coffee. More silence.

She didn't take the bait, Ian thought, 'Okay we've got a situation here', "Claire, what's on your mind?"

"Nothing." Said Claire. "I just thought I'd stop by, see how things were, here, today."

"Claire, I'm not buying it. What's up?"

"Can I talk to you Ian?"

"Claire, that's what I've been trying to do with you for about the last five minutes!" Then in a softer, friendlier tone, "C'mon Claire!"

Claire began a little more careful voice than she normally used with Ian, "I miss him Ian. I miss him so much."

Carefully he said, "I do too Claire. He was one of my best friends." Ian stopped, he wanted Claire to continue.

"It seems like yesterday, not six years. Has it really been six years Ian?"

"No Claire, it doesn't feel like it's been that long."

Claire looked up from her coffee at Ian, "Ian, how have you gone on for as long as you have?"

Ian thought carefully, he didn't want to rush this or upset Claire anymore. "I think you know why. It's Mary."

Claire knew the answer before she asked the question. Ian was being so kind. He knew that she and Charles would have loved having children. They would have been great parents. They'd waited. It never happened. She smiled at Ian.

"I've been lucky Claire. Besides Mary, I have my whole family here." He laid a hand on hers. After a moment, he motioned back towards the window at the course. "We both have."

"Ian, you're right of course. I do feel that same way."

"Claire, anything in particular bring this on?

It was Claire's turn to nod towards the window, "When you see them, you wonder …what about me?"

Ian turned to look out the window. Mary and Cletus were coming around the pond. They were holding hands, laughing.

He turned back to Claire, a large smile had returned to her face

~ 35 ~

As Mary and Cletus walked around the pond, she looked up to see Ian standing there. She nudged Cletus to look up. Cletus's immediate reaction was to try and let go of her hand. She held tight. They continued walking. She began laughing, first about Cletus, then about *them*. Holding hands like two teenagers! She didn't care.

Cletus finally broke off by saying he had to get unpacked and said he thought he'd probably see her later.

She smiled and leaned in close saying, "That likelihood is waaaay beyond 'probably'!"

With that, she was off. Dinner would begin being served in MacGregor's before long, she had to get up there.

As she came through toward the kitchen she found Claire and her father sipping coffee.

Ian was smiling at her, as was Claire. All Mary said was, "I hope you two were enjoying yourselves …up here ….*spying* on me!" As she smiled going into the kitchen.

~ Brad Leech ~

~ 36 ~

While he was unpacking in his room, Cletus heard a knock. "Anyone home?"

Cletus yelled back, "Door's open."

Teddy came in, "Good. Looks like you're getting settled in. I spoke with Robby and he says to make yourself at home in the locker room if that works out better. He's got a locker set up for you. I know what's in here is pretty Spartan."

Cletus said to him, "Thanks Teddy, really, for everything. You, everyone here has been great. I'm looking forward to working with you."

"Good Cletus. Did you have a chance to make it up the creek where all those limbs are down? I saw you out there with Mary."

Cletus responded, "Yeah, she took me up past the last hole to the waterfall. That is some mess up there."

Teddy spoke, "Well, we'll get up there tomorrow and really see what we can do. I can't spend a lot of time with you up there, but obviously, we have to get started on it. I hope we can get it all cleaned out before winter. If that stuff goes through a winter with everything getting frozen, then thawing, it'll be a whole lot worse. Get yourself some sleep. It'll be a long day tomorrow. Your day will start pretty early when everyone comes tramping through here to get their gear in the morning."

"Okay Teddy, see you in the morning."

Teddy left for his commute home. Cletus left shortly afterwards to speak with Robby about his locker in the clubhouse. When he was done there, he went upstairs. Curtis had left also. The club downplayed keeping the course open late on Sundays so everyone would get a little break, and could be home with their families for at least one evening meal during the season. In the middle of the summer they tried to rotate people in the clubhouse so everyone wasn't working constantly. It was easier then, because school wasn't in session. Most of the kids liked the extra money.

Cletus walked into MacGregor's to find it fairly empty. There were only three foursomes left, as well as some stragglers at the bar.

Claire was eating a sandwich at the bar chatting with Ian. Bill was sitting next to Claire sipping on a coffee. Cletus sat down next to Bill. Bill turned to him. "Afternoon Cletus." was all he said.

Cletus responded, "Same to you Mr. Morgan. Glad we bumped into each other so soon. I think I have you to thank for some kind words to Curtis and Teddy. I appreciate the chance you're giving me with Teddy."

Bill said, "Well, I think you and Teddy are going to get along just fine. You seem to be getting along with everyone."

As this Ian and Claire exchanged smirks.

Cletus answered, "It's not hard getting on with everyone here, everyone seems to enjoy what they're doing. They treat the golfers very well. It just is very relaxed here."

"We try hard to make it that way. Sure, it's a job and all – but we play hard here too! I think it's great that even after we've worked all day together, we can still enjoy each other's company, with our families. I've worked other places where that wasn't the case."

Bill looked at his watch. "Well folks, I'm heading home. Claire, always a pleasure. Ian, I'll leave you to it. Cletus, there may be one more chicken sandwich left in there if you're looking for supper." As Bill nodded toward the kitchen.

Cletus said, "Well I've about had my fill of chicken, but it was pretty good. Maybe one more sandwich wouldn't hurt."

Bill walked away from the bar headed out towards the desk to see if anyone needed anything before he left.

Mary came out of the kitchen with meals for the last of the golfers that had come in after their round and ordered a meal quickly before the kitchen closed. She then came over to Cletus.

"So, we're going to start cleaning up in there. Last call for supper." this to Cletus, Ian and Claire.

Claire said, "Thanks, no dessert for me I'm full. I probably shouldn't have had this meal. I ate too much last night. The chicken was good though, wasn't it?"

Everyone agreed. But Ian shook his head no to Mary's question. "I've been picking at those sandwiches all day. Nothing else for me."

Mary turned to Cletus again. "Made your mind up yet?"

Cletus paused, "Yeeees, if there's any of the sandwiches left I'll have one. But only if you join me. I don't want to eat alone, you must have worked up an appetite with what was going on around here today – and hiking up the hill with me."

Mary smiled, "Sure, let me get something from the kitchen."

She walked around the end of the bar into the kitchen. Claire stood up. "Ian, nice chatting. Cletus, hope your first day, tomorrow, goes okay. I'll see you later in the week, I'm sure. Until we get the festival dinner out of the way, I'm going to be a frequent guest." Claire nodded again at Ian, smiling, and left.

Ian looked at Cletus and said, "So, how far up the hill did you two adventurers make it?"

Cletus responded, "She showed me a waterfall up above hole number 14. Maybe a quarter of mile beyond the tool shed."

Ian nodded, "That's where I thought she'd take you. It's just about her favorite spot in the glen. Been a while since I was up there, but it is beautiful there, isn't it?"

143

Cletus nodded his head in agreement, "That it is sir."

"When you have more time, have her take you all the way up to the big pond. Wait 'till you see what that's like." Ian paused a little, stumbling perhaps, before he continued. "Our farm was up there. Just past the pond."

Cletus just sat and listened.

"Cletus, I shouldn't say it 'was' there, the buildings and all are still there. Jerry Talbot – the farmer I sold it to – doesn't use any of the buildings, just farms the land. He maintains everything though. I think he's planning to sell off the house and buildings as a residence and keep the land for farming, himself."

"It was a nice home for us. It had been in Kate's family for quite a while. But after Kate …. I just thought I needed a change. And Mary didn't feel at home there any more either. So, we sold it. Moved down here. It's nice, we're still 'home'. Just a litter further down the hill.

Mary came through the door and motioned Cletus to the booth. When Cletus stood up, Ian smiled and motioned him off. Cletus came over to the booth and sat down opposite Mary.

Mary had yet another chicken sandwich with salad facing her. Cletus looked at his plate and found a large hamburger with French fries piled high alongside it.

"I thought you'd probably had enough chicken for a while, so I brought you a 'burger. Hope that's okay with you."

Cletus looked up from his plate at her, "It's perfect. The chicken would have been great too, but thanks – I was nearing my limit on the chicken."

They ate in silence. Exchanging small talk as most of the other patrons left. Terry had been in the kitchen and said goodbye when he left. Everything was caught up, the only clean up involved what little was left on the tables.

When they finished eating, Cletus helped Mary clean up everything and dried the half dozen settings that Mary washed.

Everything was cleaned and they could close up MacGregor's after the two remaining golfers called it quits at the bar.

Ian saw that Mary and Cletus were done and motioned for them to leave. He'd close up the bar soon and lock up.

As they headed out the door Mary asked Cletus if he'd like to stretch his legs with a walk around the pond.

"Come on let's walk around the pond." She tugged at Cletus's hand.

They walked down the stairs and out onto the patio. They were alone. Only the lights from the back of the clubhouse shown out across the expanse of the course surrounding the clubhouse. They walked up to the pond then slowly followed the path they had started out on this afternoon. When they came to the fork in the path, they turned downstream, coming back close along the pond. Here the sycamores were quite large. They strolled close to the water approaching the wheel. The patio lights blinked out. The only light now was shining down from Mary's room by the wheel that looked out over the pond. The moon was coming up but it provided only a dim glow over the water.

Cletus had been watching Mary, but had leaned onto the railing along the path, to stare down at the wheel. The water was methodically plup, plupping back into the pond.

Mary reached up under his chin, to place her hand against his face and turn it towards her. She then reached to his face with her other hand and slowly pulled his face to hers.

As their lips met he was practically breathless. Her breathing was shallow and disorganized.

After a long moment, as one, they moved apart, both gasping for a little air.

The wheel continuing plup, plup, plupping.

After several moments, Cletus pulled Mary closer. As she kissed him, she pressed hard against him. Wanting to feel his body against hers as they kissed.

When they paused to catch their breath, Cletus looked into Mary's green eyes for a long moment then pulled her back into the tight embrace. Her eyes closing, as their lips came together again.

~ 37 ~

Cletus was wide awake before anyone came through the maintenance building. He had been awake since four am, and had finally gotten dressed and made some coffee up in the urn in Teddy's office next door to his room. He was on his second cup when Teddy came in. Teddy had seen Cletus's door open and gone into the office. He poured a cup of coffee and returned to Cletus's room.

He leaned against the doorframe while looking in at Cletus. He raised the cup in a salute and said, "Morning Cletus. You're going to be a big hit around here." As he saluted with the cup a second time and went back to his office.

Cletus got up and followed him. Teddy was checking to see who was scheduled to be working today. He looked up at Cletus when he came into the office.

"Why don't you head out there and find a good axe. See that it's sharp. Get something you're comfortable with. Pick out a locker too. You can store some of your gear in there. It'll save you some space in your room. Make sure you get some good gloves. You've got pretty good sized hands, like mine. Should be plenty. Most of the kids here have small hands – still growing."

Cletus walked to the lockers and found one without a name. He scribbled his on a piece of duct tape from a roll that he found on a bench, stuck it on the door.

Most of the hand tools were hanging on the back wall of the building. There were all sorts of tools. Some he'd never seen before. There were a number of axes. He hefted several until he found one that felt good in his grip. Made sure the wedge was tight. He checked it over for cracks near the head. Finding none, he headed to the large workbench that had a variety of hand tools scattered across it. In a drawer, he found a number of files. He chose one that was still in pretty good shape and even had a sturdy handle on it. He tested the edge of the axe with his thumb. It was fairly sharp. He looked the edge over. It didn't have any large nicks. It wasn't bad at all. He mounted the axe head in a vise and began lightly running the file across it. He didn't want to take much off, just get a feel for the edge. He put the file down and retrieved a stone from the same drawer. He worked the stone against the edge and brought it back into sharpness quickly.

Teddy had been watching. He was impressed. This guy knew his way around an axe.

There was a locker at the end of the line of lockers with no door, just shelving. Piled on the shelves were a variety of work clothes. Cletus tried on several gloves before finding a size that fit. He laid them on the workbench with his axe. He noticed there was a chain saw further down the bench with no chain on it. The engine was somewhat disassembled and parts were scattered about.

Teddy came up beside Cletus, stared down at the saw. "This one may be a goner. We've been working on it for a while, but we're probably going to scrap it. It's why I'm sending you out there with the axe. We've only got two saws and I need the other one on the course for a couple of days. We had a pretty big tree come down on the front side of the course and I've been working on it a little at a time. That saw makes quite a racket out there. I try to use it when there's no golfers nearby."

Cletus said to him, "Don't worry, the axe suits me just fine. I didn't see too many trunks up there that would be a problem. Mostly limbs. Probably best to go at it slowly with an axe while getting things untangled."

Teddy said to him, "When you get to something really big, just leave it. I'll bring the saw up and we'll handle it together."

While they were talking, a man came up to them. Teddy said, "Tim, you're here bright and early. Tim Davis meet Cletus Armstrong. Cletus is going to be working out there with me to get the creek cleaned up. Tim here is the greens keeper."

Tim shook Cletus's hand. "Nice to meet you Cletus. I heard someone was starting today. We could use the help around here. I lost my assistant last week, so it's just me on the greens for a while. Teddy, I need to get right out there. A couple of the greens have really had a spurt of growth over the last day or so. I want to get them cut right away."

Teddy motioned him off, "Don't let us hold you up. I'm taking Cletus up to 14, I'll be back down here after that. I'll get the mowers started on the front side."

Tim headed off for his mower/roller which was parked just inside the farthest door. He fired it up and was off.

"Grab your gear Cletus, let's get out there too."

Cletus got his stuff and followed Teddy to his maintenance cart. It was fairly good sized and had a decent engine that roared to life quickly. Cletus put his equipment in the back, including the file and stone. He'd probably need to re-sharpen during the day, especially if he was chopping around on the ground. The axe was sure to get nicked up. He climbed in and they headed out through the parking lot. They started down the road away from the clubhouse and had only gone a short distance when Teddy turned off the road into the woods. They immediately crossed over the creek on a small bridge that Cletus had not seen before. The roadway turned uphill, went through the woods, and joined the path that Mary had taken Cletus on the day before. It only took a couple of minutes to reach the area Cletus would start in on.

Teddy shut down the engine and got out. Cletus walked with him up to the creek. Teddy stared down at the mess.

He said to Cletus, "Okay then. Looks pretty self-explanatory."

Cletus stared down also. "Yup. That stuff there, shouldn't be there."

Teddy laughed, "We're going to get along."

Cletus collected his axe, gloves and tools. "I'll get this stuff cut up so we can haul it out of here. I'll throw it back far enough so we can continue to drive through here in case we don't get a chance to get it all moved anytime soon. How's that sound?"

Teddy replied, "Sounds like you have a plan. I like it. Ian said that Mary brought you up here, she showed you the shed back there?"

Cletus nodded yes.

"Well, be safe up here. Use the phone if anything happens. I'll pick you up around lunchtime. Maybe stop by later and see how it's going once I get everyone else straightened out on what needs to get done today."

With that, Teddy piled into his cart and tore off down the hill, leaving Cletus with the mess.

~ 38 ~

Mary was having her breakfast when Ian came into MacGregor's at seven am. He went into the kitchen, started some toast and came out to get a coffee. After collecting his toast, he sat down with Mary.

"So, what's on the agenda for today?" said Ian to Mary.

"Morning dad. Routine stuff. I do have to call the rental agency to make sure they'll be able to deliver all the tables and chairs we need for the dinner. What do you think about reserving a tent also?"

Ian responded, "A tent? You worried about the weather?"

"I'm not worried, we just don't know what the weather is going to be. Maybe the tent would come in handy if the weather is bad. I know we can probably get everyone inside – between here and the maintenance building – If Teddy can clean it out. I just thought we wouldn't be packed in like sardines around the tables if we had a tent."

Ian said, "You're right. It wouldn't hurt. I hope we don't need it, but if we wait, we might not be able to get one."

Mary had finished her meal and was staring out the window. Ian looked over at her, and said, "You know, I'll bet that neither one of them thought to take any water up there."

Mary turned to Ian, smiling.

Then Ian said, "Why don't you run up there when you get a chance. Take one of the coolers that Teddy uses out on the course. I don't want him drinking that creek water."

~ 39 ~

It was about nine thirty before Mary remembered what Ian had said. She was caught up with everything, there had not been many breakfasts to make. Monday was always the slowest day of the week.

She came out of the kitchen and said to Ian, "Dad, I'm going to take a cooler up to Cletus. I'll be right back."

Ian nodded to her as she left.

Mary went downstairs and crossed over to the maintenance building. Teddy wasn't around, so she lifted a cooler into a golf cart and swung back around to the patio. She took the cooler inside the clubhouse and filled it with water. The water wasn't really cold so she put some ice in it from the icemaker that was in the storage room. They had put one in there to save trips up into MacGregor's when setting up for meals on the patio.

She jumped into the cart and headed up the hill along the edge of the course. There was no one playing 18 so she was able to go right up to the dogleg on 17. She had to wait there for a twosome to play through past her. No one was on the tee at 14 so she continued up along the creek. She stopped when she saw a group putting on the green. When they left, she continued up past 14. She turned to cross the creek heading for the shed.

When she got to the path she looked downhill expecting to see Cletus. All she saw was a green mountain of limbs and leaves. She turned down the path and was near the mountain when she heard the axe.

She left the cart and approached the pile. The axe still rhythmically chopping away. She yelled out, "Hello there, anyone home?"

The axe stopped. Cletus's head bobbed up into view just beyond the pile. He was smiling. Sweating and smiling. He came around the pile.

Mary caught her breath … just a little. Cletus had taken off his shirt. His whole torso was the same golden brown as his forearms. He was glistening with a film of sweat from the exertion. She had not thought of Cletus as a particularly muscular person. She was wrong. He was not what you would call 'sinewy', the muscles were prominent. But they were not the result of a program to create muscles for show, they were the result of life.

Cletus yelled across to her, "Hey there. Don't try and come through, I'll walk around. It's a little snarly in here."

Cletus sidestepped through some of the brush, around the pile he was making, and came up to Mary.

He said, "This is nice surprise. What brings you up here?"

Mary pointed back to the cart, "I don't suppose anyone thought about bringing any water up here?"

Cletus laughed, "You know I had that thought a while ago. I have to admit I sampled the creek – it's not as good tasting as it looks."

Mary waved him back to the cart. Cletus lifted the cooler off the cart and sat it on the ground. She handed him a cup. He immediately filled it. He offered it to her. She smiled, shook her head. He drank it. Mary watched him, all of him. Cletus saw her eyes wandering over him, suddenly was aware of what was going on.

"Sorry, took my shirt off so it wouldn't get all sweaty. Brand new shirt, didn't want to ruin it on the first day."

Mary was a little embarrassed for staring. Smiling said, "Don't worry, I understand. I *have* seen men without their shirts before."

All Cletus could think was, "All I meant was …. Thanks for thinking of me Mary."

A little nervously Mary jumped into the cart. "I can't stay, dad's holding the fort down there."

Cletus waved her off with a smile, "See you later – thanks again!"

~ Brad Leech ~

~ 40 ~

Teddy came up to see Cletus at eleven. He came up to a huge pile of limbs that Cletus had cut up and thrown back in a pile that stretched along the roadway. Cletus was down in the creek wrestling with some limbs that he'd freed up. He dragged them to the bank and climbed up.

Teddy said to him, "You've been busy here." As he pointed to the pile.

Cletus nodded, "I'm making a little progress." He threw the limbs on the pile then straightened up and wiped his hands on his pants.

Teddy looked at his pants, "I see you found those slippery rocks I was telling you about!"

Cletus laughed, "Yeah, there's a couple in there that I found."

Teddy motioned him over, "What do you say about taking a break for some lunch? I'm starved, but it looks like you've got a lot more accomplished this morning than I have. You must be famished!"

Cletus grabbed his shirt and pulled it on, then sat in the cart. "I could use a meal."

They picked their way past the piles Cletus had made and went down the hill to the clubhouse. When they came around to the maintenance building Cletus saw that there was a group of people at a table set off from the patio closer to the maintenance building.

Several mowers were pulled up in front of the building. Teddy pulled up and they got out and came across to the table.

Teddy spoke out, "Everyone, this is Cletus Armstrong. He's going to be helping us out. I've got him working on that mess up there on 14. Cletus is staying in the room next to the office for the time being. We'll let you continue here, we're going up to get something to eat."

Cletus said, "Nice meeting everyone. I've met a couple of you already, when I get a chance I'll meet the rest of you."

With a wave, Teddy and Cletus headed toward the patio and MacGregor's. Cletus was conscious of how he looked, he stuffed his shirt into his pants as they walked. They walked into the clubhouse and Teddy made a beeline for the locker room. Both he and Cletus went right to the sinks. They washed up and Cletus changed out of his shirt, putting on one he had in his locker. He took his boots off and swapped them for his caddy sneakers. When they were done. They went up the stairs.

Curtis was at his station in the entry and nodded to the pair as they went into MacGregor's. They moved to the 'reserved' booth near the end of the bar and sat down.

Ian came over with two large glasses of ice water.

"You two look done in!" was all he said.

Teddy paused after a long drink of the water, "Thanks Ian, this is what I needed."

Cletus too was drinking and nodded thanks.

Teddy said, "We'll be out of here in a minute, just need to collect some food."

"Stay." Ian said, "There's nobody here, the boys outside are breaking up. No point to rush right back out there."

Teddy replied, "Okay Ian, you talked us into it."

There were already menus on this table, a permanent fixture. Cletus was looking it over when Mary came out of the kitchen. She smiled at them as she passed the booth on her way to a table with a full tray for a foursome.

When Mary returned, she paused with an order pad, looking at Teddy. All Teddy said was "Ham on rye."

She turned to Cletus who said, "The club sandwich please." She nodded and was off to the kitchen.

Ian had remained nearby and said to them, "So, Cletus, how's it going up there?"

Cletus had taken another drink of water, "Well sir, it's going to take a little effort up there. It's just a complete mess. I thought I'd get further along than I am."

Teddy spoke up, "Don't worry about it Cletus, you're doing fine. I've been in that stuff a couple of times and it's not easy work. You're making good progress, better than I would have. Course, you have a couple years on me. Back in the day I could have kept up."

Ian chuckled and said, "I've seen you out there Teddy, you haven't slowed down that much. Don't paint yourself as an old man."

Cletus said, "Well it's hard work, that's for sure. I may have to get a rope or something in there and tie things off to pull them out."

Teddy said, "Okay, let me know when you need the larger cart. I can take a small one out on the course once I get that heavy stuff moved off of number 4."

Cletus said, "Well if I can give you a hand lifting that stuff just let me know."

Ian had moved back to the bar, they hadn't noticed he'd left. He watched them. Cletus and Teddy would get along just fine. Teddy needed someone like Cletus, someone he could lean on from time to time. He was starting to slow down a little, that's good – he'd worked hard here he deserved to take it a little easier. There was always plenty to do. He should leave some of the harder work for someone a little younger.

Mary came back out with their sandwiches and placed them on the table.

"Thank you, Mary." Was all Teddy said. Cletus also said, "Thanks" as Mary bustled back into the kitchen.

Teddy got up and said to Cletus, "You want a soda or something? Maybe a coffee?"

Cletus responded, "Thanks, a coke please."

Teddy moved to the bar and asked Ian for two cokes. Ian poured them and slid them out to Teddy. Ian marked them off on the order that Mary had dropped off behind the bar.

Cletus noticed this and when Teddy returned asked, "Teddy, how does it work here at lunchtime?"

Teddy responded, "Sorry, should have explained it to you. When you're working, and come in for a meal or anything, Mary or Ian will write up an order. When you're done just sign it. The course repays MacGregor's for all the meals that the employees have signed for. I know the wages may not seem to be the best, but when you consider the meals ... well, it helps out."

Cletus nodded that he understood.

"Only thing is Cletus, nothing from the bar. Beer, wine, liquor – you know."

Cletus understood, "Of course, makes sense. I won't abuse it."

They continued their meal, mixed with plans on how to attack what needed to get done. Tim stopped by to mention to Teddy that they needed to start thinking about the fall aeration of the greens. It was an effort that usually took place twice a year. Once in the spring and again in the fall. They hadn't done the fall aeration yet and would need to start it soon.

While they were discussing this, Mary came by and caught Cletus's attention motioning him away from the booth. He followed her a short distance. She stopped at an empty booth and sat down. He joined her.

She said to him, "I didn't mean to ignore you or anything. Up on the hill too. It's just ..."

Cletus cut her off, "Mary, it's okay I know you're working. I don't want you to …."

Now Mary interrupted him, "Cletus, that's not it." She looked at him with a shaky smile. "You make me …. nervous. Sometimes."

Cletus was a little confused.

"Not in a bad way." She stumbled forward in the conversation. "It's good … I just don't understand it."

Cletus broke out into a smile, "Mary it's okay. What did you tell me? Just be yourself. I don't bite!"

Cletus noticed that Teddy and Tim were done talking, Teddy had gotten up to leave.

"Mary, I've got to go. I'm trying to make a good impression on my first day. Sorry. Have dinner with me tonight. Okay?"

She nodded and got up with him, gave him a big smile as he rejoined Teddy. The two of them nodded a goodbye to Ian as they left MacGregor's and headed outside to continue their work.

Ian had watched Mary and Cletus, he smiled to himself as he washed glasses in his sink behind the bar.

~ Brad Leech ~

~ 41 ~

Cletus worked just as hard throughout the afternoon. He had spent a fair amount of time using an axe when he was at the correctional facility. He could quickly sense when the blade was dulling and stopped several times to re-sharpen it. As much as he avoided hitting the ground with it – it was inevitable that would happen. The ground was just rough enough that the stones were taking their toll. The nicks came out easily and the breaks for sharpening helped pace him. The sun didn't seem quite so bright – or hot. He was a little surprised when Teddy showed up in the cart.

Teddy came up to him, "Cletus, what do you say we call it a day?"

Cletus looked up at him. "Already? I should keep at this."

"Cletus it's almost six. I almost forgot you were up here! When everyone else came off the course, Mary asked me where you were. Come on, let's get down the hill."

Cletus took his axe and tools to the tool shed while Teddy loaded the cooler back into the cart. He put his shirt back on and settled into the cart as Teddy headed down the roadway.

They arrived back at the maintenance building as Tim was getting in his pickup. He waved to the two of them as he left.

Teddy and Cletus went into the building, Teddy into his office and Cletus to his room. Teddy came back to Cletus's doorway and knocked on the frame. Cletus had taken his boots off and was walking around with just his socks on stretching his toes and feet.

Teddy said to him, "Stretching the dogs out huh!"

Cletus laughed, "Yeah, new boots.'

Teddy continued, "In case you get tired of the food in the clubhouse, there's a couple nice places in Jasper. There's a restaurant called Johnnie's – full menu, lasagna, fettuccini, pizza … really good food. Mavis and I go there all the time. In case you need a break."

Cletus thought about it, "You know that's not a bad idea, that might taste good tonight, I've really worked up an appetite!"

Teddy said, "Well, I just thought you might like to know. Say, it's none of my business but another thing, maybe nice to know also. Mary has Monday nights off. Just saying …." He winked at Cletus and left.

~ 42 ~

When Cletus came into MacGregor's he had put on his best shirt and pants. The logistics of using the locker room showers and the commute back and forth from his room hadn't become second nature, but he could deal with it.

Ian looked up as he approached.

"So, Cletus, how did you fare up there on the hill? Make some progress?

Cletus smiled, "I'd like to think so. Teddy will be the judge." He carefully settled into the bar chair. "I know I have some muscles that I haven't used in a while."

Ian said, "Well don't try and do it all in a day or two. The work will still be there!"

Mary came out of the kitchen and came up beside Cletus.

"You clean up nice." She said with a smile.

Ian moved away, towards customers further down the bar.

Cletus said, "Well I'm better now than I looked earlier anyways."

With a grin, Mary said, "You didn't look so bad."

Cletus blushed a little.

Mary continued, "You're all dressed up."

Cletus responded, "Well I asked you to have dinner with me, I thought you'd like to see me in something other than blue jeans or golf clothes."

Mary looked down at her waitressing outfit, then up at Cletus – smiling.

Cletus knew what she was thinking, "You look great just the way you are! I have just a small suggestion though…"

Mary gave him a puzzled look, not thinking he would criticize her.

"If we're going to a restaurant, it might be a little confusing if you're already dressed like the waitress."

Mary was stumped for a moment. She assumed that'd be eating at MacGregor's

Cletus continued, "How much fun is it to have dinner in your own restaurant, on your day off, dressed like a waitress!"

She laughed, "How did you …"

Cletus stopped her, "Hey, I have my sources. They told me about a little restaurant in Jasper called Johnnie's."

Mary said, "I know. Teddy and Mavis are there all the time. It's very nice there. I've been there also. You'll like it. I don't go there very often because this is so convenient." As she indicated MacGregor's with her hand.

Mary continued, "Betty's here now. So, just give me a minute to change. I'll be right back."

Mary poked her head into the kitchen to say that she was leaving and walked out through MacGregor's towards her apartment.

Ian returned to Cletus. Cletus looked at Ian a little sheepishly. Then he said to Ian, "I'll try to have her home by ten."

With a mock frown, Ian said to Cletus, "You better or I'll ground her." To which they both laughed.

~ 43 ~

Mary stared into the mirror. Damn, not enough time. She quickly slipped out of her work outfit and looked into the mirror a second time. Damn.

She washed in about thirty seconds. Just about enough to get rid of all the kitchen odors. No time for much else. She looked at her nails. Damn.

She chose a dark blue A-line dress from the closet. This will have to do. 'I know he's wearing blue, but I don't think we'll look like the Bobbsey Twins.'

She combed her hair out with rapid strokes. She sniffed it, damn. It smelled like kitchen grease. She sprayed some hairspray into it, not to hold it, just to improve the smell.

She squirmed into her dress and struggled with the clasp at the back of her neck. 'Why is this suddenly so difficult?'

She looked in the mirror yet again. Damn. What did she need?

She rummaged through her jewelry box and yanked out a simple gold chain and slung it around her neck.

She looked in the mirror. Good – it's starting to look good.

She went back to the jewelry box and took out a pair of small, gold, ear rings, returned to the mirror and put them on – performing a final check. OK!

She sat and put her sneakers back on and raced out of her apartment.

~ 44 ~

Cletus stood when Mary returned to the bar. He and Ian were still at the bar chatting. Cletus was not quite shocked, a little breathless maybe, but still in control.

Mary was gorgeous. How could she have changed so much in five minutes?

Even Ian was impressed. Daughter or not, she was quite a sight.

Mary came over to them. "What, what's wrong? Something dragging. Something showing that shouldn't be?" as she swung around trying to look at herself, then standing on tip toes trying to look at more of herself in the mirror behind the bar.

Cletus was finally able to speak, "No. No, Mary you look …. Great! I just … haven't seen you in a dress before."

Mary relaxed. Good. Then she looked at Ian.

Ian said, "Mary, everything's fine, really."

Mary turned to Cletus with the look 'okay let's get started', and they started away from the bar. Ian watched them take a couple steps then called out, "I especially like the shoes you picked out!"

Mary stopped, looked down, and froze. Cletus looked down. Then all three started laughing as Mary and Cletus left.

As they were almost to the door Cletus said, "I hate to ask this but, do you mind driving? I don't have a car and I don't know how to get where we're going."

Mary looked up at Cletus, "I don't mind driving, and I know where we're going" With a wink at Cletus as he leaned in close to her, to open the door for her as they left the clubhouse.

~ 45 ~

Johnnie's was on a side street in Jasper. It was a small family owned restaurant. The front portion of the restaurant consisted of half a dozen tables near the counter that offered pizzas and items to take out. After walking through this area, the room opened out wider into a more formal restaurant. The lighting was a little dimmer and the room quieter than the front of the restaurant. There were several other couples in the room, but no families with children. A waitress seated them in a booth along the far wall.

Mary slid in against the wall and Cletus sat beside her. A waitress came over with menus and lit the candle perched in a chianti bottle. She said she'd let them look the menu over and asked if they knew what they'd like to drink.

Mary said, "A small glass of rosé, please."

Cletus thought for a moment and said, "A draft beer, anything's okay."

The waitress left them to decide what they were going to order. Mary convinced Cletus to try the lasagna. She explained that it really was a family recipe here. He would like it. She chose a light meal consisting of fettuccine and a salad. When the waitress returned, she was with Nancy, the owner. The waitress took their order and left. Nancy sat down opposite Mary.

Nancy said, "Mary, how nice to see you. It's been a while, hasn't it?"

Mary nodded in agreement, "I know Nancy. I miss coming here. You know how it is. It's just non-stop in the kitchen. You should visit us more often too."

Nancy said, "I should. Do you know how hard it is to pry Russell out of the kitchen? I'm sure you do. How is your father? I haven't seen him in a while either."

"Dads good. It's been busy, but it will start to wind down now that summer's coming to an end. You'll see more of both of us then."

Mary looked at Cletus, "Cletus, this is Nancy Pagano. She and her husband Russell own the restaurant. Nancy, this is Cletus Armstrong. Cletus just started working at the course, helping Teddy."

"Good." Said Nancy. "He works too hard up there. He should spend more time with the girls."

Mary continued, "Well, I think that's Mavis' plan, I'm not sure about Teddy."

Nancy stood up, "Well, I'll leave you two alone. Your meals will be right along. Nice meeting you Cletus. And she left to visit with another couple several tables away.

Cletus chuckled at Mary, "You know everyone around here don't you?"

"It's a small community Cletus, too small sometimes."

Cletus said, "I notice you don't have any of the items on your menu in MacGregor's that are served here. Is that an accident?"

"No accident Cletus. Just two friends trying to keep it that way. I'd hate to compete with Nancy, she's practically family. And besides, do you know what a pizza oven costs? Not to mention the space it would take up. For seven, maybe eight months of the year."

Cletus nodded in agreement. Made sense. He thought for a moment, "Did you ever think about selling some of these items, from Nancy's, transporting them up to MacGregor's? It's not too far. Most of the items could be kept warm or reheated. You could probably store some small pizzas in the cooler and cook them. They'd fit in the oven."

Mary sat back and looked at Cletus. No. She hadn't ever thought of that. She tried to process this a little more as their meals were delivered. Cletus could see the wheels turning. 'Nice move genius, you've probably lost her for the evening.'

After taking a couple bites of her meal, Mary returned to Cletus.

"You know that may be a very good idea. I'll need to discuss this with Nancy in a lot more detail, but it could work. The business here falls off in the summer when we're busiest. Our slow time is in the fall and winter when the course closes down. It could work."

Cletus was making progress on his lasagna, listening to Mary. She realized what was happening and slowed down a little, began eating.

Their meal continued, and as they finished they had another drink.

When they left the table, Nancy came over to say goodbye. Cletus excused himself to pay the cashier while Mary lingered to talk with Nancy. When she rejoined Cletus, she told him that she'd invited Nancy up to the clubhouse later in the week for a meal with her.

The trip back up the hill was quieter than the trip down. Both were tired from a long day and having a larger meal than either expected when the day began.

Mary parked the car and asked Cletus if he'd like to walk around the pond. He nodded 'yes' and they started off across the lot around the front of the clubhouse. They walked around the front towards the wheel and came up around to the pond. The temperature tonight was dropping a little and there was a mist settling in over the water, spreading out onto the grass. It was hard to tell where the water ended and the grass began. They walked around the pond then the patio. Mary sat at a table beneath the windows of MacGregor's. The lights were out. Only the clubhouses' outdoor lights were on. The timer would shut them off at eleven. The lights were on in Ian's apartment, he'd be reading. As Cletus sat next to her she reached out and took his hand in hers.

"I had a really nice time tonight Cletus, really. I miss doing this. I miss *being* with someone. I'm always with *everyone*, but I'm never with *someone*. It's nice," She kissed his cheek and put her head down on his shoulder.

Cletus put his arm around her shoulders to keep her against him. He didn't say anything, it wasn't necessary. He felt the same way too. He wanted to be with someone too, he wanted it to be Mary.

~ 46 ~

The next morning Cletus began his work routine again. He talked to several of the others that worked for Teddy that he had not had a chance to meet earlier. It was a small bunch, but everyone worked hard. He had seen several out on the course and it appeared to be a well-choreographed effort.

As the days of the week ticked by, he would see them mowing. Stopping and starting as golfers played through. Being very particular when golfers were on a green. Cletus could understand what Dan meant now about being quiet. You could develop a sense about it as golfers approached. He tried to keep this in mind as his work took him closer to the green on number 14. This part of the course was right up against the thicker trees in the forest that bordered the course. The green was back in a corner, almost surrounded by trees. The trees tended to block out the sounds from elsewhere, containing and magnifying everything in the immediate vicinity of the green.

Cletus could hear most of what was said by the golfers as they finished the hole. Several yelled back in thanks when he paused his chopping while they putted.

He was now up to the small footbridge over the creek that was adjacent to the green. It had taken him four days to chop his way this far.

Someone would stop by occasionally to check on him. To see if he needed anything, to make sure he had enough water. He had toughened up a little. Not that he was out of shape, but this felt good. He liked the exercise, the sweat, the purpose of what he was doing.

Teddy liked it too. And told him so. Frequently. Cletus was just what Teddy was looking for. He hoped he wouldn't tire of the work and move on. That was on Teddy's mind when he pulled up at lunchtime.

As Cletus approached, he put his shirt on and leaned against the vehicle. "Teddy, I finally made it here." He said pointing to the bridge.

Teddy smiled, "I knew you would. Just not this fast. You're pacing yourself, aren't you? I don't want you burned out in a week!"

Cletus smiled back, "I'm doing fine Teddy, just fine."

"Well I hope so. I don't want you to think we're running a lumbering operation here." He said in response. "Let's get down there and have something to eat."

Cletus got in and they were off down the hill. On the way down he told Cletus he'd work with him in the afternoon to get the stuff Cletus had cut up, loaded and moved down the hill. There was a large chipping machine near the maintenance building that they would use to shred up most of what Cletus had cut. They would use most of it around the course. The larger stuff would be cut and used in the clubhouse. There were several fireplaces in the building besides MacGregor's, including one in both Ian's and Mary's apartments. Everything else, which wasn't much, would be hauled back further into the woods and just dropped. It would eventually decay with the rest of the undergrowth in the forest.

Cletus went up to MacGregor's and returned to the table alongside the maintenance building with their sandwiches and drinks. It was a little early yet, no one else had stopped for lunch.

They started eating. Teddy had planned this so they were alone. He gave Cletus a chance to have several bites of his sandwich before he began.

"Cletus. I need to ask you something. Pretty important. Think it over, I don't need any answer right away." He paused, waiting for Cletus to swallow what he was chewing on.

Cletus had a sip of his drink and said, "Sure, go ahead."

Teddy was looking for the right words, "Thing is Cletus, you know we close for the winter, right?" Cletus nodded.

"Well I'm in a tough spot here. Maybe you can help out. I'm sure you're going to chop your way right up that creek. Probably in less time than I can figure. But I want to keep you here." He slapped his hand on the table.

"I know this is seasonal work but I don't want you to leave. There, that's the long and short of it."

Cletus didn't have an immediate response, his throat was actually closing up a little. "Teddy I'd like nothing better, really."

Teddy could see he meant it. 'Good' he thought, 'Now I just have to figure out a way to make it happen'. He said to Cletus, "Normally, everyone is let go that's involved with the course and we start up again in the spring and everybody comes back. There's work enough for Tim and me. We do all the maintenance on the vehicles and keep an eye on the buildings. Curtis and Robby stay busy in the clubhouse too, there's work there that has to be done during the winter. Not a lot, but it's enough, so they scrape by."

Cletus was listening and he thought he knew Teddy's problem. He said to him, "So Teddy, the problem is, as I see it, that there wouldn't really be enough work to keep me on the payroll. Right?"

Teddy smiled, Cletus was sharp. "Exactly. But mainly I just needed to know that you wanted to stay. I'll try and work something out. Not exactly sure how, but I'll figure something out."

Cletus sat back taking a long sip of his drink, Teddy watched him. Slowly Cletus began. "Teddy, how much land does the course own? I mean, out beyond the course itself? Any idea?"

Teddy thought for a moment. "I don't really know. I think it's quite a bit. I can find out from Bill, I'm sure he must know what we own here. Why?"

"Well I've been into the woods a little. You know, there's quite a bit up on the hill. It's pretty thick in spots. I know you said we're not running a lumbering operation here, but a little careful thinning out, in spots, would really help maintain the woods."

Teddy was following, he'd had similar thoughts before. "So, what you're saying is, that a 'little' cutting would be good for the forest?"

Cletus nodded. He was thinking this through again. "Not a lot, certainly none of the old growth trees. But there's some in there that, if they were taken out, everything else would be better off. There's also some big trees down from that storm."

Teddy nodded. "Do you think we could make money on this?"

Cletus said, "Well it wouldn't be a lot, maybe enough to keep one person on through to next season." Cletus nervously smiled.

Teddy was relieved. He had at least one idea to go to Bill with in order to keep Cletus on. And it made sense. He'd have Cletus available on a regular basis for whatever came up.

He smiled at Cletus and finally chomped into his sandwich, which he had barely touched.

~ 47 ~

On Friday morning, it began raining. The rain on the metal roof of the maintenance building, woke Cletus up. By the time Teddy arrived, it was a solid, continuous drizzle. Teddy had been listening to the radio and the weatherman had said, this would be an all-day event. This was good. Tim had started aerating some of the greens and the rain would penetrate the greens. Combined with some selective seeding in several areas that had seen heavy traffic during the season, this would allow for some healing to begin to occur. Teddy called the kids who were scheduled to mow and gave them the day off. Tim would still come in, as would Curtis, but the course wouldn't see any play. While not technically 'closed', they would be reluctant to let anyone out on the course if the greens got much wetter. There were some small pools of water starting to appear in the number 1 fairway which was one of the lowest spots on the course. Teddy kept looking out the window in his office which looked out over number 1 fairway and number 6 green.

Cletus was drinking a coffee looking out his window which faced towards the practice green and clubhouse patio. He could also see the number 9 green that was below the patio. The water was not pooling, but the rivulets of water running off the front of the green were clearly visible.

Teddy came into Cletus's doorway. "It's a washout today."

Cletus came away from the window. "I could still get dressed up and get up there." He motioned toward the upper part of the course. "I'm back in the trees now. It's probably not coming down too hard back in there. I could move up further towards the pond?"

Teddy shook his head, "No, take a break today. You deserve it. Tim's coming in, there's a couple things he wants to work on. I know he wants to do a little maintenance on the aerator. He gave it quite a workout this week. See if he needs a hand. Otherwise you're on your own. Okay?"

Cletus responded, "Sure, whatever you say. I'll check with Tim as soon as I see him. Do you want to go in for some breakfast, since we have a little time?"

Teddy said, "You read my mind. Besides I need a break from your coffee!"

Cletus nodded in agreement, after staring down into his cup. Teddy was right.

The two of them sprinted the short distance to the lower door of the clubhouse. When they came through the doorway they had to dodge Curtis and Robby who were staring out at the course. A knowing look from Curtis said it all, 'washout'. Curtis and Robby followed Teddy and Cletus up the stairs into MacGregor's.

Ian was at the bar reading the newspaper. Alone. There was a little noise from the kitchen, someone else had made it in.

Teddy nodded to Ian and sat down at a larger table, back from the windows. Everyone else settled into chairs at the table. It was quiet, everyone was glancing towards the windows seeing if the rain would let up.

Ian got up and stuck his head in the kitchen, "Couple of paying customers out here!" was all he said. He went back and sat down. He started the crossword puzzle in the paper.

Mary burst through the doors into the dining area. As soon as she looked at the table …. "Oh, I thought we had paying customers."

Everyone at the table smiled. Nothing like having Mary start your day.

She said, "If Bill were here you could turn this into a staff meeting. I just saw Tim pull in also. Better move a couple chairs over."

Ian had his back to everyone but you could see the movement in his shoulders, trying to contain the quiet laughter.

Mary said, "As soon as Tim gets here I'll take your order. Terry came in, but I'm sending him home after he's done with the order." She left for the kitchen to tell Terry who was here. He'd probably start cooking what he knew everyone would be ordering.

The door to MacGregor's opened and Bill came in. He had parked out front and knew everyone would be in MacGregor's. He came over to the table as Tim also made his way into the room, following Bill to the table. They sat and joined the conversation about the weather.

Mary came out of the kitchen and jotted down what everybody wanted for breakfast and went back in to help Terry. Everyone had retrieved coffee and settled back into their seats.

Bill spoke to Tim, "So, is that aeration going okay?"

Tim answered, "Yeah, I think we got lucky getting as much done as we did right before this rain. I'd still like to get number 11 done. There's also a couple of tee boxes that could use a little repair work."

Teddy joined in, "Tim, what about a little trimming over the tee box up on 15? Cletus and I have been up there on 14 during the week. Take a look up there and see what you think. As long as Cletus is up there he could take a couple limbs out if you think it would help."

Several discussions along the same lines continued until Mary began bringing their meals out. Nobody had ordered anything fancy, just a hearty breakfast to start their day off. Terry came out and sat with Ian checking to see if there was anything else to do before he left. Ian had finished his puzzle and was content to just let things go for the rest of the day. There'd be some activity tonight. Terry would return, but for now it was quiet, he told him to get back home and enjoy what he could of the day with his family. School wasn't far off, so this would be a chance to do something – even if it was only getting the school 'shopping' out of the way.

The breakfast food had been finished and most had found their way back to the urn for a second cup of coffee. Bill, Curtis and Robby were at their corner of the table discussing a couple ideas Curtis had about what they'd do over the winter to freshen up the clubhouse. A little painting, maybe replacing the carpeting in the entryway.

Cletus had spoken with Tim, Tim said he could handle the maintenance on his aerator. He told Cletus that after he was done with that he was going to take a little time off too, if the rain persisted. It was getting so wet out there, that he'd damage the course if he took any equipment out.

Teddy and Bill left for Bill's office to carry on the conversation that they'd started over breakfast. Neither would go home, they still had plenty to do.

Mary came out of the kitchen and sat in the booth to eat her breakfast. She looked over at Cletus and motioned to him to join her, since it looked like he was done with Tim.

Cletus sat down opposite her with his coffee. Between bites of her toast she asked him what his plans for the day were. "So, different schedule today? I hope you're not thinking of going up there with your axe."

Cletus said, "Well, I offered, but Teddy says to stay put until it eases up out there. What about you? What's your day look like?"

Mary thought for a moment, "There won't be much happening in here. Maybe tonight it'll pick up – being a Friday. I've got everything done that can be done, for next week's dinner. That's about all. Why, do you have something in mind?"

Cletus answered, "Well 1 thought if I helped you clean up all this" he motioned to the destruction they'd just caused at the larger table, "you might have enough time to take me up beyond the falls and show me what's up there."

Mary smiled back. She liked the idea.

Cletus added, "That is if you don't mind risking getting a little wet. The trees are pretty thick up there, but by now it's dripping down through so we're bound to see some of it."

Mary said, "Sure, it'll be fun. I've got a raincoat, I don't mind risking it a little!"

~ Brad Leech ~

~ 48 ~

Cletus cleared the table while Mary finished her breakfast. He brought all the coffee cups in from the bar also. Might as well get everything cleaned up. Mary came in with her plate and they began washing. MacGregor's hadn't gotten a dishwashing machine yet. They were a little pricey and space in the kitchen was already at a premium. Mary washed, Cletus dried.

When they finished, they came out to find Ian behind the bar filling out a list of items he needed to get from the liquor distributors that he dealt with.

Mary came up to him and said, "Cletus and I are going out there. I'm going to take him up above the falls. It shouldn't be too bad out there, we'll be back around lunch time. Okay?"

Ian looked up from his list, looked out the window, turned back to her, "Well be careful up there, things get slippery in the woods. Try not to get too wet, the last thing you need is to come down with pneumonia! Same to you." As he nodded to Cletus.

All Cletus said was, "We'll be careful."

They walked out, Cletus said he'd meet her downstairs – he was going to get his hooded jacket and change his boots.

Mary went to her apartment and changed out of the work clothes into blue jeans and a sweat shirt. She slipped into boots and grabbed her raincoat on the way out the door to rejoin Cletus.

Cletus was waiting outside the door under the overhang. Mary came through. They looked at each other as if to say, 'Do we really want to do this?'

Mary started off. Cletus followed. They walked quickly around the pond to the path that followed the creek up the hill. They moved along briskly - it was normal to try and avoid the rain - although they both must have realized they would get soaked anyway.

They made it up to where Cletus had been working, before too long. The hill was getting a little steeper, they were slowing a little. The rain wasn't really that bad.

The tangled limbs slowed them more as they approached the falls. The larger trees were actually blocking the rainfall. There was a constant dripping effect but they continued onward.

Above the falls the path they were on leveled out quite a bit and the walking was easier. The creek bed was wider up here. Not so many stones, mostly larger flat slabs of limestone. They continued walking side by side with some chatter between themselves but mostly quietly enjoying what surrounded them.

Several hundred yards upstream Cletus could hear the sound of water tumbling over rocks. Not a waterfall just rapid water. Mary raced ahead to the pond.

When Cletus came up beside her, he looked out over an enormous pond. Much larger than at the clubhouse. The sycamores here were much larger too, an absolutely gigantic one perched right where the water exited the pond and began tumbling downward. Beneath the tree were several large old mill stones that were partially buried. Obviously there had been a mill up here at some time. The stones had cracked and been discarded.

It was a stunning sight. Mary took his hand and pulled him along the pathway and begin moving around the pond. They came out of the trees that only partially surrounded the pond, and Mary pointed across the pond.

There stood a modest stone house with a small stone barn just behind it.

This was Ian's and Katherine's farm. Mary's home.

The rain has eased a little, more of a soft drizzle.

Mary continued pulling Cletus along the edge of the pond. They had walked almost halfway around the pond when she stopped and said to Cletus, "Isn't this place just beautiful?"

Cletus nodded in agreement, continuing to look around the area. It was wide open here. The house and barn were near the edge of the woods, still perhaps a hundred yards away, but the expansive fields opened out away from the pond and the buildings. Corn was six-foot-high in all directions.

Cletus said to Mary, "Can we go over to the house?"

Mary shook her head no, "That's okay, I don't need to go there. Besides, I don't want to trample too much of the corn."

She looked back at the pond. Cletus turned to look also. Mary stared at the pond and the sycamore. She took Cletus's hand and led him back toward the tree. Cletus had noticed there really weren't other sycamores here, just the giant by the pond, before they also began appearing along the creek below the pond.

Cletus said to her while pointing at the tree, "Do you suppose this is the 'mother' to all the trees down along the creek?"

Mary slowly lifted her head up to look at Cletus. Tears were streaming down her cheeks. She tried to speak, but her quivering chin wouldn't let the words out.

Cletus pulled her head in against his chest, his hand across the top of her head. He could feel the silent sobbing happening against him.

Mary was finally able to take several deeper breaths and lifted her head away from him. She said, "My mother used almost the same words to describe the sycamores to me when I was about six years old."

Cletus stayed silent, letting her continue when she could.

"I miss her so much. I love it out here, up on the hill. I come up here by myself. I used to think I'd see her in the woods. She loved the trees as much as me. I'm sure a part of her is here."

Cletus still hadn't said anything. He took her hand and started her back along the path. They walked wordlessly back through the trees, down the hill, past the waterfall.

The rain had not stopped, the drizzle had thickened into a steadier rainfall.

They came off the course towards the clubhouse. Mary headed towards the steps to her apartment. Cletus turned to go to the maintenance building. Mary took his hand and pulled him back to follow her. She led him up the steps to the balcony that reached out over the pond. She opened the door and let him into her apartment, closing the door behind them.

Mary told Cletus to stay put while she checked on what was happening in MacGregor's. It was past noon but only Ian was there.

Ian said to her, "You missed the rush. I think everybody decided they had someplace else to be."

He looked at her, soaked to the bone.

"Get out of those wet clothes, and get yourself dried out. Nothing's going to happen in here this afternoon. If something develops I'll come get you."

Ian didn't expect an answer from Mary, he just motioned her out with a shush of his hand. He knew it had probably been emotional up there for Mary.

Mary didn't argue. She returned to her apartment.

~ **49** ~

Cletus stayed at the doorway, dripping, while Mary was gone. He looked around the large living room.

The room was immense with heart-of-pine flooring. Overhead were large hand-hewn beams supporting the roof. This had been the main portion of the original mill. Cletus looked at the end wall, large blocks of granite had been used. There was a pilaster projecting into the room. Several feet up from the floor was a large steel plate bolted into the stonework. Cletus knew this must be the bearing for the wheel. He could hear the wheel turning, the sound radiating through the plate. The main bearing must be housed in there. Obviously, the axle had been cut and the plate added when the milling stones and apparatus had been taken out.

As he looked around the room further, he spotted the coffee table. It was a large circular glass table. The glass was resting on a massive wooden gear, one of the gears that had been driven by the main axel of the wheel.

Mary had a variety of things in the room that probably came from the farm, but there were some newer, eclectic items that were ... well ... Mary. Like the black 'Tick Tock Cat' clock in the kitchen. This area was small, since she probably used the kitchen in MacGregor's, but still offered her the freedom of her own apartment.

He was taking off his boots when Mary came back in. Mary took their raincoats and hung them on the shower curtain rod over the tub in her bathroom.

When she came back out to Cletus he stood there, still dripping.

She came up to him and began unbuttoning his shirt. When she'd finished with it she dropped it on the floor. Wordlessly she began unfastening his belt.

After his pants fell to the floor she began undressing. She undid the belt on her blue jeans which fell to the floor beside Cletus's pants.

Cletus was silent as she pulled her sweatshirt up over her head and dropped it on the heap.

She reached behind herself to undo her wet bra then added it to the growing pile.

Cletus was looking deep into her green eyes as she took his hand and led him into her bedroom. The shades had been drawn to keep the bright, direct, sunlight from her room. Standing alongside the bed in the semi – darkness she pulled Cletus to her. She reached up around his neck and pulled him down to kiss him. Cletus put his arms around her waist and drew her up tight to him as their lips merged.

After a very long kiss. Mary sat on the edge of her bed. She removed the last of their clothes and pulled Cletus into bed with her.

The rain continued outside. A steady drumming against the roof.

Afterward, they laid intertwined on the bed, their bodies melded together as one.

Cletus tried to pull away, Mary pulled him back. She reached up with her hands to pull him down to her, to kiss him, again.

Later, she got up and threw his clothes in her clothes dryer. She quickly came back to Cletus and curled up against him.

Mary's breathing settled into a slower, rhythmic pattern.

Later, Cletus was the first to speak. Softly he asked, "Mary, you awake."

Mary nodded her head.

Cletus looked at the alarm clock on her nightstand. Three o'clock.

"Mary, I should get going."

Mary looked at the clock. "Okay Cletus, I've got to get moving too."

She rolled over to face him, "I had a great afternoon!"

"You too?" Cletus asked.

"Yup." Was all Mary said as she got up.

She retrieved a towel from her closet and wrapped it around herself. Cletus sat on the edge of the bed.

Mary turned to him, "Your clothes aren't dry yet, but they'll have to do until you get to your room. I've got to take a quick shower and get this hair untangled."

Cletus smiled and said, "Yeah I'll change and come back over for supper after I've showered too. I'll collect my clothes and let myself out."

Cletus made his way back to her laundry area, dressed and put his wet boots back on at the door. As he was leaving, he heard the shower come on.

~ Brad Leech ~

~ 50 ~

When Cletus returned to MacGregor's later for supper, the dining room was only partially filled. There were a couple foursomes that had probably booked tee times for tomorrow and shown up to confirm that they could play. From what he could overhear, the course would be open at the regular time. The rain had eased up somewhat.

He poured a coffee and sat at the end of the bar. Ian rang up a sale at the bar and returned to Cletus after returning the change to the customer.

"So, Cletus, you got a look at the upper pond? What'd you think?"

Cletus answered, "It's beautiful up there. It must have been hard to leave it."

Ian responded, "It is nice up there!" In a little more somber tone he added, "But it wasn't the same after Katherine … left."

Cletus thought to himself, 'wrong words again'.

Ian saw the look on Cletus's face, "It's okay Cletus, really. I don't mind talking about it. How was Mary, up there?" as he nodded up the hill.

Cletus's heart almost stopped …careful now

"She was okay with it. She showed me around a bit. It was nice."

Cletus's heard a little laughter from the kitchen. He glanced at the door, saw Mary looking through the porthole window in the door. Smiling.

After a moment or two she came out through the door with a plate of food for a customer sitting at the far end of the bar. Smiling at both Cletus and Ian as she walked by.

Cletus said to Ian, "I'm going to get something to eat over there." Nodding to the empty booth, "I'll leave you to your paying customers." Smiling as he moved to the booth.

Cletus moved to the booth and it wasn't long before Mary popped her head around the corner.

"Hey you." She said to Cletus.

Cletus smiled back, "How have you been?"

Mary came back with, "Well, you know - the same old stuff, just another workday." With that she plopped down beside him. She leaned in a little closer and softly said, "Way to go with dad." And she nodded back toward Ian who was still at the bar. "I heard."

Cletus said, "I know, I heard you laughing in the kitchen."

Mary jumped up. "Can't stay. Got a couple more meals that should be ready to serve." And off she went.

~ 51 ~

Later that evening the Judge came into MacGregor's to talk with Ian. The Judge asked Ian to join him in the corner booth that was his favorite spot in MacGregor's. It was away from the bar and the through traffic around the kitchen. Ian mentioned to Bruce that he would be with the Judge. Bruce nodded and said he would take care of things. As he left the bar, Ian poured a cup of coffee for the Judge and brought his own along. He sat down across from the Judge.

While they were alone Ian addressed the Judge quietly, "What can I do for you Henry?"

"Ian, it's been a while since we talked. With all this rain, I figured I wouldn't be bothering too much if I stopped in."

"It's never a bother Henry. I know it's been a while. Thanks for the kind words at the cookout."

"Just the truth Ian, I don't know what we'd do without MacGregor's"

"It's kind of you to say that Henry, but the course would do okay."

"I'd like to believe that Ian, really I would. But we're struggling with the course. We're getting by, but it would be a real stretch without you here."

Ian said, "I know this is going to sound a little strange Henry, but I had a very similar conversation with Dan last week."

The Judge looked at Ian, "I know."

Ian was concerned. He saw the look on the Judge's face. Ian continued, "Dan was concerned. He asked me about MacGregor's and I told him the same thing you just told me. We're doing okay, but MacGregor's and the course need each other."

"Ian, we go back a long way, and you're about the only one I can say this to. I'm tired. I'm tired of a lot of things but, I'm just tired. I couldn't have a better crew running the course. Charles was responsible for that. He set this whole operation up and ran it. Bill is great also."

Ian said, "Henry, I know you let these people do their jobs – they have a lot of freedom – they're good at what they do. It shows."

"Well here's the thing Ian, Bill and I have talked a lot about this recently – and this is just between the two of us – he's thinking of leaving!"

Ian was stunned. He'd known Bill for years.

The Judge continued, "He hasn't absolutely made his mind up yet. But I know people, and I can see it in his eyes. Did you know that he's a grandfather now? His daughter had a baby boy last month!"

Ian was still stunned.

"Yup. They named him William."

Ian cut in, "But …why hadn't he said anything?"

"It's complicated," Said the Judge "His daughter had already miscarried twice and they didn't know if she could carry the baby to full term. They didn't want to put any pressure on her so they've kept everything quiet. The baby was born almost a month prematurely. He's doing okay, but it's going to be tough on them for a while."

Ian was beginning to understand now.

"Bill just thinks he's ready for something else. Look how much time he spends here. Probably more than Teddy. You don't see a lot of what he does, but without him – I'd be lost."

Ian thought about this for a moment. "Does Claire know?"

The Judge said, "Yes, the three of us have discussed it. She understands, probably better than I do."

Ian spoke, "Well I can see that Claire's been a little edgy, I thought it was just this dinner coming up."

The Judge chuckled, "No, Claire's got her own irons in the fire. Some are hotter than others right now. She's made it clear that she'd support whatever I decide to do."

Ian had to say the words, "Henry are you thinking of selling?"

The Judge took a deep breath, "Ian I just don't know. As much as I'd like to, I don't know if I can. It's hard letting go."

Ian was worried for the Judge. It showed.

"Ian, I don't want to make matters worse for the course – or for you. In the past, I've had offers but never seriously considered any of them. Now ...I don't know, this is very difficult. If I can't find a replacement for Bill before next season ..."

Ian said, "Listen Henry, you do what's best for you. Don't concern yourself with MacGregor's. I only got into this on the spur of the moment. If it weren't for Mary this place wouldn't be what it is!"

The Judge looked at Ian, for the first time, he did look tired to Ian.

Ian continued, "Sometimes I think it's too convenient for Mary here. I think life is perhaps passing her by. Maybe she's letting it happen. Like Jasper. She's close to it, but not really in it."

The Judge said, "Ian you're a good friend. I didn't mean to upset you about all this, but I just felt you should know what's going on – what might be happening."

"Henry, I'm not upset. I appreciate your speaking about it with me. If I can help in any way, I will, you know that. Make sure you let Bill know also, anything, really."

The Judge replied, "I do Ian, and you already have. I feel better being able to discuss it with you."

Ian smiled at the Judge, relieved that the Judge actually looked better after having told him what might be happening.

But the Judge had one more question for Ian, "Ian, how well do you know Dan Steele?"

~ Brad Leech ~

~ 52 ~

Mary had seen her father and the Judge in the corner booth. She kept other guests from sitting nearby. Obviously, this was important to the Judge.

It wasn't long before Mary found Cletus sitting in the employee's booth. He had a beer and some pretzels from the bar. She sat down opposite him.

She said, "Hey, I missed you at suppertime."

Cletus smiled, "Yeah. I skipped a meal tonight. I think I'm putting on weight."

Mary eyed him cautiously, "Not that I can see." She leaned across the table and whispered, "Or feel."

Mary hadn't quite straightened back into her seat when Claire appeared at the table. "What are you two whispering about, anything juicy?"

Mary laughed as Claire sat down beside her. Mary said, "Cletus says my cooking is causing him to put on weight!"

Claire looked Cletus up and down, "Not possible Mary. I know you're cooking is good, but look at him."

Mary looked back at Cletus, he was starting to blush.

Claire continued, "I'll bet there is not an ounce of fat on him."

All he said was, "You two do know that I'm sitting here, right?"

Mary and Claire were laughing, "Oh, we know!" responded Claire. "By the way, I stopped into Johnnie's for a quick bite to eat tonight and chatted with Nancy while I ate my salad. What are you and her cooking up Mary?"

Mary smiled at her, "Not me, him!" as she motioned to Cletus. "We stopped in there earlier this week and Cletus wondered if it were possible to sell some of Nancy's food here in MacGregor's."

The businesswoman in Claire kicked into gear. She said, "That's not a bad idea. You wouldn't really be competing with her, but helping her out. Her volume would increase and you'd have a little more variety on the menu without all the work. It could make a big difference to Nancy in the summer. You'd probably offset your costs with the increased bar business, maybe branch out with a little wider variety of wines to go with some of the dishes that Nancy could provide."

Claire eyed up Cletus a little more critically, "I knew Mary must have spotted more than just your good looks when you came in here."

Cletus remained silent, sipping his beer and looking at Mary with eyes that betrayed what he was thinking. He just tipped his head slightly in thanks to her praise.

Claire broke off all this by asking, "What's the big conference about over there?" As she nodded back towards the booth where Ian and the Judge were still talking.

Mary answered, "I don't know, they've been at it for a while. I've left them alone, it looked pretty serious for a while."

As the three of them glanced across at the table, Ian and the Judge were chuckling about something. Ian continued saying something, and the Judge laughed harder.

'Good' thought Claire, 'He needs this, I know he's got a lot on his mind.'

Mary was still thinking about the long discussion that the Judge and Dan had carried on last week. She hadn't wanted to pry into it but she couldn't hold back any longer. "Claire, I know I shouldn't ask, but I have to. The Judge and Dan were really having some serious discussions last week. Can you tell me what it's about? Just before you came in I saw how your father looked over there. I'd never seen him like that. Is everything okay?"

Claire thought for a moment, "I had spoken with Dan earlier, before the diner. He's very interesting. We started out talking about what we'll be revealing at the dinner next Saturday and one thing led to another. Dan asked about the course, how it was doing. I know he and Ian had talked about it earlier. It's probably not a secret that we're struggling a little. I'm not heavily involved here, not like dad. But I know enough to realize we should be concerned, maybe there's steps we could take to improve the situation."

Mary nodded, "Yeah I've noticed it too. Bill's been quiet, I'm sure no one wants to say the wrong thing at the wrong time, but we're tied so closely to the course …"

"Exactly", Claire said while motioning back to the booth with Ian and the Judge.

~ Brad Leech ~

~ 53 ~

Ian got up when the Judge rose from his seat. The Judge shook Ian's hand warmly. Ian had made him feel a little better. The relief was obvious in his face. The two of them came back to the bar, they just nodded in recognition to Claire, Mary and Cletus. Ian put the coffee cups away and poured two tumblers of a single malt scotch that he held in reserve. Ian only very rarely drank while at MacGregor's, this was one of those rare occasions.

Claire got up from the booth and joined her father at the bar. Ian offered Claire the scotch also, but she shook her head. "Okay you two, what's up? I haven't seen that bottle out on the bar in quite some time."

Her father laughed and said, "Just two friends enjoying each other's company for a brief visit."

Ian backed him up, "Evening Claire. As the Judge says, just having a little nip with a friend!"

"And I'm supposed to believe that?" she said with a sarcastic, smirky, smile.

The Judge answered for them both, "No secrets here Claire. I just asked Ian for some information. He obliged. Done."

Ian looked at Claire, this might be good. He settled back against the rear counter to see how this played out.

Claire responded, "I don't think I've ever heard you lie about anything, I'm sure anyone who knows you would say the same thing. Why is it that I get this feeling you've just 'bent' the truth a little bit?"

The Judge chuckled, "You're accusing me, a former officer of the court, of lying, to my own daughter!" replied the Judge in mock horror.

Claire's response, "In a nutshell, yes. Do you want to change your story?"

Ian looked at the Judge. The Judge appeared speechless – it didn't look like he had a backup plan here.

Fortunately for the Judge, help came from Mary. She had joined them at the bar. She cut in, looking at her father, "Are you going to help him out here?"

Ian had suddenly been pulled back into this. He straightened up and said, "It's just as the Judge said."

Mary looked at him, "Pathetic, two grown men can't get their story straight!"

Cletus had come up to the bar beside Mary, but said nothing. When Mary looked at him, he was smiling. She said to him, "Given half a chance, you probably wouldn't do any better either!" Cletus's smile disappeared.

Mary grabbed Claire's arm and said, "Men! Come on Claire" She started off with Claire, as she passed Cletus she gave him a sly wink. "I'll be with Claire in her office for a couple minutes." She said as they left MacGregor's.

Back at the bar Ian and the Judge were laughing. Cletus was a little unsure of what had just happened. This was the first time he'd experienced the tandem performance of Mary and Claire. Ian and the Judge were old hands at it. Ian could see the satisfaction on the Judge's face. Claire meant as much to the Judge as Mary meant to Ian.

Two strong willed daughters. Two proud fathers.

~ 54 ~

Mary plopped onto the couch in Claire's office. Claire settled into the chair behind her desk. Claire waited for Mary.

Mary began, "Claire what do you think of Cletus? You've been around him a little this past week, first impressions of him?"

Claire answered without hesitation, "He's a keeper."

Mary laughed, "I thought you'd say something like that."

"Really Mary, he's something special. You sense it too."

Mary looked at Claire, "But how do you *know* when it's the right person?"

Claire looked at Mary, "Don't use your brain, use your heart. What do you feel?"

Mary looked at Claire, paused, smiled, "He's the one Claire."

Claire said, "I know that, so does anyone else who's seen the two of you together."

"I look into his eyes Claire, and I see it there. I don't know how to describe it any better than that."

Claire said to her, "That's the way it's supposed to be. You'll be many things to each other, but you've seen how it begins, how it's supposed to feel."

"I'm nervous Claire."

Claire came out of the chair and sat beside her, took her hands. "You're on the brink of a new life, it's normal to be nervous about it."

Mary leaned over against Claire.

"Mary, I envy you. So many good things will happen for you and Cletus. Take everything as it comes, enjoy it."

Mary visibly relaxed. She took a deep breath. Any doubts she'd had, vanished.

~ 55 ~

Ian, the Judge and Cletus were still at the bar. The drinks had turned to coffee. Cletus finally feeling at home using the urn behind the bar.

Ian said to them, "Did you two know that Dan fought in the war? Yup. We got talking about it a while back. I don't remember how we got around to it. But you know how it is, being a bartender. Anyway, he was in the Army. Fought all across Europe. From Italy, up through France and into Germany. Tough time of it."

The Judge nodded knowingly. Cletus was quiet, listening. The Judge said, "I was in France in 1918. Nasty business!" He didn't elaborate.

Ian said, "I tried enlisting when I turned 17. They took me in, but the war ended before they could use me."

Cletus nodded, "I tried enlisting too." This surprised Ian and the Judge. Cletus was quiet, but continued, "I made it through everything until the physical. They said I had a heart murmur. I said, so what? They wouldn't let me in. Our family doctor went to them, said there was no history of it in the family – that it wouldn't be a problem. They still wouldn't let me in. I tried everything."

Ian could see this really bothered Cletus.

Cletus continued, "My brother died in Korea." A simple statement.

~ Brad Leech ~

~ 56 ~

Mary and Claire rejoined their fathers and Cletus at the bar. It was getting late and Mary knew she had a full day ahead of her. The weather report was for much improved conditions, the course would be busy. Claire came up to her father and said, "If you've concluded your business maybe you should think about letting these people close up."

The Judge smiled, "Quite right. They've had a long day too, they deserve a break."

Ian said, "If anyone needs another coffee, the pots still hot."

The Judge nodded no. Claire too. Claire took the Judge's arm and the two left MacGregor's.

Cletus thought about the coffee, but he turned it down also. He didn't know what tomorrow would bring, so he said goodnight to Mary and Ian and was close behind Claire and the Judge as they exited the building.

"Well Mary, that just leaves us. I sent Bruce home a while ago." Said Ian.

Mary sat down opposite Ian at the bar. "Dad you're right, a long day today, a long day tomorrow. I'm going to turn in also."

Ian sensed a little hesitancy in Mary. He said, "Anything we need to talk about? This is Dad talking now, not the bartender at MacGregor's"

Mary smiled, "How is it that fathers *know*? Is there some gene that fathers have that others don't?"

Ian responded, "It's got nothing to do with genetics, just good eyesight!"

Mary said, "What is it you think I need to discuss with you?" she said with her cheeks dimpling up as she smiled at him.

Ian was right to the point, "Not what, who?"

Mary had to laugh, "It can't be that obvious, can it?"

"You can't tell me that Claire didn't just tell how obvious it was to everyone else around here, can you?"

Mary just shook her head. She smiled, "I never thought I'd say it, but maybe love does make you blind."

She leaned forward and put her hand on Ian's. Ian was smiling.

"Dad, I think this is real. I think it's happening to me and I don't fully understand it all. But I want it to happen. I want it to be Cletus."

Ian was pleased. She had finally let herself fall in love. He liked Cletus, he told her so, "Mary, I know he hasn't been here long, but I see him around you …I think he's going to be great for you."

"Dad, I'm learning more about him all the time. He amazes me. I've never met anyone like him."

Ian said to her, "I've only met one other person like him, …you!"

The tears slowly started coming down across Mary's cheeks. Striking the bar in little droplets.

Ian moved to brush them off her cheeks, she laid her head sideways into his hands. She was quietly sobbing now. He let this continue for a while before he said to her, "Come on now, you should get some rest. Go now, and I'll finish up in here."

Mary quietly got up and came around the end of the bar and gave her father a kiss on his cheek. Smiling she said, "Thanks dad. Don't stay in here too long, don't read too late tonight either."

With that she came out from the bar and crossed through MacGregor's toward her apartment.

Ian stood there for a moment smiling, swirling his finger around in the teardrops that had fallen on the bar.

~ Brad Leech ~

~ 57 ~

Cletus circled around the clubhouse and went down to the patio. He was sitting at a table staring out at the pond when the lights in Mary's apartment came on. It wasn't long before MacGregor's went dark, then Ian's apartment lit up.

It had been so long since Cletus had felt he was a part of a family. When his brother had died, it tore his family apart. His father had never wanted Floyd to enlist. He had seen war in France. He didn't want his sons to go through that. When word came back that Floyd had died, it destroyed him. Cletus watched him age twenty years overnight.

His mother was devastated. She was only going through the motions of living. When Cletus tried to enlist, she turned numb. He'd expected a fight from his parents but it was beyond them. After that, he couldn't stay. He couldn't seem to help them, he felt it was pulling him down too.

As he looked at the windows, he wondered. Was he going to move these two people apart? As much as he thought he loved Mary, what would it do to Ian?

Mary's light clicked out. Ian's stayed on.

Cletus got up and walked to Ian's apartment door. It was just off the corner of the patio close to the parking area. The outside light by the door was still on. Cletus softly knocked on the door.

Ian came to the door. When he opened it, he saw Cletus and said, "Cletus. I thought you were turning in for the night. Is there a problem?"

Cletus said, "No problem sir. I hope I'm not disturbing you."

Ian said, "Not at all. Come in. Please."

Cletus stepped through the doorway into Ian's apartment. The room that he was standing in looked more like a library than a living room. There were not only shelves filled with books, but books on several tables as well.

Ian said, "What's on your mind, how can I help? Sit here." Ian motioned to a sofa. Cletus sat down, followed by Ian in his reading chair adjacent to the sofa.

Cletus swallowed hard, not knowing how to begin. "Sir, I think I'm in love with your daughter." It just came out. It didn't even feel like he'd said the words.

Ian had been concerned, but broke into a smile. "Of course you are. Any damn fool can see that!"

Cletus took a breath. Relieved. There, he'd said it.

Ian continued, "My guess is that you haven't let Mary in on this secret, have you?"

Cletus nervously smiled, "No sir I haven't."

"Well if I were you son, I'd tell her!" was Ian's response.

Cletus said, "I know she likes me sir, it's just that *this* is more. What if she doesn't want, or isn't ready for it? Maybe I shouldn't be asking you, but I don't want to hurt her. I don't want to do anything …"

Ian interrupted him, "Cletus, you won't hurt her. I think you're the best thing to come into Mary's life in a long time. Be yourself. She enjoys you. I've seen the difference in her over the past several days."

Cletus was feeling better. He said, "I know you don't know anything about me, not really. I don't want to do anything to disrupt the two of you."

Ian continued to try to reinsure him, "Cletus, don't worry. Talk to her, tell her how you feel. I know men aren't great at all this, I certainly never was, but speaking as her father – I think she needs to hear it from you. I think she wants to hear it from you."

Cletus got up from the sofa, "Thank you sir, I just had to say something about it."

As he moved towards the door Ian stopped him, "Cletus, anytime you want to talk I'm here." He patted Cletus shoulder. "Now, try and get some sleep. Okay?"

Cletus nodded as he left the apartment, "I'll try. Thanks again Ian."

As Ian closed the door he was smiling. He liked Cletus, he was sure things would work themselves out.

~ Brad Leech ~

~ 58 ~

Sunday would normally have been a day off for Cletus. When Teddy came in he didn't expect to see Cletus dressed for work. Teddy was the first one to show up. The kids that worked on Sunday doing the mowing had flexible schedules to work around church and other family responsibilities. Most wouldn't be here until after ten o'clock.

Cletus came into Teddy's office. Teddy looked up at him.

"Cletus what are you dressed for? You're not going out there, are you?"

Cletus said, "Yeah, I'm going up there into that thick stuff towards the waterfall."

"Cletus, it's your day off!"

"Teddy, I just need a little time by myself. I thought I'd go up there and get a workout in. I won't stay up there all day."

Teddy said, "Well be careful, take some water too. I heard that this might be the start of a warm stretch, maybe not Indian summer, but it might get a little steamy up there in the woods."

Cletus said, "I will. Is there anything I can help you with today?"

Teddy said, "No, I've got some paper work to catch up on once I get the mowers started. Later though, we should get together and talk about the dinner next week and what we need to get done for it. Stop in and we'll chat about it."

Cletus said, "Okay, I really won't be up there all day. I'll catch up with you later." Cletus headed out the doorway.

He crossed the patio and walked around the pond to the path leading up the hill. He just needed to get away for a while and the walk up the hill felt good. He reached the shed and retrieved his axe. Heading back into the woods he moved up just beyond the bridge to the next pile of snarled limbs tangled along the creek bed.

He began trimming small limbs from the larger limbs and pulling the debris back from the path. Soon he could extricate the larger limb and cut it into sections small enough to be carried in a cart. This process continued as he moved up the creek bed deeper into the woods. He was far enough from the green where he could continually cut without pausing for golfers. He began really sweating now. The exercise felt good. The rhythmic chopping was second nature to him. It cleared his mind out.

He continued swinging the axe.

~ **59** ~

Mary was in MacGregor's at six thirty when Teddy came in for breakfast. He settled into the booth with a coffee and waited for Mary.

When Mary came out he motioned her to sit down while he went through the motions of studying the menu.

He looked up at her and asked her about some scrambled eggs, maybe some bacon. He watched as she said that wouldn't be a problem and left to cook them. With a wife and two daughters, Teddy wasn't oblivious to problems when they presented themselves. He got up with his coffee and sat at the bar opposite Ian who had just started the crossword puzzle in the paper.

As he sat down he wordlessly nodded towards the kitchen. Ian had looked up when Teddy sat down. He nodded his head in agreement.

Teddy said to Ian, "Cletus is up there! Said he needed some time to think!"

Ian smiled without looking up. "Yeah, there's a lot of that going on around here this morning." With a small movement of his head towards the kitchen.

Teddy said, "What do you think of *this?*"

Ian put the paper aside, sipped his coffee. "It's okay as long as neither one mucks it up!"

Teddy laughed, "Yeah, that's pretty much what I was thinking too!"

Ian looked at Teddy, "Boy I don't envy you having to go thru this – twice!"

Teddy looked at Ian, "Hey I'm trying to learn from the best!" and with that he returned to the booth.

It wasn't too long before Mary returned to the booth with Teddy's eggs and bacon.

She said to him, "Sure that's all you want Teddy?"

"This is fine Mary, Thanks. Have you eaten yet? Join me if you want to."

Mary thought for a moment, looked around the restaurant, and said, "Sure, let me grab something back there."

She was gone for a couple minutes, returning with a plate of eggs and a glass of juice. She sat down opposite Teddy.

They ate quietly for a couple of minutes. Finally, Teddy broke the silence, "You know a kid showed up last night to take Barbara out on a date."

Mary looked up smiling.

"It practically killed me!" was all Teddy said.

Mary let this sink in for a moment. Then she said, "I remember the look on Dads face when this boy showed up to take me out. My first date. It looked like yours does now."

Teddy said, "I think Mavis was more concerned about me than Barbara."

Mary said, "She was concerned about what you'd do to the boy. Barbara can take care of herself."

Teddy chuckled, "You know you're probably right. The kid looked terrified!"

Mary continued, "I think that's the way it's supposed to be, at least at first!"

Teddy asked, "Then what."

Mary continued, "Then everyone relaxes a little."

Teddy looked at Mary, questioning …and.

"Then it gets interesting. Then you start learning about your daughter."

Teddy looked a little puzzled.

"You start learning about what's really important to her. About the things in life you've taught her. About what she wants to do with her life."

Teddy was absorbing what Mary said.

"It can't be easy for a father to watch this happening. Having to let go a little. It's normal, it has to happen."

Teddy had to think about this some more.

Mary said, "I probably didn't make it easy on Dad, but he never protested – much."

Teddy looked over at Ian, still working on his puzzle, and said, "Ian you are one lucky guy!"

Mary laughed, "Well, I happen to think I'm one lucky girl! I not only have a father like him, but friends like you!"

Teddy smiled, blushing just a little. Then he said, "Well, from one friend to another I'll let you in on a little secret. I've got this knucklehead that works for me. Right now, he's up there chopping up limbs. He said he needed a little time to himself. I think what he really needs is someone to take him a little breakfast. I don't think he had any this morning. I also don't want him up there thinking too much! Maybe you could help out?"

Mary looked around MacGregor's. No one had come in for a meal in some time. Terry had passed by on his way into the kitchen several minutes ago.

Mary got up from the table collecting Teddy's empty plate and her own. She moved around the corner into the kitchen depositing the plates at the sink. When she came back out she said to Ian, "Dad I'm going to take some breakfast up to Cletus. Teddy said he started up there early this morning. I'll be back in a bit."

Ian waved her off nonchalantly as he continued his puzzle. Teddy got up from the booth, filled his coffee cup and once again sat down in front of Ian.

Without looking up, Ian said, "Thanks." And smiled.

~ 60 ~

Mary packaged up the last of the scrambled eggs, some bacon, sausages and fresh toast. She filled a thermos with coffee and headed out to get a golf cart.

She passed by Robby to let him know she was going to scoot up along the edge of the course to Cletus who was woing just above 14. She loaded everything up and carefully picked her way up along the creek on the edge of 18, 17 then 14. She moved across the bridge and immediately turned up the path towards the falls. When she reached the pile of cut limbs, Cletus was not there. She got out of the cart and looked around. As she moved down into the creek bed she found the axe laying on the ground. This wasn't right. Cletus would not leave it laying on the ground like this. He would have taken it with him or stood it up, not lay it on the ground. She panicked, yelling out his name "Cletus!" No response.

She jumped back into the cart and went down the hill, turning off the main path to go to the shed.

Cletus was there sitting in the doorway. Bleeding.

"Cletus what happened?" Shouted Mary as she jumped from the cart and rushed to him.

Cletus said, "Mary, it's okay I just scratched myself. Really, it's nothing."

Mary looked at him. He'd been scratched deeply across his chest and he was trying to bandage himself.

She took control. She took some of the gauze from the first aid kit that was open and dampened it with water from the cooler that Cletus had brought to the shed. She cleaned everything up as best she could and saw that the cut itself wasn't really that bad. The blood had mixed with his sweat and the result was that the wound looked much worse that it really was.

"Why didn't you call?" was all she said.

Cletus said, "It didn't really seem too bad. It's not really a cut, just a scratch."

"How did it happen?"

Cletus explained, "I was taking a small limb out, and a larger limb rolled forward. This small branch just whipped across my chest. Really, it's not serious. It doesn't hurt."

"Well I'm worried about an infection. Come on, you're done here. We're going back."

She quickly put some gauze across the wound taping it in place. She said, "This is good for now. I'll clean it out at home. Get in."

As Cletus got in he said, "Just get back there so I can get the axe and my shirt."

Mary drove back to the pile and retrieved the axe and his shirt throwing them in the cart and going back down the hill to the clubhouse.

When they pulled into parking area they left the cart and came around into the lower entrance off the patio into the locker room. There was a full medicine cabinet there and Mary handled getting Cletus cleaned and bandaged.

Curtis came down when he heard what had happened. He could see that the injury was actually minor, but he stayed out of Mary's way. When she had finished, Mary left Cletus so he could change out of his work clothes into clothes that he'd stored in his locker. Curtis also left.

When Cletus came up into MacGregor's, Teddy and Curtis were in the booth – obviously discussing him. He sat down next to Teddy with a guilty look on his face.

Cletus said, "I know, I know. I should have called – but it's really not very serious. It really is just a scratch."

Teddy looked at him, "You're sure, it's just a scratch? Do we need to get some stiches, maybe get you checked out at the hospital?

Cletus said, "Teddy, it's not serious. Mary got it all cleaned up. I'm not bleeding. It looked a lot worse when she showed up. I'm fine, really."

Teddy said, "Okay then. Just take it easy. Nothing up there until it's healed. Agreed? Seriously now."

"Agreed Teddy."

Mary had changed after leaving the locker room. She came back into MacGregor's and joined them in the booth. She sat down next to Curtis.

"I don't know why you didn't call. That's why the phone is up there." She began.

Cletus said, "I'm sorry – everyone – I should have called. I didn't think it was serious, but I should have called. Next time I'll call."

Mary said, "Next time! There'll be no next time!"

Cletus looked at her, "Mary I'm sorry I didn't call. I'm careful up there. It was an accident. As careful as I am, it may happen again. If it does, I'll call. Please, I'm okay. Thanks for coming up when you did, thanks."

Mary was beginning to calm down, the adrenaline wearing off.

Teddy looked at Mary, "Mary, we've agreed that Cletus is done up there for a while. He's going to stay down here with me until he's healed up. There's more than enough to keep us busy. I want that to heal up before he tackles anything else up there. Besides, that stuff is getting bigger, we'll probably both have to get in there with saws to get through it. We'll just let it go until after this harvest dinner thing next weekend."

Mary said, "Well keep an eye on that" as she nodded towards Cletus. "If that gets infected ..."

Cletus said, "I'll keep it clean. If you can help with the bandage, I'd appreciate it ..."

Mary said, "We'll keep it clean."

Mary got up, with a friendly scowl she pointed her finger at Cletus – a warning – stay seated. And she headed back into the kitchen.

Curtis and Teddy exchanged looks, Teddy said, "Boy, I'm glad it's you and not me!"

Curtis laughed too. "I've got to go" he said as he got up to leave. "She said it all." And he left chuckling as went.

Ian had heard all this but said nothing. Teddy and Cletus repositioned themselves at the bar. Cletus had retrieved a coffee before he sat.

He looked up at Ian with a 'phew' look on his face.

Ian's comment was, "Hey, you think it's easy living here?"

Teddy laughed, "Mavis is the same way, any little nick ...but she's right of course. It could have been worse. I know you're careful, I've watched you. It could have happened the same way to me."

~ 61 ~

Cletus went back to his room when he left MacGregor's. He needed to do some laundry so he gathered up everything and went back into the clubhouse. In the basement area of MacGregor's was the utility room for the clubhouse. It contained the furnace for the clubhouse and also had a washer and dryer that both MacGregor's and the club, used to launder all the clothes the workers used. These were heavy duty machines to handle the course worker's clothes which got soiled beyond the ability of their washers at home. His clothes only half filled the giant washer. He started the cycle and went back to his room.

While he was cleaning his, almost new, boots – he thought back about how Mary had behaved this morning. This was something new to him. He'd been away from home so long that he'd almost forgotten about what it was like to have someone really care about him. This was different than family, they were supposed to care about you.

With Mary, it was different. He asked himself if it would be any different if he were to come into the kitchen and find Mary bleeding from a serious accident. How would he react?

It was a mistake thinking like this. His mind was swimming with thoughts of how often Mary was alone and how easily an accident might take place. Is this how it is when you love someone?

~ Brad Leech ~

~ 62 ~

Mary had worked by herself during the afternoon in MacGregor's. At five Betty came in expecting there would be more customers than there were. By six o'clock Mary could see there would not be a flood of customers. She hated to have Betty turn around and go back home so she asked if she wouldn't stay and work. Mary would, in turn, work Monday night and Betty wouldn't have to come in. Betty agreed, it would give her an extra evening with her family before school started.

Mary went back to her apartment and changed out of her work clothes into some casual clothes. She sat down on her sofa for a few minutes, thinking about Cletus.

She got up and collected her purse and left her apartment to walk across to the maintenance building. She walked in through the main bay to the office areas. As she came up to Teddy's office the door was open. He looked up to see her standing there in the doorway.

As he looked at her he nodded his head in the direction of Cletus's door.

She took a couple steps to the door and knocked softly.

"Doors open." yelled Cletus as was the usual case when someone knocked.

Mary opened the door, Cletus looked up.

"Sorry ..." he started to say.

"Hey, can we talk …" she began.

She closed the door and crossed the room to sit beside him on his bed.

He put down the boot he'd been polishing and hurriedly tried to clean his hands up.

"Sure" he said, "Sorry I didn't answer the door, I thought you were one of the guys"

"Cletus, I wanted to apologize …"

Cletus cut her off, "For what, I'm the one that should apologize. I should have called. I'm fortunate you thought of me and came when you did. I'm sorry."

Mary said, "Well I shouldn't have made such a big deal about it. Especially in front of everyone."

Cletus said, "It's okay, I think they understand."

Mary looked at Cletus …

"Mary, they know you care about me. I think they also know I care a lot about you. They may even suspect that I love you. I probably can't hide it very well. I also am going to be terrible at telling you very well. But I do love you. I have since I first saw you. There hasn't been one thing that I haven't adored about you since I met you. I'm nervous when you come into the room, and I can't wait to see you again when you leave the room.

Cletus did not wait for a response. He drew her close and kissed her.

Mary didn't try to speak, she pulled him closer and returned his kiss.

They remained locked together for several moments, as Mary pulled back from him a little there were tears on her cheeks.

She said to him, "I just couldn't bear to see you hurt. I knew it was just a scratch. I knew it was nothing, but it just hurt to see your blood. I'm not like that. I've seen others around here hurt. Some really seriously. But not like today. I was afraid."

Cletus pulled back a little more to look into her eyes.

She continued, "I know it's crazy, but the thought of losing you made me really afraid. I don't know how it's possible from a scratch like that but …"

Cletus said, "Don't worry, I'm not going anywhere, not if you want me to stay."

"I do Cletus, I do. Don't leave. I love you. Please stay."

And Mary pressed her lips back against Cletus's as more tears came.

~ Brad Leech ~

~ 63 ~

Teddy had left when Mary closed Cletus's door. He was through for the day. The mowers were done, he'd kept their work to a minimum. They would be out in full force on Monday.

He walked across the patio to the clubhouse, came upstairs past Curtis and told him he was leaving. He looked into MacGregor's and saw Ian alone at the end of the bar. He came in and sat down in front of him.

Ian looked up from his paper as Teddy sat down. He could see that Teddy's workday was done. No coffee now.

Teddy said to him, "Well, I'm out of here."

Ian nodded in agreement. "Yeah, it's been slow today."

Teddy said, "If it were me, I'd keep an eye on them." He said nodding towards Cletus's room.

Ian said, "The fathers curse, ever vigilant"

Teddy said, "I know, see you tomorrow." As he left.

Ian glanced at the maintenance building, but turned back towards his paper, smiling.

~ Brad Leech ~

~ 64 ~

Not long afterward, Mary came into MacGregor's. She came up to Ian who had given up on his paper.

Mary said to him, "Dad, I swapped with Betty tonight. I'll be here all day tomorrow. I'm going to make Cletus dinner in my apartment. If you need anything just give a shout okay?"

All he said was, "Sure Mary. It'll be quiet here. Enjoy your evening, okay?"

"We will Dad, I'll see you later."

Mary left MacGregor's and went into her apartment. She had a trout in her refrigerator that she'd frozen and she decided she'd cook it for Cletus. She didn't keep a lot of food in her apartment because she rarely cooked there. She wanted this meal to be from her kitchen, not MacGregor's. She had some potatoes and several ears of corn that should be used up. She also had enough fresh lettuce for some salad.

While the oven was warming up and the fish began baking, she quickly showered and did her hair. She got the water for the corn started on the stove, and washed the vegetables for the salad while waiting for the water to come up to a boil.

Cletus hadn't shown up yet, so she tried to reach him by calling Teddy's office. Cletus picked up on the second ring and said he'd come right over.

She had just finished dressing when Cletus knocked at the door. She let him in and told him to sit while she finished things up.

He dawdled in the kitchen area until she got him involved in moving things to the table. Her table was small, and was rarely used.

They finally sat down and Mary encouraged Cletus to start before the fish started to cool. Mary was an exceptional cook. He had tasted the food in MacGregor's but this was really something else. She obviously enjoyed cooking, it showed in all the details.

As they ate, Cletus asked her how she had learned. Mary explained that it was mostly from her mother, as Cletus would have expected. But also from the several cooks that had worked at MacGregor's. Terry had been here the longest and was more formally trained than the others. Mary had been around Terry long enough to pick up most of his skills. He liked teaching her when they both had the time and the opportunity to tackle foods beyond hamburgers and French fries.

For dessert, Mary brought out an apple pie that she had baked in MacGregor's several days before. The apples were in season now and she would bake several more while the apples remained available.

Cletus was enjoying himself. The food had been great and Mary had continued chatting during their meal. Not about MacGregor's or the course, but small things that a family would discuss around the dinner table. It had been a long time since Cletus had experienced a meal like this. He had almost forgotten what it was like. When he was living at home, this was his favorite part of the day. His father and older brother would discuss all sorts of topics that he and his mother would listen in on. It's not that they were excluded, it's just that both his father and brother were passionate in discussing their viewpoints and it was tough to get a word in edgewise.

It was as World War II was winding down and all the talk was about the Russians and what would happen next in Europe. His brother would soon be old enough to enlist and that was what he was planning to do. His parents didn't discourage him, but wanted him to really think it through thoroughly. In the end, his brother had prevailed and went off into the army.

That's when Cletus's turn came at the dinner table. They discussed everything from politics to religion to farming. There were no boundaries at the table, everything was fair game. Including Cletus's first girlfriend. Her name had been Sally. Both his parents really liked her, so did Cletus. But Sally didn't want to get serious, and actually, neither did Cletus. With what he was expected to do on the farm, he didn't have a lot of free time for anything, or anybody, else. When Sally and Cletus broke up after several months of dating, his parents understood and helped him through it. His mom told him he would meet someone that was right for him, probably when he least expected it. She had been right.

Mary had asked him if he wanted some more pie, and was waiting for a response. He snapped back into the moment and politely declined.

"Mary, it was great, but I can't eat another bite. I'm stuffed."

She said, "Well you're welcome to more. I have a problem keeping anything here because I eat so frequently in the restaurant. I wind up throwing quite a bit out."

She got up and began clearing the table off. Cletus helped. He told her he would do the dishes while she dried, since he didn't know where anything went. They made quick work of it since there were so few dishes to clean.

While Mary was putting away the last of pans, Cletus examined the bookshelf that stood in the corner of the living room. There was a wide range of material, mostly historical but some newer fiction and authors that Cletus had heard of but not read yet.

Mary came over beside him. "Dad keeps giving me books, but I never have the time to really sit down and enjoy them. He reads all the time. I don't know how he does it since MacGregor's stays open late so often."

Cletus hadn't really taken the time to read much of anything in the last several years. Most of what he read consisted of newspapers and periodicals. Life and Look magazines were his favorites. With so much emphasis on current events, these kept him occupied. A weather satellite had been launched earlier in the year and there was talk of perhaps sending a man into space sometime in the future. It was incredible to think about it.

Mary asked Cletus what he liked to read, "So, who's your favorite author?"

Cletus thought for a moment, "Well I haven't really read too much recently, but I liked a couple books by Ian Fleming about a secret agent. They were exciting, pretty believable considering the Cold War and all. What about you?"

Mary reached up on the bookshelf and pulled down 'Peyton Place' and handed it to Cletus. She said, "Here's one I finished a while back. It was good, probably a novel women find more interesting than men. But it's set in New England, I've never been there. It's interesting to see how things affect everyone in the small community."

Cletus turned to look at the coffee table. The four-foot diameter glass surface rested on a large wooden gear.

Mary said to him, "It's from the mill that was here. It was going to be thrown out but I saved it. Downstairs there's more of the mill. They kept all but what was beyond repair. The large room was actually some sort of machine shop. They used power from the wheel to also drive the equipment down there as well as the mill in this room."

Cletus looked down at the gear. Pegs were driven into the side faces of the main cylinder to create the 'teeth' that meshed with other gears to drive the mill. The cylinder was made of many laminations of wood built up to create the two-foot thickness that the pegs were driven into. Each peg was, in turn, locked into the cylinder with smaller pegs. Then the entire cylinder was wrapped by a hoop, in much the same way as the metal bands that secured barrel staves.

As Cletus looked around the room some more, Mary moved into the kitchen and turned out the light. The only light still on was a small light on the far side of the room by the fireplace. Curtis turned to look at the light. 'This must be the light I see at night when everything else is dark.' He thought.

Mary moved into the bedroom saying, "I'll be right back."

Cletus moved over to the windows that looked out over the pond. On the table with the lamp was the book Mary was currently reading - It was a large book - 'Doctor Zhivago'. There was a small, high backed, wing chair next to the table. A nice place to snuggle in to read a book during the winter, next to the fireplace.

When Cletus looked up as Mary came back into the room he caught his breath.

Mary has changed into a long shear nightgown that was a very pale green. As she came towards him he could see she had nothing on except the nightgown. Her hair was down and combed out, free of the barrettes she had been wearing. She came over to Cletus and put her hands up to his face to draw him forward and kissed him.

They remained standing for several minutes in front of the fireplace, their lips caressing each other.

Mary broke free and led Cletus to the sofa. She pulled him down onto the sofa to sit beside her as she stretched out. As she lay there she drew his hand to her chest. The nightgown had no buttons, it was open half way to her waist. Cletus lifted his hand and moved it inside the nightgown. Mary pulled his hand down tight against her. As she closed her eyes, Cletus bent forward and kissed her.

Their tongues met, exploring each other. Mary broke free to capture a short breath and returned for more.

Later they got up. She moved to turn out the light, and returning, led Cletus into her bedroom.

~ Brad Leech ~

~ 65 ~

It was one o'clock when Cletus carefully got up from the bed to leave for his room. Mary was quietly sleeping and he didn't wake her as he dressed and left. As he walked across the patio the moon was up high. It was nearly full now, as Mary predicted, it would probably be a real harvest moon on the night of the dinner.

As he let himself into his room his mind was swimming. What a woman! How could he have been so incredibly lucky to meet her?

He pulled off his clothes and collapsed onto the bed. He was exhausted but couldn't force himself to go to sleep.

~ Brad Leech ~

~ 66 ~

Teddy was sitting in his office when Cletus returned from MacGregor's with a plate containing several pastries. He motioned Cletus in and said to him, "You're up early."

Cletus responded, "I didn't sleep very well last night. I had a bigger dinner than usual. It's just not my habit."

"You sure you're okay? How's the scratch?"

"It's fine Teddy. I'm okay. What's on the agenda today?"

"Well," Teddy said, "Mostly stuff concerning this dinner coming up. Everything on the course is under control. We've just got to do some work around the clubhouse to get everything in order. I talked with Curtis yesterday and we've got a good idea of what needs to get done."

Cletus said, "Just point me in the right direction."

Teddy began, "Okay, for starters – How are you with a paint brush?"

Cletus responded, "Just call me Rembrandt! – at least until you're able to see what I've painted."

"That's the attitude." Teddy smiled. "Curtis mentioned a couple spots around the entranceway that could use a little sprucing up. Let's take a look and see what's involved. We've got all the colors here in the storage room, I'm not sure how involved this might get but let's get it out of the way first, in case we get wet weather!"

With that Teddy and Cletus were off to tackle Curtis's list of Clubhouse items. During the next couple days Cletus and Teddy trimmed everything back and touched up the paint around the clubhouse. The results were impressive.

They were having lunch in MacGregor's on Wednesday when Claire came in. She came over to the booth and sat down opposite Teddy. "Teddy, it's very impressive out there as you come in. I'd forgotten how lovely this place can look."

Teddy smiled at Claire, "Claire, thank you. An artist appreciates having his work recognized. Wouldn't you say Cletus?"

Cletus nodded in agreement as he swallowed a bite of his sandwich. "Thank you Claire, we're trying our best."

Claire continued, "Well it looks just great. I'm going to have to wander around and see what else you two have spruced up!"

Claire quickly looked around the room, looking for Mary. "Have either of you seen Mary? I need to have a word with her."

Teddy stayed silent. Cletus answered, "I think she's downstairs. She had a big delivery come in and she's getting it arranged in the cooler."

Claire nodded, "Thanks, I'm off to see her then." And she whirled away to leave Teddy and Cletus to finish their lunch. As she left she waived 'hi' to Ian at the bar.

Teddy looked around to see how many people were in the restaurant. When he could see that there really was not a lot going on, he waved over to Ian to join them.

Ian came over to the booth. "What's up Teddy?"

Teddy said, "Well I was just wondering if there was anything here that needs looking into while we've got the painting supplies out. Anything you need done?"

Ian thought for a moment. Nothing came to mind. "I don't really think so Teddy. Nice of you to ask though. Let me do a quick search through here. If I find anything I'll get right back to you. Okay?"

Teddy said, "Sure Ian, just let us know. Otherwise we'll put all that stuff away and get on with something else. No rush."

Ian nodded and left on his mission.

Cletus said to Teddy, "I know there's been some talk of using the maintenance building for cooking in case it rains. Do you want me to pick things up in there? There's quite a bit of stuff laying around that could be hung up or stowed away so nobody trips or gets hurt in there."

Teddy said, "Yeah, I've been putting that off, but we should get started. I'm as guilty as everybody else for using something then not putting it back where it belongs. Why don't you get on in there and start. I've got to touch base with Bill and make sure we're not missing anything he needs to have done."

Cletus said, "Okay, I'll catch up with you later." He got up and left MacGregor's to start the cleanup in the maintenance building.

Teddy got up and went to the bar where Ian was making a list of several items he thought could use a little paint. As Teddy sat down Ian said, "I'm almost through here. Just a couple items really. Shouldn't take too much time."

Teddy looked at him, "It can wait Ian."

Ian looked up from his list to face Teddy, "What's up?"

Teddy chose his words carefully, "Does Bill seem okay to you Ian? He's been pretty quiet, barely spoken to me this week."

Ian thought for a moment. "He's got a lot on his mind Teddy. I wouldn't crowd him too much."

Teddy said, "Anything I should know about, anything I can do to help?"

Ian thought for a moment.

Before he could say anything, Teddy continued, "Ian what's going on?"

Ian decided Teddy should know. He came from behind the bar and stuck his head in the kitchen, "Terry, can you cover for me out here for a couple minutes?"

Terry came through and said, "Sure, I've got it here."

Ian led Teddy outside the clubhouse where they'd have some privacy. He walked around to the front of MacGregor's as if looking at the painting that had just been done there.

Ian began, "This is just between the two of us okay?"

Teddy nodded and said, "Mums the word and I didn't hear it from you anyway"

Ian went on, "The thing is, Bill's thinking of leaving."

Teddy was stunned.

Ian continued, "The Judge has spoken to me about it, and it was hard for him to talk about it. Bill's got his reasons and we should support him. I think he's having a rough time making his mind up, but I think he has to leave."

Teddy listened carefully expecting Ian to elaborate some more.

"What I think is happening is that the Judge is also questioning keeping the course. As hard as it would be for the Judge to lose Bill, I'm not sure the Judge can keep going on here the way it is. He's feeling old Teddy. I think we all are, but with Bill leaving I don't know that the Judge wants to continue."

Teddy nodded his head agreeing with Ian.

"Don't get him wrong Teddy. You're doing a great job here – and he's the first one to tell everybody that, always has. I think the Judge is just having trouble accepting what might happen."

Teddy continued thinking about Ian was saying.

"Teddy, from my point of view I don't see Claire taking over either. She's great, I know she could handle it, but ..."

Teddy said, "You're right Ian, she's never made a secret of it. I'm sure she could take over, but after Charles ..."

"Exactly." Said Ian. "I can't blame her. Would you want to take it on if you were in her shoes – probably not – would be my guess."

Teddy said, "So what will happen to MacGregor's Ian?"

Ian said, "I'm not sure Teddy. But I told the Judge to not worry about that, he's got to do what he feels is right. I'm sure he'll find someone to manage the course."

Teddy agreed, "You're right Ian, he's held this place together for so long. I wouldn't second guess any of his decisions, Bill's either. They've made this place."

~ Brad Leech ~

~ 67 ~

Claire found Mary in the basement cooler. Her suppliers had delivered forty frozen turkeys and two hundred steaks. It would be a tight fit but she was going to get everything packed away. There would not be any room left at all in the freezer. She came out after finishing and there was Claire.

"Claire, you startled me!" said Mary as she slammed the cooler doors closed. "What can I do for you?"

"Just checking." Said Claire, "Looks like everything is on schedule."

Mary agreed, "Yup. We've got some more deliveries coming in this afternoon, and tomorrow the extra tables and chairs are going to be dropped off."

Claire was relieved, "Good, I'm getting nervous about everything coming together, but as usual, you're on top of everything."

Mary said, "Thanks, I'm trying – but you never know what might happen."

Claire said, "Take a break, I need to talk to you."

Mary said, "Okay. Let me check upstairs, I've been gone a while. Come on up with me."

The two of them walked back through to the lower entrance and up the stairs to MacGregor's. Mary saw Terry behind the bar, he nodded toward the front windows where you could see Ian and

Teddy, outside talking about the painting. Mary nodded in return and led Claire to the corner booth.

Mary said, "Claire, do you want something to eat or drink? I'm going to get a soda."

Claire said, "Please, a club soda. Thanks."

Mary went to the bar, "Terry had already poured the club soda and added a lime. Mary retrieved her coke and went back to the booth.

Claire began, "A couple days ago I gave you some advice about a man." Claire said smiling.

Mary said, "I do remember that, pretty good advice I think."

Claire said, "Well now I need some advice about a man."

Mary looked a little puzzled.

Claire continued, "Dan."

Now it was Mary's turn to smile.

Claire said, "He intrigues me Mary. I've known a lot of men. Some better than others. I've never really taken any of them seriously. I've already had the love of my life."

Mary studied Claire. She'd known Claire forever, in a sense she'd grown up with Claire.

Claire went on, "I'm a flirt!" she smiled, "I admit it, I think everyone knows that. I enjoy being around men, maybe more so than women. I think I like being in charge – which I always am with men."

Now it was Mary's turn to smile at Claire, she had to also chuckle. This was Claire.

"But I didn't feel that way around Dan last weekend. I suppose he behaved the way he did when I ...well you know, when I behaved the way I always do." She paused, "The truth is, I think he was just acting the part."

Mary could see that Claire was really concerned about this.

"The more we talked Mary, the more I felt drawn to him. I think there's a lot more to him that being a car salesman who likes to golf every weekend."

"Each time we talked – about anything, I think he was speaking to me on a couple different levels. I just have never met anyone like that."

Mary paused before saying, "Claire, he's an awful lot like you!"

Claire looked at Mary, "You're probably right. I'm not sure of anything. I know I want more, I just don't know how far down the path to go."

Mary said to her, "Claire, you'll handle it just fine. I know you've got a lot going on this weekend, but things will settle down. You'll have a chance to take a breath and sort things out."

Claire said, "Well, I called Dan and convinced him to come back on Friday. I wanted a chance to talk to him before Saturday. We'll be dealing with chaos then and I'll be in no shape to talk to him."

Mary said, "I can't wait to see him also. I like flirting with him too! Don't worry, I know when to stop!"

Claire laughed now.

Mary said, "I've learned from the best!

~ Brad Leech ~

~ 68 ~

Ian came back into MacGregor's and saw Mary and Claire in the corner booth still working on plans for the dinner. Terry headed back into the kitchen as Ian walked over to the corner booth.

"Well ladies, is everything under control?"

Claire and Mary both started laughing. Claire said, "I think we've got everything done that needs to be done, right Mary?"

Mary smiled at her, "I think you could say we're handling everything that needs handling!"

Claire returned the smile.

Ian looked at them, "I'm sure there's more going on here than a dinner, but I don't need to know anything more. It usually gets me into trouble when I ask."

Ian smiled at them, "Ladies, enjoy the rest of your afternoon." And he retreated to the bar.

~ Brad Leech ~

~ 69 ~

Cletus spent the rest of the afternoon in the maintenance building. While he was moving things around to find where they belonged, he took the opportunity to really look at everything in the building. He had spent almost all his time outside working since he began at the course. This break allowed him to really explore.

It's not that everyone was particularly messy, it's just that, in always rushing around, the place had wound up being messy. Most items had a pretty obvious 'home' where they should be hung or stored. He found that there was about three of everything – one where it belonged and two laying around someplace else.

When he got to the large workbench he stopped. This was just a disaster. There were not only tools scattered all over, but bits and pieces of broken equipment mixed into the stuff. It took more than an hour to separate things that needing repairing from tools, and to put the tools away. When he was done, he had to admit that maybe some of the things could actually get repaired.

He was studying the chain saw when Teddy came in.

"Wow." was all Teddy said.

Cletus looked at him. "Some difference huh?"

Teddy looked at the bench. "This looks like it could actually be worked on now." He said pointing at the chain saw. "When you see it like this, maybe it will run again."

Cletus had his doubts, "Maybe. I'll ask Tim to take a look at it. Maybe he can give me a couple pointers, I'll take a crack at it."

Teddy said, "Well we could use it out there, that's for sure!"

Teddy looked around the floor. "Looks as though you got all the small stuff back where it belongs. I'll pass the word around to keep it that way. I know we have this dinner coming up, and we may be in here if it rains, but I'd like to keep this place looking like this."

Teddy said, "Ian's only got a couple small things for us to look at. It won't take long. Why don't you head back in there? The only painting is some white using a smaller brush than you were using. I brought it around front for you."

Cletus said to him, "Just let me get my hands cleaned up and I'll take care of it." He left Teddy to go clean his hands.

Teddy looked around again. Cletus was a hard worker. He was glad he'd been able to hire him. It looked like they both had a lot of hard work ahead of them

~ 70 ~

Claire had left MacGregor's and Mary had returned to work. She and Terry had a master list of everything they would need for the dinner. There was barely room to turn around in the kitchen. Terry was keeping up with the usual activity while Mary was looking at all the flatware. Some of it was in pretty bad shape and she had decided to buy an extra one hundred settings to replenish what she was discarding. She had already decided to do this and was in the process of removing the flatware that was in the worst condition.

Ian poked his head into the kitchen and said to her, "Got a minute?"

Mary stopped what she was doing and followed Ian back to the bar.

Ian poured her a coffee and sat next to her with his ever-present cup of coffee. He began, "I know everything is coming along fine with the dinner ... is Claire okay?"

Mary smiled at her father, "You don't miss anything, do you?" She laughed. "Claire's fine, just needed someone to talk to."

Ian looked at her, "A good guess would be that it was about Dan. Am I right?"

Mary laughed again, nodding her head.

Ian said, "I thought so. He's a popular topic. The Judge asked me about him also. I think it's more than something about Claire. Claire can take care of herself."

Mary said to him, "Well I'm sure the Judge is concerned about Claire. Any father would be concerned. I know we've known him for a couple years but, how well do we know him? Maybe Claire's looking for something else?"

"Well, as I said, Claire can take care of herself. How about you?"

Mary looked at him, "I'm okay, I apologized to Cletus last night for over reacting. I know it was foolish. I didn't mean to embarrass him or anything. I was just really worried."

Ian nodded, letting her continue.

"Like I told Cletus, when I saw him bleeding it just …well I've seen injuries worse than that. It just really bothered me."

This didn't surprise Ian, at all.

"Dad it's simple, but it's complicated, I love him."

There was some movement behind them and they turned to find Nancy Pagano standing there.

Ian immediately got up from his seat. "Nancy, what a surprise. Please sit, let me get you something."

Nancy said, "Mary I hope I'm not interrupting, but I thought I'd better come up here before you got busy with the dinner. You don't mind, do you?"

Mary said, "Of course not. This is perfect. Please sit. How about some coffee?"

Nancy nodded okay and sat down next to Mary while Ian got her a coffee. He sat it down and leaned back against the rear counter.

Mary began, "Dad, Nancy's here to discuss an opportunity we may have. I didn't want to say anything to you without having Nancy here so we could all discuss it together."

Ian was curious, where was this headed.

Nancy was curious too, Mary hadn't really said much about it in the restaurant.

"Here's the thing. When Cletus and I were having supper with you last week, he wondered if you could prepare and sell to us a couple items on your menu that we could in turn cook and sell here at MacGregor's."

Ian and Nancy listened closely.

"I had explained to him that we really didn't have the equipment to offer the kinds of items you have on your menu. Besides, I don't want to compete with you Nancy."

Nancy smiled, she felt the same way too. MacGregor's had a few items unique to the restaurant, but she wouldn't think of trying to offer a similar item on her menu.

Mary continued, "I've given it a lot of thought and it could work. What I'm thinking about are things like some small pizzas, perhaps lasagna. We could purchase the pizzas from you, all made up and store them in our cooler. There wouldn't be a big quantity until we see how it works out, but it might work. Most golfers come off the course and stop in here for a drink and a quick meal. We could handle cooking a smaller pizza here in our ovens with no problem. We could also re bake lasagna without too much trouble. It would give us a little more variety on our menu."

Ian had been thinking this through while Mary was speaking, "I agree Mary, this might work out nicely. Nancy, it would mean a little more volume for you without the entire effort of everything involved with serving it. We'd promote it as a product of yours. It might give you a little more exposure to the visitors that come in here that might not otherwise be aware of your restaurant."

Nancy liked the idea, "Mary, Ian – I agree, this might be a nice arrangement. We struggle a little in the summer, our business tends to be better at other times in the year. Since summer is your season, you'd be helping us when we need it most. Russell and I will discuss it, but

I'm sure he'll agree. We've been trying to come with some ideas to bring some business in, this seems like a very good one."

Mary was smiling. Then she had another thought. "Dad, Nancy – here's something else to consider. Nancy, do you like the game pie we have here? I know you order it when we see you and Russell here."

Nancy said, "I love it. If I thought I could make it, I'd ask for the recipe."

The words were just out of her mouth when she realized what Mary was suggesting. The same with Ian.

Mary said, "When we've closed for the season, I could continue making the pies. You could sell them at your restaurant. It would be something your customers might like. I know a lot of people that come in here like it, and many of them are locals, they can't have it when we close for the season."

Now everyone was feeling good about this arrangement. As Mary said, "After this harvest dinner is out of the way we'll get back together with you and Russell. If you think it makes sense, we'll give it a try. Okay?"

Nancy agreed, "Let me talk this over with Russell. Plan on getting together sometime soon. Oh, and bring that cute Cletus along!"

~ 71 ~

After Nancy left Ian said to Mary, "Cletus came up with this idea?"

Mary nodded, "Yup. We had just sat down and he asked me why we didn't have any Italian food on the menu at MacGregor's. I explained that I didn't want to compete with Nancy."

Mary said to Ian, "You're not upset that I'm suggesting something other than 'Scottish' food for the pub, are you?"

Ian laughed, "If you want this to be a restaurant you're going to have to broaden the menu a bit."

Mary chuckled, "Well I just thought it might help out."

Ian said, "It will, trust me. Everything helps out."

While they were talking, Cletus came up to the bar. Mary turned to him. "Looks like you've gotten into the paint."

Cletus looked at himself, "Yeah, I'm not the neatest painter. I don't have any on my boots, I checked. But I better not sit down anywhere. I just wanted to make sure that I painted what you needed outside, Ian. When you get a chance, look out there, let me know if I've missed anything. I'm going to get all this stuff back into the maintenance building, out of your way." Cletus nodded as he left. Backtracking to make sure he hadn't left any paint on the floor.

Ian looked after him, "He really is something, isn't he?"

Mary looked at Cletus also, "Yes he is dad, yes he is."

~ Brad Leech ~

~ 72 ~

Friday morning found Cletus still working around the clubhouse. He and Teddy were putting the final touches on the whole patio area. They had moved some of the smaller tables with the umbrellas down onto the grass surrounding the practice green. They needed the space on the patio to set up the larger tables that had been rented. They would wait until later in the afternoon to do that, as the golfing would be winding down. On Saturday, there would be a minimal crew working. Bill had encouraged everyone to try attend the parade and festivities in town. He and Curtis would stay at the course.

Today, however, was still about a normal day at the golf course. At lunchtime, Teddy and Cletus came into MacGregor's and ordered hamburgers. Cletus got their coffees and settled into his seat to find out what Teddy had in mind for the afternoon.

Teddy said, "Well Cletus, we've got most everything wrapped up except those tables on the patio. Once they get that tent set up down there we'll finish with the tables and chairs."

Mary brought their lunches out and sat down next to Cletus. "Hey you, how's it going out there?"

Cletus smiled, "We're doing okay. Like Teddy say's, once the tent is up we'll finish with the tables and chairs."

Mary looked at Teddy, "Thanks so much for helping with all this. We couldn't have done it without you."

Teddy said, "Not a problem. I just hope it doesn't rain. I don't know how many we'll fit under that tent. Once we get the tables set up we'll have a better idea."

Mary said, "The people with the fireworks will be here soon. They'll be out there just beyond the practice green. They're not setting up any fireworks until tomorrow morning, they just want to set up the rest of their equipment. They asked about storing the fireworks in the maintenance building. Would that be a problem?"

Teddy said, "Nope, not once we move the rest of that equipment out of there. We're going to pull it around down by the driving range for the time being."

Mary said, "They'll have it cleared out sometime tomorrow morning so we can set up the grills in there. Terry's coming in early to help with all that. I'm glad we got the tent. The weather report says that there is a good possibility of thunderstorms tomorrow night. I just hope it holds off until later."

Teddy said, "Well then, until that tent's up, you're on your own Cletus. I have to find Bill. I'll catch up with you later. When that tent's up come get me." With that, Teddy got up and stalked off in search of Bill.

Mary sat there for a moment then said, "You know Cletus you could do me a big favor."

Cletus said, "Name it."

Mary asked, "Could you go into town and pick up some glassware for me at Bartlett's? I called yesterday and they're holding it for me. I looked over what we've got here and some of it should be replaced."

Cletus said, "Sure, no problem."

Mary said, "Take the truck, the keys are in it. I really appreciate it."

~ 73 ~

Cletus pulled onto the side street alongside Bartlett's and parked the truck. He was on his way around to the front and happened to look down the street past the square towards Delancy's. The square was bustling with activity. Two large tents had been set up and workers were moving extra trash barrels into the square around the edges. Just beyond the square, parked outside Delancy's was a fire engine red, 1959 Chevy convertible. Dan.

He hurried into the store and found Ralph who helped Cletus carry the glassware out to the truck. Cletus went back in and signed the receipt for Ralph. And quickly returned to the truck, he wanted to stop and say hi to Dan.

When he looked back down the street however, the car was gone. Cletus swung the truck around and drove to Delancy's. Dan's car was not in the rear parking area, it was nowhere to be seen.

Cletus parked the truck and went inside. He found Mrs. Delancy in the front parlor.

"Why Mr. Armstrong, I didn't expect to see you back so soon. How are things up at the course?"

Cletus said, "They're fine Mrs. Delancy. Everything's working out okay. Say, I just saw Mr. Steele's car out front a couple of minutes ago. Is he staying here?"

"Why, yes he is." She said. "You just missed him. He dropped his bags off and left in a big rush."

Cletus asked, "He didn't say where he was headed did he? I wanted to say hi."

"No dear, he didn't. I'll make sure I tell him you stopped when I see him though."

Cletus said, "Thanks Mrs. Delancy, I'd appreciate it. He knows where to find me."

Cletus got back to the truck and started off back to the course. He had to skirt around the square past the courthouse. Maple Street, in front of the church, was now blocked by a large truck delivering tables and chairs. He continued past the courthouse on Second Street before attempting to turn back towards Main and the way to the course. As he passed the rear parking area for the courthouse he saw Dan's car parked near the rear entrance. It was parked next to a large Lincoln.

Cletus turned onto Elm and then back onto Main and left Jasper. The drive back to the course didn't take long. Along the way he thought about Dan and what Dan had done for him.

He was still smiling when he got back to the course. He brought the first case of glassware into the basement storage room, giving up where to neatly place it and just deposited it on the floor. The room was jam packed with everything imaginable. He went back for the second case and returned with it. He found Mary staring at the situation in the storage room.

She looked at Cletus and just shook her head.

She said, "We can't just leave all this here. Help me take it upstairs. I've got to wash all this before we use it."

Cletus moved the cases into the elevator and rode up with Mary. Upstairs he moved everything into the kitchen. Terry looked up as if to say, 'Not in my kitchen' but Mary quickly jumped in – "Cletus can you help me wash these up? We'll get them out of here as soon as possible Terry."

Terry nodded moving around them as they went to the sink. This was going to get crowded in here until the dinner was over with.

As they were unpacking the glasses Cletus said to Mary, "I saw Dan's car in Jasper. I missed him at Delancy's but he was over at the courthouse. Just how long does it take to fix a ticket around here anyway?"

Mary laughed, "Yeah, Dan's back alright. He probably brought the Judge all the brochures on the new Cadillac's."

As they began washing the glasses, she thought to herself, 'This doesn't involve tickets or Cadillacs or anything like that'.

~ Brad Leech ~

~ 74 ~

Claire met Dan as he was leaving the Judge's office. The Judge had retired several years ago, but still kept a small office in the courthouse. From time to time he advised some of the local attorneys on technical legal issues. His opinions were valued and he was also sought out occasionally for his thoughts on current cases by his replacement as well as the sheriffs' department.

Claire came up to Dan and said, "Dan, I'm glad I convinced you to come back a day early." She hooked her arm into his as they headed back outside. As they came up to their cars she motioned Dan to jump into hers.

"Hop in" she said, "I know a quiet spot where we can have a quick chat. Have you eaten yet?"

Dan said, "No, I skipped lunch on the road so I could get here early. I figured that this place would start hopping earlier than normal with all that's happening here this weekend. I wouldn't mind getting a little something to eat, if you'll join me."

Claire said, "Perfect. The place I'm thinking of is just a block or two away."

Claire pulled out of the parking lot and headed toward Main Street. She crossed it and passed the movie theatre and turned left on Washington Street. As she passed the parking area behinds Bartlett's she pulled up in front of Johnnie's restaurant.

They got out and entered the restaurant. There weren't any customers in the front part of the restaurant that they passed through, and only a couple tables were occupied in the rear, main, dining area. Nancy was handling everything this afternoon, all the help would be on duty for the evening crowd.

She came up to Claire, "Claire, what a nice surprise. Follow me and I'll get you seated."

Claire said, "Thanks Nancy, we're just going to have something light and I thought it'd be quiet enough here to do some business. Nancy this is Dan Steele, Dan, this is Nancy Pagano. Nancy and her husband Russell are the owners. You'll love Nancy's food."

Dan said, "Nice to meet you ma'am. This is my first time in here. I've driven by before, but I'm usually coming or going to the golf course."

Nancy smiled, "Let me guess, you eat there all the time. I can't blame you. I love Mary's food too. Do you know how hard it is to eat somewhere else when you own a restaurant?"

Nancy said, "I'll put you over here in a corner booth so it'll be nice and quiet for you, okay?"

Claire nodded her head, "That will be perfect Nancy, thanks."

Nancy continued, "Let me get some water for you while you look at the menu Mr. Steele. And I'll let you think about what you'd like to drink, unless you're ready now?"

Claire looked at Dan – who nodded yes, he knew what he'd like. Claire said, "How about a white wine for me. I'm not going to have a meal. Dan?'

"I think I'll just stick with a coffee for now, please." Was all he said.

Nancy said, "I'll bring them right back." And left.

Now that they were alone, Claire asked, "So, have you thought about what we discussed?"

Dan was anxious too, "It has crossed my mind now and then over the past couple of days." he said tentatively.

Claire looked a little disappointed, "And ..."

Dan broke into a smile, "You convinced me."

Claire was now all smiles, she leaned up against Dan and kissed his cheek. She said, "Good, I'm glad you made your decision."

Dan said, "Well you were pretty persuasive." He smiled. "But I did some more research and I agree with you, this'll work out nicely. I spent some time on the phone with both Jim and Dave, they gave me some good information. I still have quite a bit more to do, but it's safe to say that I can make it happen."

Claire relaxed now, "Oh Dan, you won't regret it, I'm sure."

Nancy came back with their drinks. She had waited until she saw what looked like a break in their conversation before returning. She sat them down on the table.

Claire realized that she hadn't given Dan a chance to look at the menu. She said to Nancy, "Dan will have the lasagna Nancy, okay?"

Dan nodded in agreement, as Nancy left with the order.

Claire said to him, "Don't worry, it's the best. It's made from a family recipe. Trust me. You should try some wine too, they have a nice selection here."

Dan smiled, "I could get used to this kind of treatment!"

~ Brad Leech ~

~ 75 ~

Back at the clubhouse, Teddy and Cletus were finishing moving the last of the chairs into place around the tables. Mary had recounted the seating about three times before realizing that everything would work out. There were just two hundred seats under the tent. They had just under three hundred responses that guests would attend. The balance of the guests would be seated outside the tent scattered in several locations. They had about twenty guests that they needed to keep together in the tent, they would be speaking and Claire wanted them to be seen together as a group.

As they set up the last of the chairs, Teddy left to begin moving the equipment out of the maintenance building that wasn't already in use on the course. Tim was still out on the course and had reminded everyone to return their equipment to the area adjacent to the driving range when they were done in the afternoon. It only took Teddy half a dozen trips before the building was empty.

Cletus joined Teddy and the fireworks manager who was about to bring his two trailers into the building. Teddy directly him as they backed the trailers inside.

Teddy said to Cletus, "Now all we have to do is hope nobody drops a cigarette in here and blows everything up!"

Cletus laughed, "That would kind of spoil everything, wouldn't it?"

"Absolutely ", said Teddy.

The fireworks manager came back from his truck. He was carrying several signs. He handed them to Teddy. Teddy looked at them – "Danger – Explosives – No Smoking!"

The manager looked at Teddy, "Hey no joking, I've seen it happen."

Teddy handed them to Cletus. He said thanks to the manager. Cletus retrieved his roll of duct tape and fastened a sign on each of the doors.

Teddy told the manager, "We'll keep the place locked up also. No need to take any chances." He handed his keys to Cletus. "Cletus, keep these. I should have given you your own keys, but I just forgot to do it."

Cletus pocketed the keys. The manager said he'd see them in the morning and left. Teddy asked Cletus if he could buy him a soda. Cletus nodded yes, and they headed up to the restaurant.

Mary was talking with Ian at the bar. Teddy came up to them. He said, "Okay we're done out there for today. You see any problems, anything we missed?"

Mary looked at him, "Everything looks great I think we're all set. All we have to do is set the grill up in the morning."

Ian agreed, "Thanks Teddy. You've done a great job out there. Everything looks terrific. You two guys look like you need something wet, what'll it be?

Cletus said to him, "A couple of cokes would be great Ian, thanks."

Ian pulled two from a cooler and opened them for Teddy and Cletus. They had seated themselves at the bar since there were only a couple of golfers in the pub with them.

Teddy said to Mary, "Cletus here was telling me that he almost bumped into Dan in town. Saw his car. Just thought I'd warn you so you could thaw out a steak for later!"

Ian laughed, Mary said to Teddy, "He should have fewer steaks and eat more of a variety of foods."

Teddy said to Mary, "Sounds like you've been talking with Mavis. She says the same about me."

Mary continued, "Well it's true. I think men eat too much meat when there's other foods that are just as good." She stopped for a moment. "Teddy, would you eat pizza here if it were on the menu?"

This was a no brainer as far as Teddy was concerned. "Absolutely. If I could get it with sausage and pepperoni." He smiled.

Mary looked at Ian smiling.

Teddy added, "And if Nancy made it." He chuckled expecting a rise out of Mary.

Mary and Ian began laughing. Even Cletus had to smile at Teddy who didn't have a clue as to what was going on.

~ Brad Leech ~

~ 76 ~

That night Dan came into MacGregor's at about eight o'clock. Mary had expected to see him much earlier. Dan came up to the bar near Ian. He nodded towards the coffee, Ian wordlessly filled a cup and sat it on the bar in front of him and moved down the bar to wait on another customer.

As Dan sat there, Mary came out of the kitchen and crossed behind him saying, "The steaks are all gone." And continued to a table with four dinners on a tray.

Dan swiveled back around towards her and said, "Wasn't hungry anyway!"

Ian just chuckled, his look said it all 'Good to see him back here!'

As Ian came back to Dan, Dan said, "Cletus still around or did Teddy fire him already?"

Ian looked out the window, "Probably in his room, light's on."

Dan looked out the window, "Pretty convenient being able to keep an eye on him out there, isn't it?"

All Ian said was, "Would be, if I was, I'm not."

Dan looked at Ian who was smiling, and said to him, "It appears that things have changed here just a little." And he finished it with a smile as he searched for Mary.

Ian looked at him, "Probably for the better."

Dan said, "Thought that might be the case."

Mary came by and stopped, close by Dan, she leaned in closer, "Don't keep him out all night, okay?"

Dan gave her his best 'I don't know what you're talking about look' and said, "And whom might you be referring to ma'am?" Mary just scowled at him and returned to her kitchen.

When Dan looked at Ian he was holding up his bar towel. Ian looked back toward the entrance which caused Dan to also turn his head. In came Jim and Dave. They came straight across towards Dan.

Jim began, "Dan, Great to see you again so soon." And shook his hand. Dave leaned in and shook his hand also, just nodding a 'hello' greeting. "Come on let's grab a table."

Dan got up and moved to a table with Jim and Dave. They had just sat down when Cletus came through the door. Dave stood up and waved him over to the table. Cletus settled into a chair next to Dan.

Dan looked at him, "Hey kid, how's it going here? You look great. They keeping you busy?"

Cletus said, "Yeah I'm okay here. How have you been? Did you get your inventory issues all straightened out?"

Dan said, "Yeah, it didn't turn out to be a big problem. Everybody gets nervous when you even hint that there might be a delivery problem. We've got a lot of back orders already. The last thing we need to hear is that Detroit can't ship on time."

Dave said, "You boy's putting together a foursome for tomorrow?"

Dan looked at Cletus, Cletus shook his head, Dan said, "I'm pretty sure we've seen the last of Cletus on the course, as a player. That right Cletus?"

Cletus said, "That would be a good bet Dan."

Dan said, "Well I don't know about you two, but I'm going to hold off until Sunday. I'm going to the parade tomorrow and I think golf can wait a day."

Jim's plans were the same. "I'm with you Dan. I can wait another day to take his money." As he nodded toward Dave. "I see too much of him as it is."

Bruce was working with Ian and he came out to the table to see if anyone needed drinks. Dan asked for a pint of bitters, Cletus thought a cold beer would taste good and Jim asked for two Scotch and Sodas, Dave had apparently worn him down – it was just easier to order two.

When Bruce left, Dave looked at Cletus for a moment, then Dan with a slight questioning movement about Cletus. Dan nodded slightly. Dave said, "So did you get things worked out?"

Dan quietly said, "Yup."

Then Dan turned to Cletus, "Cletus, Dave and Jim here have made me aware of an investment opportunity that I'm looking into. Won't be a secret much longer, I don't have everything worked out yet – let's just keep it under our hats for a while longer. Okay?"

Cletus said, "Whatever you say Dan."

Dave relaxed a little more. Jim said, "Dan, after we talked last week, I checked with a couple friends and everything in Bingley is falling into place. I think the whole plan is really coming together."

Jim too, seemed upbeat. This was something Cletus hadn't seen in them when they'd first met. While Cletus could see that Dan, Jim and Dave felt at ease with each other at the course, they had also sized one another up and felt comfortable with some sort of business dealing. Cletus sensed that had become a lot closer since he'd 'caddied' for Dan.

Dan said, "Nuff business talk fellows. Let's find out what Cletus here, has been up to."

Cletus answered Dan, "Well Dan, it's been pretty simple. A lot of work with an axe up on the hill pretty much covers it."

Dan laughed, "Come on kid you're not getting off that easy. We need some details." Jim and Dave were laughing now. Even Cletus had to smile.

"Okay," he said, "Everyone here has been great to me. Teddy is probably the best boss I've ever worked for. Really. Everyone here works hard and gets along. I couldn't be happier. And I have you to thank for all this. If you hadn't stopped to give me a ride, none of this would have happened."

Dan got a little red in his face, "Nonsense kid, if it was meant to happen, it still would have happened somehow."

Mary stopped at the table on her way past with a tray full of food. She stopped between Dan and Jim.

"Are you sure you wouldn't like something to eat? Maybe some fries or onion rings? Terry could make up some sandwiches, you really should have something to eat."

Cletus turned to Dan and said, "It's too bad they didn't have some pizza here don't you think?"

Dan beamed, "You know kid that would be a treat!" Jim and Dave both looked like they'd be interested.

Mary scowled at Cletus, "I'll bring some fries" and stalked off.

Dan chuckled and asked Cletus, "What was that about?"

Cletus said, "Nothing Dan, just taking a little survey."

Dan said, "Looks to me as though you've exhausted the menu and need something else."

Cletus saw Ian, perched at the end of the bar – obviously following their conversation. Cletus smiled, answering Dan, but looked at Ian, "No Dan, everything I need is right here."

Ian returned the smile.

~ 77 ~

Claire came into MacGregor's about nine o'clock. She sat down with Ian at the bar. Ian gave her a club soda.

Ian looked at her. She seemed tired, not as upbeat as usual.

He said to her, "Claire, it'll all be over with tomorrow. Things will settle down."

Claire looked at Ian, "I wish it were that simple. I'll be glad when the dinner is behind us but, it's not going to settle down anytime soon."

Ian stayed quiet, waiting for Claire to continue. She had to get this out of her system.

"I know dad has talked to you about Bill. I'm glad you talked with him. He's worried. I think he's feeling his age a little more than usual.

Ian said, "Well I told him to do what was best for him, and you. Claire, I mean it. Don't concern yourselves about us."

Claire smiled, "Thanks for understanding, Ian. I know that dad will do what's best, but I also know he won't do anything to hurt you or Mary. Neither would I. We'll work things out. Trust me."

Ian said, "Well I certainly wouldn't worry about Mary." He smiled. "I'm glad she met Cletus, he's good for her."

Mary smiled also, "I know. She's excited, happier about herself than I've seen in a long while."

~ 78 ~

Mary brought two large plates of French fries out to the table and said to Cletus, "No pizza, just fries." Depositing one in front of him with a clump and carefully sitting the other one down in front of Jim.

They thanked her as she moved away from their table. She'd spotted Claire at the bar.

As she came up to Claire she said, "Claire. One day left and we're done."

Claire nodded in agreement." I just thought I'd stop by to say thanks in advance. Tomorrow is going to be crazy and I know how much you and Ian, everyone at MacGregor's, are putting into this. I appreciate everything you're doing."

Mary said, "We're glad we could help out. I know everything is going to be perfect tomorrow. Even the weather reporter is saying the rain won't be until later in the evening. We'll probably even get through the fireworks without any problems."

Ian said, "Claire, go home get some sleep. Everything's under control here. Okay?"

Claire nodded, "You're right Ian. I'll say goodnight, I just have to say hi to everyone over there.", as she nodded towards Dan's table.

Mary tagged along as Claire went to the table.

Claire said, "Gentlemen, I just wanted say hi and thank you all for coming back for our dinner tomorrow." They had all stood when she approached the table. Claire motioned for them to sit.

"I can't stay. It's going to be a long day tomorrow. I know it's important to all of us. As Ian just said, everything's under control. Have a good evening. Try to catch the parade tomorrow morning, Okay?"

Dan got up as Claire started to move away from the table. He said to her, "Let me walk you out to your car Claire."

As they left MacGregor's there were some smirky smiles exchanged at the table.

At her car, Dan held the door open for her as she climbed in. After he had closed the door, he leaned in and kissed her on the cheek. She started the car and Dan moved back slightly so she could back up. As she pulled back around to pass by Dan she stopped and leaned out the window.

"Don't stay here all night, okay?" She pulled back into the car and opened her purse. A moment later she leaned back out the window. "Here.", she said handing Dan a key. "Don't be too late, we've got a big day ahead of us tomorrow."

With that, Claire left Dan standing in the middle of the parking lot as she left the course.

~ 79 ~

Ian was alone in MacGregor's. Few had stayed late. It was earlier than usual when Ian began turning out the lights. It would be a long day tomorrow, he appreciated being able to turn in early. As he came back behind the bar one final time, he looked out towards the maintenance building.

Cletus's light was still on. Ian thought, 'wait till you get a little older, you'll have no trouble falling asleep' and he had to chuckle to himself.

As he looked far around to the right, he could just see the light on in Mary's apartment. She must be reading – 'wonder why she can't get to sleep after the day she had put in?'

'Yup' he thought, 'glad I'm, not their age. Well …No, just glad I'll get some sleep tonight!'

~ Brad Leech ~

~ 80 ~

When Dan walked out onto the veranda at Delancy's on Saturday morning, there was no movement anywhere in sight. The newspaper boy had come and gone. Delancy's was filled, but no one else had come down for coffee yet. Mrs. Delancy would be the next one up. She left the coffee pot all set for the first person up to turn it on. It was usually her habit to start breakfasts at six. After a lifetime of earlier breakfasts on the farm, she felt like she was 'sleeping in' when her day began at six.

Dan sat down on the veranda and read the entire newspaper. He was on his second coffee when the first guest to get up, joined him. He sat down opposite Dan at one of several, small, tables strung out along the veranda.

"Morning", he said to Dan extending his hand. "Name's Bill Weaver, came down from the capital for the festivities."

"Dan Steele, nice to meet you. I golf here pretty regularly and thought I'd come back for the festival too."

Bill said, "I golf, but I've never played the course here. How is it?"

Dan said, "It's a great course. A little hilly on the back nine, but the layout is great. You have to try it. You'll keep coming back, like me."

"I didn't bring my clubs, but I will next time. Maybe we can put together a foursome."

Dan said, "I'd like that. They're great at pairing up golfers. Just call ahead and let Robby, or Curtis know when you're coming in. I've always wound up with a good bunch of golfers. I have a GM dealership up north and come down here pretty often. What line of work are you in, if you don't mind me asking?"

"Heavy construction Dan." I've got some prospects opening up here and there's a good chance I'll be down here pretty frequently."

Dan said, "Well, keep in touch with them at the course, our paths will probably cross again and we'll get that round in up there. I gotta get moving, it was nice meeting you Bill."

Dan got up and shook Bill's hand again as he left. Bill said goodbye and he'd make a point of checking out the course later today when he attended the dinner.

Dan got to his car and drove back to the outskirts of the town to the Gulf gas station he passed each time he came into Jasper. They had a car wash bay there and he needed to wash his car. He pulled up in front of the bay and parked. The attendant was coming out to meet him, expecting a gas customer.

Dan said to him, "I didn't know when you opened. Is it too early for a car wash?"

The attendant answered, "If we're open, it's never too early or too late for a wash."

Dan went back to the car to make sure all the windows were rolled up tight and that the top was secure. He got out and handed his keys to the attendant, named Mark.

"Here you go Mark." Mark got in and pulled the car into the bay. He got out and came back to Dan with the keys. He said, "This make take a little while. If I get a customer at the pumps I'll have to come out and pump. It's just me here now, and no one else will be in for a while."

That's okay", said Dan, "I just wanted to get it cleaned up for the parade this morning. Name's Dan, by the way."

"Well Dan, this won't take long."

Dan walked around the service station looking at the tires on display in the waiting room. There was also an impressive pyramid of oil cans decorating the front window. He browsed through a magazine but didn't finish it. He couldn't sit any more, he just wanted to keep moving. He went back to the bay where Mark had finished washing the car and was rinsing the soap off it."

"This is a real beauty Dan. I've seen one on TV but haven't had one in the bay until now."

Dan said to him, "I'm a dealer up north so I get my hands on them early. I get a new one every year."

Mark finished rinsing it. Dan handed him the keys so he could back it out of the bay.

When Mark had parked it, Dan got back in the car and lowered the top. He snapped the cover down over it and looked the cover over.

Mark said to him, "I'll get a towel and we can clean that down and get the marks off it."

Dan thanked him and continued examining the car while Mark got the towel and cleaned the cover. When Mark was done, Dan thanked him, "You did a nice job there, Mark. I appreciate it." He handed him the money for the wash as well as a ten-dollar tip.

Mark thanked Dan, "Thanks Dan but this tip is too much."

"Nonsense", said Dan. "You did a great job. I'll bring this back here again."

"Anytime Dan, my pleasure."

~ Brad Leech ~

~ 81 ~

At the golf course, everyone there was hard at work. The fireworks technicians were moving the fireworks to the shooting stations. They had roped the entire area off to keep everyone away from the explosives. It was being set up out beyond the practice green in an area that didn't normally have any golfers in it.

Now that the maintenance building was emptied out, Tim and Cletus were helping Terry set up the large grill. This would allow for all the steaks and most of the other cooked food to be prepared.

The kitchen in MacGregor's was going to be used exclusively for the turkeys and other smaller dishes. The ovens would be filled with all the turkeys they could handle during the afternoon. Mary and Terry had decided that they would also cook as many turkeys as possible on spits that could be used on the grill outdoors. The trick was timing all this to happen so all the meals could be served at the same time. There would have to be some staggered serving, however, since there were just too many items to all be in the ovens or on the grills at the same time. Some of the turkeys would be done sooner and kept heated while others cooked. The steaks would be cooked and served directly.

Terry was in his element now. He had everything in control and enjoyed the challenge of juggling all the aspects of preparing meals for large groups. Mary usually just tried to stay out of his way and helped only when he needed it. She liked to watch him at times like this, he really was a pro.

Teddy and Cletus had been hovering nearby, ready to take on whatever needed to be done. Mary looked around and realized this was it, they were all caught up until the cooking started. She checked with Terry for about the fourth time, he told her everything was fine. Terry looked at Teddy and Cletus, obviously, they were just looking for work.

Terry said to Mary, "Do me a favor, would you?"

Mary jumped on it, "What do you need?"

Terry said to her, "See that guy over there", he nodded in the direction of Cletus.

Mary said, "Yes"

Terry said, "He needs to go see a parade, why don't you drive him?"

Mary laughed, "I'm in your way, I'm bugging you, aren't I?"

Terry laughed, "Just go, get out of here for a while. Take him with you. We've got everything covered here."

Mary looked at Terry, "You're a dear, thanks." Terry motioned her off.

Mary walked over to Teddy and Cletus. She said to Teddy, "My chief cook just told me to beat it. He told me to go see a parade. Any chance that Cletus could get a little time off?"

Teddy smiled, "Take him. He's been bothering me about as bad as you've been bugging Terry."

Cletus turned to Teddy, "Teddy I should stay. There's more that needs to get done."

Teddy said to Cletus, "Cletus you're a great worker, but you've got a lot to learn about women. When one of them asks you to go see a parade, you go see a parade. Now get out of here or I'll take her."

Cletus smiled, "Thanks Teddy, we won't be gone long." He made a bee line for his room to quickly change, shouting back to Mary that would be back in just a minute.

Mary turned to Teddy, "Thanks Teddy, I appreciate this. We won't be long. He'll be all yours for the rest of the day. She leaned close and standing on her tip toes gave Teddy a light kiss on his cheek.

Teddy said to her, "You better get a move on. I don't want him to see you kissing anyone, especially me. Now scoot, have fun at the parade!"

By the time Cletus had washed and changed, Mary had already changed and was waiting for him by the station wagon.

They got in and roared off to Jasper for the Harvest Festival Parade.

~ Brad Leech ~

~ 82 ~

Mary and Cletus found a spot to sit on the steps of the old Courthouse. The parade route would come through town on Main Street and loop around the square before ending at the square and breaking up. It was a small community so no one expected the parade to be a long one. The Memorial Day and 4th of July parades were usually longer because they included all the little league teams and other school groups.

The Harvest Festival parade was different because it focused on farming. There would be wagons pulled by tractors that contained 4H clubs and FFA clubs, as well as Girl Scouts and Boy Scouts which were as involved with farming as they were with other civic activities. There would also be wagons displaying some of the crops grown locally, pulled by mammoth John Deere, International Harvester, Fords and other impressive tractors used on the farms.

Leading the parade was the mayor and his wife in a new Lincoln convertible. Other local officials followed, banners on the sides of the cars indicating their government positions. Behind these sedate cars with equally sedate, distinguished looking figures came Dan.

His brilliant red convertible contained three people. Dan driving, the Judge in the passengers' seat, and Claire sitting atop the rear seat – waving to the crowd. The banner on the car identified her as Chairwoman – Jasper Chamber of Commerce.

Mary turned to Cletus, "Claire knows how to make an entrance doesn't she?"

Cletus was laughing, and applauded with everyone else. "She certainly does." Was all Cletus could add.

Dan was politely waving and smiling. When he spotted Mary and Cletus he broke into a huge smile and began wildly waving at them. This caused everyone nearby to increase their applause and become more vocal with their cheering. All the cars pulled onto the edge of the green as their route ended, allowing the passengers to get out and move to the bandstand on the square. All the trailing vehicles let their passengers out after they had passed the courthouse and continued on to a parking area beyond the central part of the town.

The square filled fairly quickly, he spectators were joined by the high school marching band. The mayor made some remarks about the occasion. This was not an election year so the speeches were short. Things were kept directed at how the farming had been this season. The harvesting that had taken place so far was proving that it had been a good season. There was still a lot to do, but it looked like they had made it through another year.

In closing, the mayor reminded everyone about the events happening all day long. After the luncheon in the square there would be some sports events at the school to raise money for the FFA. There was also going to be some demonstrations in the fields where the tractors had parked that had towed the wagons in the parade. Several farm equipment dealers had brought more of their equipment out so it could be looked over. They might even make a few sales.

The mayor also reminded everyone of the fireworks at the school, starting at eight thirty. There would be a simultaneous display at the golf course. He said both sets of fireworks should be visible to everyone, it was only several miles to the course. Finally, he reminded them about the dinner at the course. Although everyone had been asked to reserve ahead of time. He was sure that the course could still accommodate more guests. There was more than enough parking for anyone just wishing to see the fireworks at the course.

As the crowd around the bandstand dispersed, Cletus and Mary headed back to the car. Mary dodged most of the traffic leaving the square, taking several side streets before getting back on the road to the golf course.

That had only been gone about an hour when they returned to the course. Things were quieter. Everything that could be done had been done. There were not many golfers out on the course.

When they came into MacGregor's, only Ian, Teddy and Terry were visible.

Ian held his arms up, "This is it. Rush hour."

As Mary had suspected, nothing would happen until late afternoon. By then everything would be cooking, guests would start filtering in and it would be non-stop work until the fireworks.

She sat down next to Terry. "So, we're all set?" Terry just nodded.

The five of them sat at the bar, waiting for everything to begin.

~ Brad Leech ~

~ 83 ~

As Mary predicted, by four thirty, guests started arriving. Teddy had several of the kids that normally mowed, directing parking in the lots. Much of the main lot up close to the clubhouse was being reserved by Claire for guests of the Chamber of Commerce. She had supplied them with parking stickers so they could move up to the front of the lot when they entered. The two other lots were back further from the clubhouse and rarely used.

All this was moving along smoothly when Claire, her father, and Dan came into MacGregor's. MacGregor's was nearly filled. Ian had set up Bruce on the patio with a complete bar and he was doing a brisk business there also. The Judge came over to sit at the bar next to Cletus while Claire went into the kitchen to find Mary. Dan plopped down next to the Judge.

Ian looked at the Judge, "So Judge, how did it go down there?"

The Judge said, "About as expected, I've been to a couple of these. It's nice to see all the kids involved."

Ian looked at Dan. Dan smiled, "It was great. The kind of thing you think of when you think about a small town. Everybody getting together. Kids having a good time."

Ian looked back at the Judge, "How are you Henry?"

The Judge smiled, "I'm fine Ian, really." Ian studied him. He looked more at ease. Settled. "Things are fine Ian, you'll see."

Claire and Mary came out of the kitchen and headed across the floor to exit MacGregor's. Dan looked at them as they disappeared down the stairs.

Ian said to him, "You better get used to seeing that a couple more times tonight."

Dan said to Cletus, "What'd you think of the parade? You seemed to be enjoying yourself."

Cletus agreed, "It's been quite a while since I've been to a parade. It was nice. Like you said, the kids were having a great time. I'm glad I had a chance to see it."

The Judge looked towards the door and recognized several people that were coming to the dinner. "I better get out there and socialize. We'll talk a little more, later on, Ian."

Ian nodded as the Judge left. He said to Dan, "So, no golf today?"

Dan said, "The parade was better. I'll bet you never thought I'd say anything was better than golf, did you?"

Ian replied, "Well that might be so, but you've never seen a parade like the one you saw this morning have you."

Dan chuckled, "Well I've seen some parades. I've seen some big ones, even been in a couple. But you're right Ian, this one was better."

~ 84 ~

The tables under the tent were filling quickly now. Everyone was encouraged to begin eating whenever they wanted. Claire had made an announcement that there would be some guest speakers at about seven which would give everyone a chance to eat before that began.

The arrangements worked out nicely. There was no mad scramble for any of the food. Everything was cooked when it needed to be, the potential chaos had been kept at bay.

Terry seemed to be everywhere. Alongside Mary, they were unstoppable. Cletus kept to MacGregor's with Teddy. Teddy was a bachelor tonight. Mavis had stayed with the girls who wanted to be with their friends in Jasper for the fireworks.

From their perch in MacGregor's they could see almost everything happening down on the patio. The head tables with the guests were closest to the clubhouse, only the tables in the far rear of the tent were hidden to them. The weather was warmer than usual, Ian had opened the windows in the bar.

As Cletus looked down, he noticed that Dan had taken a seat at the end of the head table next to Claire and the Judge.

At seven the mayor got up and tapped the microphone at the lectern that had been set up in the corner of the tent, to get everyone's attention. The talking quieted down. The mayor began, "On behalf of everyone here in Jasper I want to thank everyone for coming to this dinner tonight. We've had a great day for our festival. I hope everyone enjoyed the parade this morning. I know I did." There was a good round of applause. "I also hope everyone was able to try some of the food at the luncheon." More applause. "Now we've had a chance to get together up here at this wonderful facility. I hope we can stretch out the evening a little longer, and have some more fun together." Once again, there was some applause. "But before we do, I have some news for everyone. It's good news, trust me." It had definitely quieted down quite a bit.

"We have some guests with us that'll speak to us about some changes that are going to happen around here. I think we'll all agree that this is good for Jasper after you've heard what they have to say. All I ask of you is to listen to them and when they're done, well ...just listen for now."

"First I want to introduce Dick Anderson. Some of you may know Dick. Dick is our State Highway Commissioner. Also, joining us tonight is Ted Billings. Ted is the Director of Planning with Continental Rail. Dick, do you want to go ahead?"

Dick moved to the lectern, "Thanks mayor. I asked Ted to join me here tonight, along with some others that you'll meet later, to bring everyone up to date on some developments that I think you'll want to hear about."

"Now, we all know that when the Federal Government put the Interstate highway system planning together, it bypassed Jasper. We were told they couldn't justify the expense of an interchange near Jasper at that point in time. We were told they would reconsider it in the future. Well, this is the future, they've reconsidered and it's going to happen."

At this there was a tremendous amount of applause. Most people under the tent stood and applauded as well as those out further on the patio.

"Now we don't have all the details worked out yet, but I can tell you the planning has started and it's moving forward. Construction will start in the spring. I know this may sound like it's happening pretty quickly considering how long we've had to wait, but you'll understand when I tell you of some of the details."

"The reason we asked Ted to join us is so he can explain how Continental is involved in this. Ted, come on up here."

Ted moved to the lectern as Dick stepped aside.

"What Dick is asking me to explain to you is how most of this actually came about. Our company approached your chamber of commerce with some ideas on how we could expand our facilities in Bingley and how that would, in turn, affect Jasper. Now, Jasper is a lot closer to the interstate, and we were exploring how we could use the interstate to improve access to the yards we plan on building in Bingley. During our discussions, we realized that the right of ways that Continental already owns in and around Bingley and Jasper might be the answer. Instead of building our rail lines from Bingley through to Jasper, what we'd like the government to do is use our right of way to bring the interstate to us at Bingley. They agree with us. That's how we plan on making it happen. Our right of way past Jasper is on land that was never the best for farming. That's how we acquired it in the first place. It's wide enough for what the government calls a 'spur', which is somewhat smaller than the interstate system. It's still a four-lane road but the speed will probably be kept to 55 miles an hour rather than 65. There probably won't be interchanges like on the interstate. We'll be able to plan on all the access that's needed without involving the federal planners. I won't go into all the details here, but we want you to know that we think this is a good solution to the problem about interstate access."

Dick moved back to the lectern. "Claire why don't you come up here for a moment." Claire came to the lectern.

She began, "Thanks Dick. What I think is important for all of you to understand is that this is just the beginning. The State is setting up an office in town, so is Continental. You're going to have a lot of questions. There will be people available to answer them. As you learn of all the details, I think you'll like what's going to happen. We wanted everyone to learn of this at the same time. We didn't want to see a bunch of speculators come in here and tear our community apart. We've had some preliminary meetings with some investors, several of them are here with us tonight. Nobody has started anything yet. We're going to offer space to those we've already met with, in the chamber of commerce building. Feel free to stop in and we'll help you understand how all of this might impact you. While we're speaking here, Continental is holding a similar meeting in Bingley – explaining the same issues to them. The folks in Bingley have been aware of Continental's plans to enlarge the yards in Bingley for some time. It's been in the planning stages for a very long time, it just wasn't feasible until now."

"What I think may happen, is that with the easy access to both the interstate and the railroad, we'll see some new businesses spring up here. I've asked several people that are guests here tonight, to look into it. They have experience putting together trucking and housing businesses and have been very helpful to us. They've seen good things come from events like this, as well as bad things. They're on our side and can help us. One thing they've mentioned is that we should think about starting a Farmers Collective. I know we don't have one, maybe it's something we should consider. It would mean sharing resources to get all our crops into the market more efficiently. With the interstate now being more accessible, the trucks can come here, rather than each of you having to truck your own goods at your expense."

"There's still much to discuss but there's plenty of time for that to happen. Please stop into our offices in town and we'll help. Mayor, I'll let you continue."

Claire stepped back to her seat at the table and the Mayor returned to the lectern. He said, "Well folks, that's what we wanted to pass on to you. I know my predecessor fought hard to get an exit for Jasper built. We've all wanted it to happen. These people up here with me have worked hard for us to make this happen. I don't have much more to say, but they deserve some recognition!" The mayor began applauding as did everyone else. When the applause finally died down all he said was, "Now, let's enjoy the rest of this evening, and make sure you stay for the fireworks!

There was some more applause as the mayor returned to his table, and as he sat, the applause turned into a furious buzzing of conversations at all of the tables.

Ian, Teddy and Cletus had listened in from MacGregor's.

Teddy turned to Ian, "Did you know about all this?"

Ian chuckled, "Not really. Claire has obviously had something in the works, but she kept it to herself."

Teddy shook his head, "Well this is really something. I never thought we'd see them do anything about the interstate. This could be something really big for us, couldn't it?

Ian nodded, "Yeah, Claire has really pulled something off here. No wonder she's been a little distracted lately."

Cletus hadn't said anything. He was looking down at the table. Dan had moved closer to Claire and had his arm around the back of her chair. The two of them were close, discussing something.

Teddy continued, "Mavis' brother works at the yard in Bingley and he was getting concerned about all this. He'd told Mavis that unless the yards could be expanded, Continental was thinking of moving the yards north where they could handle the increased truck traffic that's involved in moving those containers that they're using now. This'll be a load off his mind, Mavis' too."

~ Brad Leech ~

~ 85 ~

Mary had been with Terry in the maintenance building helping with the cooking when the Mayor began speaking. There wasn't anything she could help with, so she moved to the edge of the patio to listen.

As the speeches unfolded she grew as excited as everyone else. This was huge for Jasper as well as the other nearby small communities. Her mind raced ahead envisioning all that would happen. There would be work to keep everyone employed that wasn't already working. There would be more people coming in with their families, if there was more work than the residents here could handle. New businesses would become established.

For the golf course and MacGregor's, there would be more customers. They might need to expand if the demands were great enough. This could really help the course financially. Memberships would increase, there would be more visitors to the course from outside the area. It might not happen overnight, but things would really improve.

She looked across to the table where Claire and Dan were seated. Dan had his arm around Claire's chair. The two of them were giggling about something. Claire looked happy. Dan also looked happy. Dan was always happy. To Mary though, he looked like he was really enjoying himself. He seemed oblivious to everyone except

Claire. Mary began to understand. She felt the same way around Cletus.

It had started slowly and she didn't really understand all of it, but she liked it. She had seen Claire with a lot of men, but this was different. Maybe Claire had found the same thing in Dan that she had in Cletus.

~ 86 ~

The sun had set just after eight. The sky was spectacular. There were some thunderheads forming, and as the sun dropped behind them, they were brilliantly highlighted in shades of red and orange. The clouds rose thousands of feet and flattened out, looking like anvils at their peaks. There was no wind at all. As the sun was dropping below the horizon, the moon began to rise. It was coming up quickly and was also dramatically affected by the sun. It began as a faint pink disk until it cleared the horizon. While it appeared slightly larger in size, it turned dramatically orange then red as the sun completely dropped from sight. As it began to climb above the horizon it seemed to grow in size, seemingly doubling in a matter of minutes.

At eight thirty the fireworks began. The first shell startled everyone as the round thumped out of the launcher and blew into a spectacular array of oranges and reds when the arcing shell exploded. The force of the report reverberated back from the hillside toward the clubhouse noticeably stunning everyone.

There were arrays of roman candles mixed in with low altitude shells that lit the entire hillside.

The high shells were visible in Jasper when they exploded. The show was set to allow a little difference in the launches at the two sites which would spread the entire display out a little.

As the night darkened, the higher shells became more dramatic, several bouquets were set off simultaneously and drew oohs and aahs from throughout the guests scattered about, below the clubhouse.

The show went on for about twenty minutes before the grand finale. Multiple barrages of shells provided a nearly continuous explosion of brilliant bursts of light for over a minute.

When it was over, everyone broke into applause. Not just for the fireworks, but for the overriding sense of joy that everyone felt. Joy that they had succeeded with the farms for the season. Joy that the community would prosper in the future.

The air was filled with the smoke from the gunpowder. It didn't drift away but settled down close to the ground. The moon was now taking over, lighting the landscape with its glow, shifting from the red seen earlier, to a brilliant white.

The clouds were thickening and some of the higher ones were crossing in front of the moon. Their movement traced by fleeting shadows that moved across the fairways.

Cletus had drawn Mary away from the others, wanting to see the fireworks with her on her deck perched over the pond. The lights had been turned out during the fireworks and they stayed off. The torches were lit around the pond as well as additional ones set up around the patio. These provided enough light, the moon provided the mood.

Cletus drew Mary close and kissed her deeply. They were probably visible to anyone looking back towards the clubhouse, but neither cared. They only cared about each other.

As they looked back out across the patio and across the pond, they weren't the only ones sharing their feelings in this manner.

~ 87 ~

MacGregor's had filled after the fireworks. The families with children had left. By ten o'clock the dining area contained primarily the guests that Claire had invited. She mingled throughout the several tables, frequently joined by Dan. As Ian had told Claire, Dan was the one person you needed to invite to your party for entertainment.

Dan had done a lot of this. He had the knack of bringing people together by sheer force of his personality. He could tell an amusing story just as easily as asking about how children were doing, away at college – and genuinely caring. Most of the people that Dan knew, or met Dan at the course, knew Dan the golfer, but tonight they were seeing the real Dan.

He had come up to the bar for a drink for Claire, and Ian was going to give Dan a pint of bitter. But Dan waived him off, taking a Club Soda for himself as well as Claire.

Dan said to Ian, "I have to stay sharp with that crowd back there." As he nodded back towards Claire.

Ian nodded, understanding.

When Dan returned to the table, Claire was still holding court. While most of the talk centered on the interstate announcement, Claire was attempting to familiarize as many of the locals with people such as Jim and Dave who were beside her.

Claire continued, "As I said at dinner, Jim thought we should look into a co-op for the farmers. Jim, do you want to add anything?"

Jim said, "Well I only came down here to golf." several people laughed. "But when I got here, and saw how things operated …well it just seems like you should look into it. I'm a trucker, always have been. I've dealt with co-ops, some are more effective than others. But it definitely gives you more clout when you're taking your crops to market. I never had any problems on my end dealing with a co-op. It makes my life a lot easier. Co-ops can supply me with more business, on a bigger scale, than dealing with individual farmers."

The Judge interjected, "Jim, you make it sound like you own a single rig and are always on the road."

Jim laughed, "You're right Judge, I should explain. Right now, my company has two hundred rigs on the road. I own the rigs and the drivers are hired. The business has been good and the drivers have a union." Jim raised his hand, several people were going to jump into this. "The union has been good for my business. They're reasonable, they only want what's good for the drivers. I happen to think they're also good for me. It saves me a lot of effort dealing with drivers. Most are great, those that aren't, don't last long – with the union and with me."

Jim looked at Claire, Claire nodded for him to proceed. "I'll let you in on a little secret." Everyone seemed to pay a little more attention as Jim went on. "I'm thinking of retiring here to Jasper! No, really, I am. I'm moving my family down here. I love it here. I want to move a little further south and I love the golf here. I'm looking to buy a house here before winter. Next year I'll be putting together a facility in Bingley for my fleet. I want to expand it to as many as five hundred trucks. I'm keeping my existing setup in place but need to provide for the rest here, probably in Bingley. But I'm also retiring. My son will be taking over. His family is already in the process of moving here."

Dan was listening to Jim, impressed by him.

"I'm going to be your neighbor, not an investor. I don't want to change anything here. I want to help you grow *our* community. There will be a lot more businessmen coming into town, I hope they feel the same way I do. All I ask, is to give me a chance to show you about my business. I think you'll like what I can do."

Dave had not said a word, but stood up, "I've known Jim here for a while. He's been kicking my butt all around your golf course for quite some time." There was general laughter all around the table. "But I have to say, I don't think I've ever met anyone as honest as Jim. When he says something, you can take it to the bank. I have, several times. We don't discuss a lot of business, but I listen when he speaks. He's pointed out some opportunities to me and I've acted on a couple of them. Maybe I could have made more money someplace else, but I don't think I've ever felt I was accomplishing something as beneficial as I have when I've worked with him."

Jim tried to cut him off ...Dave raised his hand to stall him, "Jim, I want these people to know about you. They'll learn, if they have any dealings with you. I've already learned. And another thing Jim - I know your wife, Judy, has been talking with Jane, and she's convinced me to move down here also. She didn't want to see me run up a tab at the liquor store because I wouldn't have you around for drinks after golf."

Dan began laughing at this.

Dave continued, "I've been retired for some time now. The thing is, my son-in-law is a pretty good contractor. He was a foreman for me until he struck out on his own. He's become a fine builder. He's wanted to expand some, and between him and Jane they've convinced me to get back in the business ...a little. At least enough to help get him set up down here. We've got a couple lots on the way up here to the course and we'll start construction in the spring."

Dan said, "So what the two of you are saying is that when I come down here I'll have to watch myself more closely on the course so I don't get hit by any of your stray shots!"

This started Jim and Dave both laughing, but maybe not quite as hard as everybody else.

~ 88 ~

Ian, Mary and Cletus were the only ones at the bar. The only others in MacGregor's were at Dan's table listening to a story. Dan knew he had to wrap this up. When he finished, he stood and said he was calling it a day, he had an early tee time in the morning. Everyone else had similar excuses to cut the evening short and left. Claire and the Judge followed Dan to the bar to say goodnight to Ian and Mary.

Claire gave Mary a hug and thanked her again for everything she'd done.

The Judge came up to Mary and gave her a kiss on her cheek, also thanking her for all her hard work. He turned to Ian, "You have to be one of the luckiest fathers on earth." He said with a twinkle in his eye.

Ian responded, "I could say the same about you Henry. You've got some daughter there."

Claire was blushing. "Come on Dad, let's let these people get to bed. It's getting late." She said as she looped her arm through her father's.

Ian said to her, "Just be careful out there Claire. It started raining a little while ago and it's coming down pretty good out there now. The wind's picked up too. Take one of the umbrellas from the closet out front, maybe it will help."

Claire thanked him and started to the door with her father. When she opened the door, those left in MacGregor's could hear the wind until the door slammed shut.

Dan went to the window and looked out. It was getting nasty out there. He poured a coffee and came back to the bar and sat down.

He said, "You folks going to be okay up here? It's starting to look a little sporty out there!"

Ian responded, "We'll be fine. Even if we lose the power, it never stays out very long."

Mary agreed, "Dad's right, we're okay up here. It gets a lot worse in the winter when the roadway ices up. We have enough turkey left over to feed us until spring and Cletus has cut enough wood for us to make it through the winter."

Dan chuckled, "Yeah I heard he's been pretty busy out there with his axe. Hopefully he doesn't have to use it as the result of all this." As Dan pointed to the window.

Cletus said, "We're fine Dan. I'll take care of things here."

Dan said, "I don't doubt you kid. Just be careful with that axe, I don't want to hear that you've got yourself scratched up again!"

Cletus said to him, "You heard huh?"

Dan said to him, "She's not the only one around here who cares about you!"

Ian said to Dan, "He can take care of himself. Now you better get on the road before this gets any worse!" Just as Ian said this there was a brilliant flash of lightening that lit up the sky above the hill. A couple seconds later thunder rattled the windows in MacGregor's.

Dan said, "You've convinced me, I'm off."

Dan shook Ian's hand, "Until tomorrow." He then leaned to Mary and kissed her cheek, "You throw a pretty good party, thanks for inviting me."

Mary said to him, "Be careful out there Dan, okay?"

Dan said, "Always."

He got up and shook Cletus's hand. "Nice seeing you again kid. Sure you don't want to caddy for me tomorrow?

Cletus said to him, "Never!

Dan headed toward the door and turned back, "Last chance Cletus, I won't ask again?"

Cletus waved him off, "Get a good night's rest for your round tomorrow!"

With that Dan was gone, the wind blowing the door loudly shut behind him.

Ian said to Mary and Cletus, "I'm done. Turn out the lights behind you okay?"

Mary nodded yes. Ian patted Cletus's shoulder as he passed him, "You need some sleep too. If this keeps up, you may be busy tomorrow." As Ian pointed to the window.

Cletus said to him, "Yes sir, I'll be ready."

Ian left. Mary closed up the kitchen and came back out turning out the lights. Cletus was still sitting at the bar when she came past him, taking him by the hand and leading him out of MacGregor's. They silently walked through the clubhouse to her apartment.

~ Brad Leech ~

~ 89 ~

When they entered the room, Mary didn't turn on any lights. The lightening outside had increased, the room was sporadically lit by the flashes. She walked across to the fireplace and lit the kindling in it.

She said to Cletus, "Watch that and put something bigger on, once it catches."

She went into her bedroom.

Cletus waited until the kindling was fully on fire and added some small cut wood to the fire. It didn't take long to catch on fire, when it did, he added several larger pieces of wood.

When Mary returned, the room was lit by the fireplace. It was roaring along nicely. The room wouldn't heat up immediately because of the immense open expanse above the roof's supporting beams.

The rain was coming down much harder now, along with stronger gusts of wind.

She came over to the fireplace where Cletus was pulling a screen across the hearth. She was wrapped in the large quilt from her bed.

As Cletus watched, she unwrapped herself from the quilt and spread it out in front of the fireplace. The light from the fireplace danced across her naked body. Deep shadows accentuated the lovely curves of her body. She came to him and began undressing him.

When she was finished, she pulled him down onto the quilt and joined him. The two of them lay there holding each other and looking into the fire. The sounds of the storm fading for the two of them. She gently pushed him down into the quilt and moved to straddle him.

As she lowered herself onto him, the increasing storm outside ceased to exist for them. Her hair came forward, cascading from her shoulders down onto his chest.

She began rocking against him, in rhythm with him.

~ 90 ~

During the night, the heavy showers turned into something more. The rain pelted down hard onto the pond outside Mary's windows. The pond was boiling now as the rain drained off the course, down through the stream towards the wheel. The wheel was turning faster now, churning, the blades biting deeply into the pond as the water raced through. Down along the entrance road, limbs had broken off the sycamores and fallen in haphazard piles that would block anyone from entering or leaving.

Mary was lying in Cletus's arms, safe from the storm, unable to sleep. Cletus could feel Mary trembling as bolts of lightning flashed out several times and flinching when the thunder reached them. He wondered how she must have felt lying here in her room when the wind roared, such as this. He wanted to tell her that she would never have to go through it again, alone. But he didn't have the words for it. He drew her up against him a little more tightly and the trembling stopped. She knew already. Her breathing became more regular and she drifted off to sleep. For her, the storms would never return.

Eventually, he too, nodded off to sleep.

~ Brad Leech ~

~ 91 ~

Mary opened her eyes and looked towards the windows below the wheel, listening to the rain that was steadily falling – something was different. The wheel. It wasn't turning. She quietly got up and moved over to the edge of the window nearest the wheel and looked down. The wheel was stationary. A large limb had made it down the sluiceway and locked itself into the wheel. Then she went to the doorway and looked out over the pond.

Mary moved back to the bed and gently woke Cletus. "Cletus. Cletus please …" she softly said, "Look outside."

Cletus rose from the bed and walked out to the windows, looking out over the pond. It had flooded, and then some. There were pools of water scattered across the entire area extending out across the practice green and the expanse of the first several holes that were visible through the trees. The wheel was locked in place. The water roared as it blasted around the wheel in the sluiceway. Cletus moved quickly to the windows that looked out, downstream of the wheel, the scene was much the same. There were no pools of water, but limbs were down everywhere. Not just small limbs, but some of the larger limbs, limbs that normally arched outward, high up in the sycamores. No trees were down nearby, but this was going to take quite some time and effort to clean up. There would be no golf today, or maybe several days. Even if the road had not washed out.

They dressed and went into MacGregor's to find Ian on the phone. As he replaced the receiver he said, "No phone. I've tried a couple places. We have a tone, so our line's okay. I'm glad they decided to move the phone and power lines back out of the sycamores after that last big storm. Since we have power, maybe it's not too bad out there." Mary and Cletus looked a little skeptical. Mary said to her Dad, "Curtis and Teddy should have been here by now, some of the others too. There's got to be a tree down somewhere on the way up here."

Nobody had to tell Cletus what to do. He was already moving to the door. He turned back to say, "Stay put until I make sure there's no power lines down. I'll try and get down the road and see what's happening."

Before he'd gotten out the door the phone rang. Ian grabbed it. "Hello? Curtis?" With that, he waved Cletus back into the room. Cletus came back to Ian as Mary moved closer also.

Ian was quiet as Curtis talked. "Yes, I understand." After some further explanation by Curtis, Ian thanked him and hung up.

Ian began, "Curtis says there's a big limb down across the road right at the entrance. He can't get through. He's been trying to call, but the lines in town were also down in a couple of places and they've just got some them up, temporarily repaired."

Ian paused and a little more carefully began, "He says there's a car in that mess down there and someone's in the hospital. He's on his way over there and will call back as soon as he knows more."

Cletus headed back for the door, running, bursting outside. He had parked his utility cart in the maintenance building and circled around to get it. There were small limbs down all over the place but nothing that would stop him. He sped back across the parking area in his cart, keeping away from the creek. There was enough open area along the road for his cart to make it down the hill with some difficulty. Twice he had to move some larger limbs by quickly cutting them in half and dragging them to the side with the cart. While he was working on moving one of them, an already broken limb further back from the road came crashing down through the trees – taking out the phone and power lines. Cletus kept his distance, no chance of a fire yet as everything within sight was so wet.

~

In MacGregor's, Mary had answered the phone and had only heard a few words from Curtis when the phone went dead.

~

Cletus continued down the hill, the entry road had deteriorated into a washed-out creek bed encompassing the nearby stream. It was worse down here. He had to hack through larger limbs to continue down the road.

Then he came upon the last sycamore, at the course entrance. He saw the ensnarled mess of the tree and a car. A huge limb had torn free and fallen on the car. It was a mass of leaves and jumble of smaller limbs that had come down with the larger limb. It was difficult to see clearly, but it looked as though the big limb had hit the hood. The smaller limbs were everywhere. He moved around to the side where the driver had been removed – and he lost his breath.

A bright red door lay open to the driver's seat. The rescue personnel had pulled back more limbs to look in the back seat. All Cletus saw were the fins on the car.

The drizzle of rain was picking up in intensity. He stood there numb. He looked up to see Mary standing across from what was left of the roadway. Sobbing. She hadn't even put a coat on. Her long hair was matted down. Shaking. Trying to find something to say to Cletus.

Stumbling, all she could get out was, "He's gone. Curtis called to say he was ... *gone* ...", no more words, just violent shaking.

Cletus softly walked back to Mary. Nothing to say. Just held her. The rain pelting down harder now. Cletus took his coat off, wrapped it around Mary, and put the hood up over her head. He walked to the cart and returned to the tree with his axe.

He started swinging. Swinging at the tree, swinging at life, swinging at everything, swinging ...

~ 92 ~

The golf course closed after the storm. There was just too much damage. MacGregor's stayed open until the first snowfall. There was never a lot of snow that fell, but it would get cold for long stretches, and the roads would ice up. Nobody wanted to risk a ride up the hill.

If you walked up the hill to the course you'd see the wheel still locked in place, frozen in time. You might see a light on in the rooms over by the wheel. But maybe not. Too many things had changed too quickly for everyone to keep pace.

In time, the stream would return to its' natural course. The sycamores would heal, and their overhanging branches would fill out the canopy in the glen.

Most would forget the storm, others would never let it go.

Life moved on….

~ Brad Leech ~

~ 93 ~

As the days began getting longer, the ice on the pond melted and the wheel began turning. The stream began flowing more normally past the wheel, under the bridge, down the hill. The boys from school began working out on the course. You could hear mowers cutting the grass and the raspy, nonstop, noise of chain saws attacking the windfalls from the storm

Cars began accumulating in the parking lot. You could hear the golf carts struggling with the terrain, carrying golfers on their journey around the course.

In MacGregor's, Ian was behind the bar having a coffee, looking through the morning paper. Cletus sat at the bar with his coffee, looking out over the pond at the course. Neither spoke. Both - either weary from the extended effort of getting everything up and running, or just trying to wake up, maybe both - stayed silent.

The door from the kitchen burst open and Mary strode in with some eggs on a plate that she slid in front of Cletus. Directing herself toward him she said, "I thought you had some trees to cut down this morning, or something else to do that would spoil this otherwise gorgeous morning."

While Cletus was salting his eggs, he looked up at Mary, then Ian. Ian didn't lift his head from the paper just slowly shook it. 'Here we go.'

Mary directed her attention to Ian. "And you, you're just as bad. I thought we were going to establish MacGregor's as a restaurant. Not just a 'pub'!" This got Ian's attention.

"Now Mary, you know just as well as I, that a 'pub' *is* a restaurant. I can't help it if not everyone in this country is as refined as the people of Scotland."

Cletus looked up from his eggs at Mary, who continued to glare at Ian. He then quickly refocused on his eggs.

As Mary turned back to the kitchen Cletus said, "It's red pepper isn't it Mary?"

Mary stopped and turned back to face Cletus, taking a couple steps towards him and carefully saying, in a tired, measured voice, maybe even a little bit somber - "No. I did not add red pepper to your eggs." She turned and moved back towards the kitchen.

Before she'd gotten through the door, a voice from the booth just around the corner from the end of the bar, boomed out – "Paprika! I'm telling you kid it's paprika. I've known it all along. She can't deny it! It's red, isn't it?"

Mary wheeled around out of the doorway and came back around the corner of the booth. Facing Dan, she said, "And you - I thought you had an early tee time this morning?"

Dan politely said, "Now, Mrs. Armstrong, there's no need for getting surly with me. Just because things are becoming a little hectic in your life, is no reason to take it out on a paying customer … Such as myself. Besides. I own the course … I can tee off whenever I like!"

"Mr. Steele. While anyone who runs a business knows the customer is always right, I haven't seen you actually paying for any meals recently. Have I? Am I wrong?"

Ian, smiling, was holding up the bar towel for Dan. Dan was considering using it. Ian flipped it across his shoulder, waiting for the next volley.

She continued, "If you *were* actually a paying customer I'd rescind my comments. You're not. So, I won't."

Dan said, "Now Mary, you know that the storm was an act of god. That the limb falling on the phone lines was an act of god. Believe me, I was the one in the car, under the tree, and that was an act of god. You can't go on blaming me or Curtis for all the confusion. I tried calling here from the hospital to tell you I was going home, Curtis tried calling here to tell you I was going home. My calls never got through before they took me home, his call got through, well ...sort of. At least he got a couple of words out before the limb fell on the lines."

Ian looked at Dan and had to smile. Dan was actually making progress on this never-ending argument with Mary.

There was a hint of a smile on Mary's face as she said, "Well, at least you survived. All I'm saying is, you could have handled it better."

With an exasperated look on his face, Dan got up from the booth he was seated at with Teddy and walked over towards Cletus, to whom he said in a stage whisper out of the corner of his mouth that everyone could hear, "Kid I'll bet you can't wait for Cletus junior over there to be born." But Dan could see that there would be no support here.

Cletus wasn't changing the topic. He looked up at Dan and said, "Hey, I learned, when I'm hurt, I call."

Dan had to smile at that. Then, with a nod back towards Mary - "I ...have a golf course to run. And I'm sure you have better things to do than ...pester customers." Dan leaned across towards Ian and pulled the towel from Ian's shoulder, laid it on the bar, carefully folded it, and slid it back across the bar in front of Ian. "Now, where's Curtis? Where's he *gone* to? We've *got* to work on his people skills – especially communication." And with that, he left the pub.

~ Brad Leech ~

~ Epilogue ~

Cletus came down the hill from the clubhouse in his cart. He pulled up at the entrance to the course and got out. He went around to the back of his cart and retrieved a sign to replace the one destroyed in the storm. He walked past the newly planted sycamore that was set back a little further from the road than its predecessor. There was a hole already dug for the sign. He positioned the sign in the hole and began backfilling around the post and tamping the ground down to keep the post vertical. When he was done, he stepped back to make sure it looked straight and proper. It read:

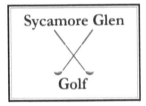

Then he went back to his cart and returned with a smaller sign. This he hung beneath the fixed sign it read:

> **MacGregor's Pub**
> (A Fine Restaurant)

On the back of this sign were the simple words:

Please Revisit Us Soon !

~ Brad Leech ~

~ Characters ~

Cletus Armstrong
Dan Steele – car dealer, golfer
Mary MacGregor – manager MacGregor's restaurant
Ian MacGregor – owner of MacGregor's Pub
Katherine MacGregor – deceased – Ian's wife
Curtis Aldridge – manager of clubhouse
Jim Robinson – businessman; trucking, farm co-op
Dave Jeffries – businessman; housing, construction
Jeffrey – works around the clubhouse
Robby – assistant clubhouse manager, manages locker room
Terry – chef at MacGregor's
Bruce – bartender at MacGregor's
Judge Henry Osborn – owns 60% of course
Claire Osborn Townsend – owns 40% of course
Charles Townsend – deceased – Claire's husband
Bill Morgan – director of operations at course
Steve 'Teddy' Trasker – on course manager
Mavis Trasker – Teddy's wife
Barbara Trasker – Teddy's daughter, twin to Susan
Susan Trasker –Teddy's daughter, twin to Barbara
Tim Davis – head greens keeper
Jimmy – starter at clubhouse
Ralph Bartlett – owner of Bartlett's store in Jasper
Jerry Talbot – farmer who bought Ian's farm
Betty – works in the restaurant
Golfer #1 – Steve Kennedy - in Judges' four some
Golfer #2 – Ed Timmons - in Judges' four some
Nancy Pagano - owner of Johnnies
Russell Pagano – owner of Johnnies
Mrs. Delancy – owns Delancy's boarding house
Dick Anderson – State Highway Commissioner
Ted Billings – Continental Rail, Director of Planning
Floyd Armstrong – Cletus's brother
Bill Weaver – out of town guest for festival

~ Brad Leech ~

~ Afterword ~

John Barmonde came to me with the idea of someone with a perfect golf swing. As you've read the novel, realize that I didn't use, or follow, any of his ideas exactly the way he intended. Our discussions concerning all this were based on the idea of John finding someone to write a screenplay using his concept. When I offered to give it a try, he thought I was insane. I quickly realized that it would be easier to first put the story together in the form of a novel rather than a screenplay. I also convinced John to let me fly solo concerning the writing effort. I did not want to have Sycamore Glen be compared to other popular golf stories or movies. So, what John intended to be a Golf Movie for guys, may have accidently turned into a Romance Novel for women. I guess I don't follow instructions very well.

Actually, all I've really tried to do is write an interesting story that anyone might enjoy. Thanks John for dropping the breadcrumbs in front of me. Now I'll get to work on the screenplay – and I'll try and work more golf into it.

~ Brad Leech ~

Sycamore Mill

What follows is a sample from the sequel to Sycamore Glen that I'm working on:

October, 1859

Henry came through the area like many others. Pushed off the family farm by older siblings, he was forced to strike off on his own. He headed west, like many farmers, to try to make a new life for himself. He had little money, all he could do was offer a full days' work in exchange for meals, a place to sleep, and maybe some money. He hoped, in time, he could become a sharecropper. He would then be able to profit from his efforts and perhaps start a family.

All he had to his name was a mule that had seen better days. Henry had farmed with the mule at home. When he left, there was no debating that the mule would leave with him. The problem was, that the mule liked Henry – and no one else. The two worked long hours together and were accustomed to each other's temperament. Right now, Jack wanted to stop and have a drink of water from the stream he'd spotted nearby. Henry was thirsty too. He'd noticed the stream tumbling down the hillside and nudged Jack in that general direction.

He had Jack pull up beneath a towering sycamore that arched out over the stream. He jumped to the ground and let Jack wander into the water. He walked upstream a couple of paces and knelt down to drink the water. The water was cold and quenched his thirst quickly. When he looked over at Jack, the mule had also finished drinking and was just standing in the water.

The two of them looked out into the valley that was spread out below them. There were a couple of farms established in the bottom of the valley, probably along a larger stream. He'd passed through a small village a couple of days before and was told that there were some farms in the next settlement, west of there. The town was called Jasper.

Now what kind of name was Jasper for a town? He and Jack had mulled over that question all morning. While Henry discussed the pros and cons of Jasper being a good name, Jack listened closely. In the end, Jack agreed with Henry that Jasper was as good a name as any for a small town. Henry was always patient with Jack, the two never rushed into anything without thinking it through carefully.

The land certainly looked like it would be good for farming. Not as flat as some parts that he'd passed through recently, but still, good land. He'd need to find work soon. His money was starting to run out. Jack was having to browse for food and Henrys' supplies had dwindled. He was now hunting for each meal. He was a good shot so he wouldn't starve, but he needed other provisions. Jack needed some proper feed and they both needed a little rest. They had been traveling almost non-stop for the last two weeks.

Henry called Jack back out of the water. He wanted to make it into Jasper by nightfall. He started walking west with Jack by his side. He'd give him a break from the additional weight for the next hour or so.

When he arrived in Jasper late that afternoon, he went straight to a stable. The rates were reasonable, so he boarded Jack there. Jack would get several good meals and a stable hand would give him a grooming after scrubbing him down. Henry cautioned the boy - Jack was a bit of a nipper and he should stay alert when handling his flanks at all. The boy thanked him for the warning and led Jack into the yard behind the stable where he could wet the animal down.

Henry left the stable and walked across the street to what looked like the only dry goods store in the small town. He bought some small quantities of coffee, sugar, salt and some other things he'd run low on. As he paid the clerk he asked about finding work in Jasper.

"So, Mr. Bartlett, do you know of any farmers looking for help?"

"Well son, there are a couple around here that are stretched thin right now. Let me think on this for a minute."

The clerk was wrapping up the purchases in an oilcloth and knotting it so it would stay sealed.

"You know. There's a farmer up on Sycamore Hill. Ezekiel Jennings. He's got a pretty big place up there. Problem is, he has no sons, just two daughters. Twins. One of 'ems married. But I don't know how much work her husband does on the farm. They're pretty private up there. Ezekiel, he's usually looking for some help. His farm would be a good place to start looking. What'd you say your name was?"

"Henry sir, Henry Hawkins. Say, do you have a newspaper? I've lost touch with what's going on since I got on the road."

"Sure Henry, here's one. It's not local. Someone passing through a couple of days ago left it, just take it. Our paper, The Gazette, only comes out on Fridays."

Henry took the sheet of paper from the clerk and looked at the headlines.

"Harper's Ferry Under Siege"

Henry looked up at the clerk. "What's this all about?"

The clerk glanced at the paper. "It's all over with. Troops came in and recaptured the arsenal. They've got that lunatic Brown and his sons. They're going to put him on trial – probably hang 'em all."

~ About the Author ~

Being not only the author, but the editor and self-publisher of Sycamore Glen, I find it impossible to write about myself in the third person to inform you, the reader, of my background. What might qualify me to ask you to purchase my work and perhaps spend several evenings to immerse yourself in the world of Sycamore Glen?

I'm retired from a satisfying engineering career essentially as a designer of HVAC equipment and similar mechanical work in other fields. I've been awarded several patents for ideas I've had that provided solutions to problems my employers have presented me with. I have a wide variety of interests including woodworking and photography, as well as a love for the game of golf.

Being an avid reader, as is my wife, I've often thought I could put together an interesting story - at least for her and myself as a test of my abilities. Approaching the task of writing a novel is unlike anything I've ever been involved with. Engineering work tends to be an organized, structured effort with milestones and defined end goals. My writing process is far from that. Even minor references to events or historical figures have led to tangential research that I would have never otherwise gotten into on my own. Most of Sycamore Glen poured out of me in a short, three-week period, during the summer of 2016. Over the next several months I refined the story in several places after having a small group of relatives and friends read the story as I continued to make minor changes to it.

Since then I've delved into the world of self-publishing to be able to distribute the novel. I hope you can look past any minor technical errors I may have committed - and overlooked - in my editing, that professional editors and publishers would have found.

Brad Leech – July, 2017